GOODFELLOWE MP

Michael Dobbs

PARAGON

CHIVERS PRESS
BATH

First published 1997
by
HarperCollins Publishers
This Large Print edition published by
Chivers Press
by arrangement with HarperCollins Publishers Ltd
1998

ISBN 0 7540 2073 8

British Library Cataloguing in Publication Data available

For Isabelle and John

CHAPTER ONE

Thomas Goodfellowe made a grab for the brakes, only narrowly avoiding a fall to the pavement. He wasn't yet in full command of his machine, an ancient bicycle with a scratched green frame and a mind of its own. He hadn't ridden a bike in thirty years and if he hadn't exactly forgotten how to ride, it was certainly taking time to make contact with the memories. Something had worked its way loose. He hoped it wasn't him.

The streets of London's Chinatown were congested with early-evening traffic. Obstacles were everywhere. Travellers rushing, tourists crushing, grubby urchins begging, lovers with blind eyes and revellers whose eyes if not blind were distinctly blurred, with every one of them apparently intent on tumbling from the pavement and falling directly into his path. A kamikaze run, he reckoned, this stretch of Little Newport Street that led to the tube station, but it had been entirely his fault. His eyes had wandered from the road as he waved to Madame Tang. Mind you, since he'd moved into Chinatown some months earlier he'd learnt that it was worth taking a few risks to be on the good side of Madame Tang. She was not so much a feature of the neighbourhood but *was* the neighbourhood. Of incalculable age and all but invisible wispy hair, she was draped in an ancient woollen cardigan so worn and full of holes that she might have been mistaken for a destitute, shuffling along the pavement pushing a shopping trolley in search of a few fresh vegetables. She had always shuffled, even at the age of thirteen when she had tramped across China, her

1

family's few possessions strapped upon her back, trying to keep from the clutches of Chiang Kai-shek's retreating Kuomintang hordes. Black days those, with memories drawn in burning charcoal. Yet nowadays the winds of fortune blew more kindly for Madame Tang. Her eldest son had a degree in engineering from Cambridge, her second son possessed a still better degree from Yale, and beneath that misshapen cardigan dangled a huge bunch of keys which marked Madame Tang as one of the most powerful landlords in Chinatown, with an empire that embraced legitimate commercial premises, dens of impropriety and assorted short-lease apartments which she controlled with considered ruthlessness. And she understood ruthlessness. The soldiers of the Kuomintang had taught her everything there was to know, a lifetime of lessons crammed into one endless weekend in Wuhan when she passed through their hands. It was the last occasion she had seen her two younger sisters and mother, and the last occasion she had ever cried. After that she never indulged in sentiment, and never gave a second chance. Yes, it was worth taking a few risks to be on the good side of Madame Tang.

With a show of reluctance, she acknowledged his wave and shuffled by, clearing her throat in the traditional Chinese manner, which sounded as though she were scraping barnacles, while Goodfellowe's attentions were drawn to the doorway behind her, where another female figure stood in shameless, almost indecent contrast. Young, barely nineteen but with older eyes, weary from spending too long off her feet and dressed in Lycra hot pants which left not even her moles to the imagination. It was Loretta, longingly watching the world go by just as, she hoped, it lustfully watched her. Two floors above was the room she called her cockpit, rented from Madame Tang, who retained the only key to the premises. It was where Loretta entertained her clients. Loretta described herself as an ordinary working girl, commuting each day from Brighton where she lived with her young daughter and ailing mother, on whose behalf only last week she had sought Goodfellowe's advice. Something about a housing allowance. He couldn't be of much help, but at least he had listened, which was more than most. She owed him. From her catwalk on the doorstep she caught his eye and mouthed a few silent words in his direction. He puckered his brow in concentration, unable to catch her meaning, so she repeated the message, her rubied lips shaping the words in the slow and deliberate manner, almost like a nun at devotions. Now he caught her drift and found he was smiling in spite of himself, before quickly glancing away, afraid his cheeks were showing colour. Wouldn't do accepting such an offer, even if as she was suggesting no money changed hands. The *News of the World* wouldn't understand and neither, he suspected, would his constituents. Nor the Chief Whip. Didn't he know it but the Government was in enough trouble without enforced resignations, even from the obscurity of the backbenches. Still, he reflected, casting a final, fleeting look in Loretta's direction, he could think of worse reasons to burn and sometimes, particularly of late, burning seemed an almost attractive fate.

He pedalled on. Loretta was scarcely a couple of years older than his own daughter Samantha. No, wouldn't do, not by any stretch of his middle-aged imagination. Thoughts of Sammy pressed upon him, even more troublesome than the traffic on Charing Cross Road. Oh, Sammy. How much he owed her, how boundless was the part she played in his world, and how stupidly insignificant were the things which nowadays seemed to deplete their lives and form the focus of their row. Row. Not rows, not several of them, but one seamless collision of Goodfellowe stubbornness that felt as though it had lasted without pause since the last summer holiday when, at the age of fifteen, she hadn't come home till two. The youthful anger that poured out had seemed relentless, like a river in flood. No sooner had he found some means of damming it than it found another, still more unpredictable and chaotic course. What was it last weekend? Yes, of course, her mother's locket.

He pedalled more energetically, trying to work off his anger. She'd come home on *exeat* from school, that cripplingly expensive palace of teenage entertainments where they appeared to focus all their energies on finding new ways of extracting money from parents, to announce that she was organizing a charitable fashion show. To him it had seemed yet another excuse to raid his wallet; for her it had been little less than a moral crusade. 'Fashion Against Famine!' or some such nonsense. If her words had been sentimental and naive, his had been inexcusably dismissive. But it hadn't been just the money. She had asked for her mother's locket. Not to borrow, not just for the fashion show, but for keeps.

'She doesn't need it any more. Won't even know it's gone, Daddy!' Sammy had protested.

4

And that's what had hurt, scraped open wounds that had never properly healed. Of course she was right. He had bought Elinor the locket to celebrate their wedding anniversary, a lifetime ago when Sammy had been almost twelve and her brother Stevie almost fourteen. Sammy had helped him choose it, had wrapped it for him and admired it from first sight with such an intensity that her mother had promised that, one day, it would be hers. None of them had understood how quickly that day might come.

So he had said no, refused her, not yet willing to let go. Sammy had shouted and argued that it was what her mother would have wanted, and then it was his turn to raise his voice and demand to know how the hell she knew what her mother wanted. They used their anger as shields. Hurting each other, because they were family. Goodfellowes. Sammy had returned to school on Sunday, early and in silence, leaving him to feel as though he had been stranded on an ice floe. That's what he liked about his rented apartment in Chinatown, not just that it was small and cheap and close to Westminster and because the streets offered impulse and inspiration to rouse the dullest of wits, but even more because you could never be alone in Chinatown, not in the way you could on an ice floe.

The next few moments were to amount to a minute and a half of intense and potentially dangerous confusion. He was preoccupied by lingering thoughts of Sammy, and distracted by the small band of buskers playing jazz on the steps of the Garrick in the half-hour before the theatre doors opened. His new shoes were rubbing raw, which didn't help when you were about to launch yourself upon Trafalgar Square in the teeth of the rush hour. And if he had to carry his mobile phone along with copies of Hansard and a bottle of Bulgarian Cabernet in the battered wicker basket on his handlebars, he really should have switched the damned thing off. But it started to burble just as he passed South Africa House, just as the traffic lights changed, just as dusk began to muster her forces and take control of the sky—and just as a retired actuary from Margate, jaw defiant beneath uncompromising NHS horn-rims, and driving his treasured Vauxhall in town for the first time in twelve years, came to a complete halt in the middle of the intersection while he attempted to locate the switch for his sidelights. Cabbies shouted, traffic weaved, Chaos Theory took the entire east side of the square in its grip. Butterfly wings had nothing on retired actuaries from Margate. Goodfellowe, caught off guard while scrabbling for his phone, lost control.

The chauffeur in the Rolls-Royce behind had witnessed both the mounting confusion and the changing lights. He had also seen what he thought to be a gap, a window of opportunity, a chance to beat the muddled masses. And his passenger was in a hurry. So he had put his foot down, only to find the leap for freedom suddenly barred by what appeared to be an attempted suicide. His foot slammed from accelerator to brake. Turbo drive to rodeo ride. From the back seat of the wildberry-red Silver Dawn, an exasperated and freshly rumpled passenger bent down to gather up his scattered documents. Then he turned to mouth an unmistakably personalized oath at the cyclist.

Thomas Goodfellowe, tribune of the people and

6

Member of Parliament for Marshwood, had had his first brush with Frederick E Corsa, a man who took pride in representing no one but himself.

*　　　*　　　*

At almost the same moment as he was staring into the storm-whipped eyes of Freddy Corsa, another confrontation was taking place which was to have an equally significant effect on Tom Goodfellowe's life and reputation.

Scarcely more than a moderate stone's throw from Little Newport Street could be found 'Zhu's Apothecary'—but only if one knew where to look. The entrance stood in a covered alleyway off one of Chinatown's back streets, and nothing but a small window presented itself to the street. The pseudo-Shanghai lamppost which had once illuminated the end of the alleyway had been moved—at the insistence of the local *feng-shui* man and at the considerable expense of the City of Westminster—ten yards farther down the pavement, leaving both alley and apothecary in the grey shadow of evening. All sight of the frugal herbal emporium inside was blocked by display cases packed with the strange wares of the Oriental pharmaceutical trade—weirdly shaped roots, seeds, exotic barks, deer tails, dissected life forms of indeterminate origin, sun-dried sea horses and absurdly twisted ginseng, forces of herbalism that offered restoration and renewal from an extraordinary range of ailments, many of which Western medicine scarcely pretended to understand and some it hadn't even heard of. Chinese doctors, as Mr Zhu was fond of remarking, had been at it a long time, surgically removing abdominal tumours under anaesthetic while Boadicea was still bathing in pig shit and knee-capping Romans.

'Westerners strange,' he reflected in his castrated English. 'Pay doctors when sick. Chinese punish doctor when sick, pay to keep healthy.' And so from a hundred different bottles and a score of rosewood drawers he would dispense herbs and potions, weighing out the ingredients in his hand-held scales and wrapping them in twists of brown paper, while above him a bright brass ceiling fan turned slowly, mixing the peppery aromas and pushing them gently around his unpretentious shop.

Mostly his customers were, like Zhu himself, from Hong Kong, with a scattering of regulars from the other Malay, Singapore and Vietnamese Chinese communities which were threaded through the fabric of Chinatown. Western customers were few, and usually ignorant, ripe for picking. Often they had little idea of what they wanted and no idea of what they were getting; they were there to experience the atmosphere rather than the herbal cures, most of which required lengthy boiling and smelled foul. So he would mix ingredients like a short-order chef, a pinch of this and a handful of that, anything which could do little harm and which would smell inoffensive to the squeamish Western nose. Much of the bulk was made up of used tea leaves from his brother's restaurant in Gerrard Street, which his niece and receptionist, Jya-Yu, dried in the kitchen out back. 'Every ingredient tested,' he would promise with a grin, although his teeth protruded and his accent was so bad that few Westerners would understand, happily lost in the performance as his hands moved like a magician's above the piles of strangely coloured herbs. They

8

would smile, Mr Zhu would smile and give a little bob and bow, and on most days everyone would be happy. But not today.

The previous night had been a long and difficult one for Zhu, locked in a fevered game of *pei-gau* in the basement room beneath Madame Tang's cake shop. He had emerged at three a.m. with a savage headache and without a penny of the two thousand pounds he'd had in his pocket at the start of the evening. 'Fate', as Jya-Yu had pronounced caustically, trying to put the disaster behind them, but Uncle Zhu was the type of man who always believed in giving Fate a little helping hand. So when the callow corporate-image executive shambled into his shop after an extended lunch, demanding tiger bone as a pick-me-up for his manhood and digging in his suit pocket for a handful of notes, Uncle Zhu was not slow to see the possibilities.

'Tiger bone not legal,' he warned, unable to scrape his eyes from the cash.

'Neither's not paying your VAT,' the young man responded gruffly and dug out yet more crumpled notes. 'Come on. Tiger bone. The real stuff.'

Jya-Yu muttered a warning but Uncle Zhu spat back, his judgement temporarily impaired by poverty and his inability to cure his own headache. 'Fate,' he snapped, and proceeded to rummage in a drawer at the bottom of the counter, out of sight of the customer. He reappeared with a twist of silver paper, which he opened with considerable care on the counter to reveal a small spoonful of pale grey-white powder.

'That all?' rasped the image executive, swaying slightly. 'Give me more. Tonight's a big night.'

Zhu ducked down again and bobbed back up with a second twist. 'Plenty strong, even for big man like you,' he chuckled. He exposed the additional powder before carefully rewrapping both parcels. He looked deep into the executive's eyes, which were glazed, focusing in a laboured manner. The breath smelt desiccated, dried by too much red wine. Uncle Zhu decided to add another fifty per cent to the first price he'd thought of.

'Hundred and fifty.'

Surprisingly, Uncle Zhu's accent coped with figures far better than any other aspect of the English language and it appeared to be the first part of the transaction the customer even partially understood.

'A hundred and fifty what?'

'Pounds. Hundred and fifty pounds,' Uncle Zhu responded.

'What? For two tiny packets?' the customer continued, picking up the twists in the hand that was not holding the money.

'Very genuine. Very rare.' Zhu extended his hand for payment, a gesture which the customer, a man of overactive imagination and Bruce Lee fantasies, somehow translated as a demand with menace.

'You're ripping me off, you little yellow bastard. You're not getting me. Shouldn't be here in the first place.' He began to back out towards the door. 'Bet you're an illegal, no work permit. You wouldn't dare call the police.'

At this point Uncle Zhu let forth a minor hurricane of untranslatable Cantonese but made no move to come out from behind the protection of his counter. Instead it was Jya-Yu who chased after the fleeing customer, catching hold of his sleeve as he

10

reached the end of the alley and was about to disappear into the crowded street. A shouting match ensued as Jya-Yu continued to tug at his arm and a small crowd rapidly gathered, although no one attempted to intervene, not even Uncle Zhu who had at last left the protective custody of his apothecary and stood remonstrating from the end of the alleyway. The noise level grew.

'What's going on here, then?' A new voice had entered the fray. 'All right, all right. Cut it out or I'll nick the both of you.' The local constabulary had arrived but, at first, seemingly to little effect. Uncle Zhu maintained his stream of abuse, gesticulating at the man, while Jya-Yu, whose English was normally at least passable, found her control of the language falling to pieces in the excitement. Around them the voluble gathering of Chinese traders and foreign tourists offered noise but no greater understanding. Puzzled, the constable turned to the image executive. 'Perhaps you can explain, sir?'

The sight of the blue uniform had had a remarkable effect upon the young man. His voice had lost all trace of its contemptuous tone while the glaze had disappeared from his eyes, which were now sharp, calculating. 'Damned if I know, officer. I was just walking back to my office for a meeting when this girl comes up. Says for a hundred and fifty she'll give me anything I want. When I said I wasn't interested she starts having a go at me.'

The youthful constable examined Jya-Yu. She didn't look much like a tart. Very little make-up, a vigorously coloured silk jacket that was perhaps a little gaudy. Anyway, most Chinese vice was kept very much to themselves, not paraded out on the streets. Maybe she was an amateur, doing a little

11

freelancing. 'You're saying she propositioned you for sex, sir?'

'Absolutely. Anything I wanted, any way I wanted it. She's a hooker.' He sniffed righteously. 'But I don't go in for that sort of stuff.'

At that point Jya-Yu, unable to express herself in any other fashion, launched herself at the man, clubbing at him, scratching. Uncle Zhu resumed his screaming and the crowd began to press closer. It was the sort of situation where a young constable might lose both his helmet and his reputation. He radioed for back-up.

It was as the constable stepped in to separate Jya-Yu from the executive that he noticed a small packet fall to the ground. A silver twist which, on closer inspection, contained a white powder he couldn't identify. Not for certain, at least, not until it had gone for testing, but he reckoned he was already way ahead of the forensic lab at Lambeth.

'Yours, sir?' he asked the executive.

'Mine? Never!'

'Miss?' the constable turned to Jya-Yu, but all he got was a stream of untranslatable abuse and a further indiscriminate pounding of fists. He was still holding her wrists when the wagon arrived and a WPC took control of the struggling girl. Jya-Yu was led to the cover of the alleyway where she was searched. That's when the police discovered two things.

The first was that, in the confusion, the executive had disappeared.

The other was that in Jya-Yu's jacket pocket, where the executive had thrust it during the struggle, was the second twist of powder.

*   *   *

12

The retired actuary from Margate had still not budged, mesmerized by the swaying of the windscreen wipers, still desperately surfing his switches, wits dulled by the insistent horns of complaint which surrounded him. Up to this point he'd always been censorious about drink-driving; now he considered it might be the only option.

Meanwhile the Silver Dawn had eased away and already Corsa's attentions had been dragged elsewhere. There were always reasons for his attentions to be dragged elsewhere. As Chairman of the Granite News Group ('one of Europe's most rapidly expanding and profitable newspaper publishing companies', as his annual report proclaimed), he lived on a diet of distractions. A headline on a front page. A detail in a corporate report. Finance. His charitable works, or perhaps an engaging woman, both of which he used for public effect. Then there was the new headquarters complex in Docklands. And more finance. Much More Finance.

The newspaper world had changed almost beyond recognition in recent years, somehow skipping over several stages of the industrial revolution. A world that had once been centred on the Gothic wine bars and union chapels of Fleet Street had, in the shadows of night and through the legs of wild-eyed pickets, been shifted out into several large cakes of concrete scattered along the banks of the Thames. Printing presses and distribution operations, traditionally run by the Spanish practices of the union fathers and manned by phantoms and cartoon characters, were now run by New World Control Systems Inc of Korea and scarcely required manning at all.

Corsa had been a prominent rebel in this revolution—'a modern-day Merchant of Venice who has fallen upon more refined table manners,' as the *Investors Digest* had once jibed. The sensitive souls over at the Commission for Racial Equality must've been out to lunch that day and missed the point, but anyone of consequence in the newspaper industry understood. Corsa wasn't 'one of us'. Could never be. Bad blood. His father, the founder of the Granite Group, had been an Italian and a prisoner of war who had lost patience with his countrymen's predisposition to chaos during his one-sided battle with Montgomery and sandflies in the deserts of North Africa. His flight from the true path had been encouraged still further by his POW indenture on a Norfolk farm, where he had come to admire the English, their inherent reserve and particularly the fair-skinned daughters. So Papa had stayed on. His admiration, however, was not always reciprocated in a country still struggling with food queues and black-market nylons. Many simply took the view that Papa Corsa was and would always be a first-generation wop and, still worse, an uppity wop at that. So he'd been cautious, conservative, bought a share in a failing local newspaper and slowly created what became a modest-sized yet comfortably successful newspaper operation. But no knighthood, certainly no peerage, none of the public respects normally accorded to newspaper proprietors and not even much of the fear, not even after he had rescued the ailing *Herald* and restored it to significance amongst the Fleet Street dailies. But Papa wasn't bitter. 'If we'd gone back to Italy to run newspapers there,' he would explain in his pasta accent to his Winchester-educated son, 'we'd

14

probably be sweating in a prison cell along with all the rest. Be happy with what we have, Freddy.'

Yet Freddy never was. He'd resented being two inches shorter than all the others at school, no way was he going to have others look down on him after he'd joined the family firm. 'I bought my manners in Winchester,' he would later relate with his habitual smile, 'but I bought my boots in Naples. And neither place sold much scruple.' Freddy developed an appetite as sharp as a flensing knife and, at the age of thirty-five, pushed his way past his ailing father to usurp the Granite chair, vowing that the Corsas would never again be ignored. In less than five years Freddy had been as good as his word. He had turned the starched and stuffy *Herald* into a tabloid, added an evening edition and several hundred thousand to its circulation, and bought a series of regional and magazine titles to support it until Granite had matched its corporate claim about being 'one of Europe's most rapidly expanding newspaper publishing companies.' Still not in the premier league, perhaps, but well on the way. Trouble was it had not, in spite of the hyperbole, also become 'one of the most profitable.' He'd borrowed dear and floated the new Granite Group in a sea of debt, only to see interest rates rise and paper costs spiral. Advertising revenues had shattered, while his competitors took him on in a series of desperate price-cutting wars.

And then it got worse. Just as all the froth and fizz was leaking away from the newspaper market the Government had announced, at the insistence of its masters in the European Commission, that it would introduce a new Press (Diversity of Ownership) Bill designed to break the stranglehold

15

which in the view of Monsieur Bourgeois, the Commissioner, was enjoyed and abused by the largest newspaper groups. 'Competition, not cartel!' Monsieur B had declared with Gallic fervour and the British Government, almost alone in Europe, had taken him seriously. So the legislative knee was bent. Observers, unused to the inverted logic that a Government should push around the media, predicted conflagration. Having lit the blue touch paper, the Government would now be expected to retire.

But the expected open warfare failed to materialize. The biggest players, already frustrated by the diminishing returns on their investments in newspapers, were growing increasingly distracted by new adventures. 'I've packed my rucksack,' one of Corsa's fellow moguls had muttered over lunch in the Savoy Grill, explaining his decision to desert the rock face of Fleet Street for the fertile ground of cable television. 'This ledge on which we press barons live has given us a great view, but it's grown too damned draughty for my comfort. Time to find a new perch.'

They'd had their fun and now the big boys seemed almost content to dump a few titles—to the advantage of the second-rank players like Corsa. Or so it seemed. During the first week of the announcement he'd vociferously supported the new Bill and the opportunities it represented to pick up still more titles and move into the big time. By the second week, however, the prospective sales had served only to drag down share prices across the sector, including the price of Granite shares. Shares that Corsa had used to guarantee his huge bank borrowings. Whoops.

The bankers. Let me die alongside my bankers! That way I'll be sure to take the bastards with me . . . They'd called a meeting for next week, wanted to discuss the covenants he'd given them for the most recent thirty million pounds. No problem. Not yet at least. He'd get through that one as he'd got through all the discussions with his bankers over the last eighteen months. Encourage them with praise, confuse them with inflated prospects, weigh them down with paper, above all allow them to be deceived by their own voracious appetites and ambitions. Corsa had added so many new companies and newspaper titles to the Granite chain that there had never been two consecutive balance sheets that were comparable. Assets, valuations, hypothecations and depreciations, he'd moved them all around the financial chess board with a speed that left his opponents, and occasionally even himself, bemused. No one knew that so much of the bottom line of the Granite accounts which he proudly proclaimed as profit existed only on paper. No one knew, not yet. But they would. In those silent moments at the very end of day, when sleep eluded him and darkness allowed ghouls and hobgoblins to prey, he knew his time was running out.

They were passing the statue of King Charles I which stood at the end of Whitehall looking down towards the parliament buildings. The Killing Field, where they had taken the King one freezing January morning, paraded him before the crowd and chopped off his head. Where so many others had found their ambitions and abilities dragged in the dust behind the baying mob. The men of the media were kings now. But here of all places he knew that

17

even kings could fall. Torn to pieces and hurled onto the rocks which lay below the crumbling cliff face. He needed a lifeline. And in a hurry. He glanced at his watch. Already he was late.

'Downing Street,' he prompted his driver impatiently.

*   *   *

By the time Goodfellowe had parked his bike in the rack at the front of Speaker's Court he was out of breath and the third toe on his left foot was developing a blister. It was almost seven o'clock, a series of votes lay ahead of him stretching into the night, and he knew he was in danger of being late. He couldn't remember what they were voting about but there would be trouble if he didn't make it to the division lobby in time, so he was trying to hurry. Even on a good day the Government's majority stretched only to nine and there had been few good days recently. Two colleagues on the Government backbenches were recovering from heart attacks, another had had an attack of conscience after his constituency association failed to reselect him, while a fourth was under attack from the tabloids for multiple philandering. She hadn't been seen in Westminster since the last issue of the *Sunday People*, hoping in vain that colleagues and correspondents would lose interest in her reported non-culinary uses of lo-fat banana yoghurt. It was at times like these that Whips lost their sense of humour. He wondered whether in another life Madame Tang had been a Whip. Or merely a cat castrator. He'd better hurry.

Then the phone started warbling again. It was getting to be a dangerous distraction. He should

18

switch it off. *Would* switch it off. Next time.

'Goodfellowe,' he panted.

'Mr Goodfellowe MP. Help. Help. Help!' The voice was thin, perceptibly stretched by tension. 'I am arrested. This is Jya-Yu. You know, Zhu's niece. In prison. Help me. Please!'

The phone was handed to someone else. 'Detective Constable Ferrit here at Charing Cross. Is there any chance that I'm talking to Mr Thomas Goodfellowe MP?' The policeman sounded deeply sceptical. When he'd offered the prisoner the one phone call, he hadn't expected a Chinese girl whose anxiety had reduced her command of English to little more than gabble to suggest that she would phone a politician rather than a solicitor. She didn't know any solicitors, she had struggled to explain.

'What's going on, constable?'

'Lady here's been arrested. Had your number and says she wants your help. I can always call a duty solicitor if it's a pain, sir. Do you know the lady?'

'Sort of. Her uncle's herbal shop provides me with fresh tea. Gave her my number because I'm expecting a new supply to arrive. What's the problem?'

'Soliciting and being in possession of a controlled substance, sir.'

'You're joking.'

'And we might throw in a charge of resisting arrest and assaulting a police officer. Actual bodily harm unless his nose stops bleeding in five minutes.'

'She's only—what—eighteen?'

'Old enough, sir. You coming or not?'

'Ple-e-e-ase Minister Goodfellowe.' Jya-Yu's fear was all too evident.

19

The bells of Big Ben directly above him were already announcing the hour and the first vote. He'd miss it unless he started for the division lobby now, and his vote might make all the difference. Yet she was sobbing. He was wondering if he could find an excuse that might satisfy the Whips, rather like when he had failed to sign his last Inland Revenue cheque, but that hadn't worked either. Perhaps if he hurried to the police station he might miss only the first couple of divisions, be back for the rest almost before anyone had noticed. Yet this was a running three-liner, a summons by the Whips which only death might excuse, and even then it had to be certified. There again, why should he bother with her? He scarcely knew her, no more than a passing smile and a request that she call when the tea came in.

'They lock me up!' she was wailing.

He knew what it was like to be locked up. Arrested. To know the stench of fear and humiliation. That's why he was riding a bloody bike rather than driving a car. You didn't need a licence for a bike. He'd only been a little bit over the limit but it was during the pre-Christmas purge and whereas twenty years ago they might have made an exception for a Member of Parliament, nowadays they made examples of them, All over that Christmas his constituency had been plastered with the Government's drink-drive posters—'Don't Be An Idiot', the posters had warned. 'And Don't Vote For One Next Time!' his opponents had added in huge yellow graffiti across every single one.

He had to go.

'I'll be there in fifteen.'

His arrival at Charing Cross police station in

20

Agar Street turned out to be less than authoritative.

'You're an MP?' the reception constable had asked dubiously. The intervening fifteen minutes between phone call and arrival had not been kind to Goodfellowe. A sudden spring shower had ambushed him as he passed Downing Street, as though the Chief Whip were using his occult powers to give him one last chance to change his mind and turn. He had arrived at the police station red in cheek, dripping slightly, with his suit crumpled and his trousers still tucked inside his socks.

'You sure you're an MP?' the constable repeated.

'Used to be a Minister. Home Office,' Goodfellowe responded, but this only served to make his appearance all the more unconvincing. His suits, even when dry, seemed to suggest faded elegance, memories of better times and evidence of several dry cleanings too far. His age lay somewhere in the late forties, that point in a man's life which is neither young nor yet old, when ambition's flame has begun to flicker if not yet die, when many a man grows preoccupied with the stretching of his waistline rather than his intellect. But not Goodfellowe. The hair at his temples was beginning to show grey in a manner which could seem distinguished when not frizzing in the rain, although it normally looked as if he had just been roused from a nap on the sofa—unruly, a little battered, much like Goodfellowe himself. But nothing about him suggested either sleepiness or indolence. He was a man of enthusiasms, sometimes excessively so, with a mind so open to possibilities that it worked best only when it was almost too late. A mind that had not always commended itself to party managers who preferred discipline and routine.

21

They compared him to a great tanker, very difficult to turn or manoeuvre once set on his course, often in bad weather refusing to answer the helm, and as he glanced at the station clock which showed twenty past and the first two votes missed, he knew there would be more rough sailing ahead. But it was in his eyes that the depths of Goodfellowe were revealed. They were dark, almost blue-black like the night sky. Sometimes they would sparkle as though filled with a thousand stars and captivate all who were allowed close enough to see, yet at other times they would darken as though great clouds were passing and threaten the most violent of storms.

He had once, until four years ago, been part of the constellation himself, one of the brightest and most rapidly promoted politicians of his time. A junior Minister who, although he did not hide his ambition, had sufficient sense to wear it with a smile and was regarded by an increasing number of colleagues as good Cabinet material and possibly, one day, even more. But at that time he had had a wife and a son, as well as Sammy. There had also been a driving licence and a Government driver too—all the trappings of success which, piece by piece, had fallen away, leaving him in a rain-sodden suit with his trousers tucked inside his socks standing in Charing Cross nick.

He reached into his pocket for his wallet. He didn't have his House of Commons pass on him, couldn't remember where he had left it, but his credit card had become one of his closest allies in his battle against misfortune, never leaving his side. 'Thomas Goodfellowe MP' it announced, and the constable at last seemed satisfied.

'We have to be careful, you understand,' he

22

offered by way of apology, opening the heavily secured door that allowed Goodfellowe into the heart of the police station.

'I understand all too well, Constable,' he replied, bending down to release his trouser cuffs from captivity.

He was led downstairs to the Charge Room, which resembled the ticket counter of a bus station, except that the boards behind the reception desk carried duty rosters and charge sheets instead of timetables. It seemed to be rush hour.

'Sarge, I've got one for the Chinese girl,' the constable announced.

'You her solicitor?' the custody sergeant enquired, continuing to give his attention to a large batch of forms in front of him.

'A Member of Parliament.'

'Ah, you must be Mr Goodfellowe.' The sergeant looked up. 'She a constituent, sir?'

'No. A friend, I suppose.'

'Your . . . friend'—the policeman tested the term cautiously—'is in a spot of real trouble, Mr Goodfellowe. Soliciting. Possession. Punching an officer. We're all going to have to be rather careful about this, if you take my meaning.' Goodfellowe took it to be a friendly warning. 'We tried to get her to call a solicitor but she insisted it should be you. I can still call the duty solicitor, if you want. If you're too busy. Got more important things to do.'

'Thank you, Sergeant. Might as well see her while I'm here, don't you think?'

'Up to you. Entirely up to you,' the sergeant pronounced, washing his hands of any further advice. Rush hour was well underway, the Charge Room was getting backed up and it was going to be

23

a long night.

'Are you going to charge her, Sergeant?'

'Depends. Haven't got her side of the story yet, she's having trouble explaining herself. And we're running a check through Clubs & Vice and through the Immigration Service to see if they've a handle on Miss Pan . . . Chou-you. That her real name?'

'*Zsha-yu*,' Goodfellowe pronounced phonetically. 'I think so.'

'Know the young lady well, do you, sir?'

'Not really.'

'I see.'

'I doubt very much whether you do, Sergeant,' Goodfellowe responded, more than aware of what was swirling through the policeman's excessively stimulated mind. 'I think perhaps I'd better see her now.'

All this time Jya-Yu had been sitting in a detention room. Less than ninety minutes beforehand she had been a carefree, bright-eyed eighteen-year-old looking forward to a night out with friends. Now she was rigid with terror, sitting on a plastic mattress on a concrete bunk in a cell whose painted brick walls were covered in crude graffiti and scratchings which seemed like the claw marks of animals. The room had been designed so that prisoners could do no harm to themselves, yet Jya-Yu, simply by sitting here, felt more harmed and in more pain than at any time in her short life. The scuffle, her arrest, the ride with head bowed in the back of a police wagon to a basement car park, with policemen and women shouting at her (or so it seemed), thrown amidst all the dregs that collected in a busy Charge Room. And then the strip search, the violation, to her the most profound humiliation

24

of her life, almost as Madame Tang had described it to her, as though the Kuomintang army had marched right up Charing Cross Road and started to lay waste. When she was led from the cell and into an interview room to discover at last a familiar face, the emotions she had kept caged within at last escaped her control. She stood to attention, hands by her side, head bowed, and began to sob inconsolably. Instinctively Goodfellowe crossed to her and placed his arms defensively around her, trying to bury the tears in his embrace. The constable smirked.

'Ah, could we be left alone to talk, Constable?' Goodfellowe enquired when at last Jya-Yu had regained her composure.

''Fraid not, sir.'

'But I thought . . .'

'Not a privileged conversation, sir, not unless you're a solicitor.'

The first battle lost. And so they had talked and Jya-Yu, calmer now and with better control of her English, had tried to explain, and the arresting constable, nose no longer weeping, had come in and recorded a formal interview during which he had displayed a plastic bag containing two twists of silver paper.

'Are these yours, miss?' the policeman had enquired, still slightly nasal.

She had nodded.

'For the record, the prisoner has indicated that the silver packets belong to her. And what is the off-white powder inside them?'

She looked at Goodfellowe, her eyes flushed with confusion and torment, then sat with her head held low and would say no more.

25

'Miss Pan Jya-Yu, it seems to me probable that this powder is a controlled substance, cocaine I would guess. Have you got anything to say?' The constable sounded a little bored and began to make patterns on the table top with the rings left by his plastic coffee cup. 'OK. For the benefit of the record, the prisoner refuses to answer. And you do understand, don't you, that your refusal to say anything can be used against you in court?'

'Yes. I do,' she whispered.

They were taken back to the Charge Room, now in a state of controlled bedlam, where an inspector appeared. They had run Jya-Yu's name through their records but had found no sordid past, no vice conviction, she was not an illegal, her presence in the country was entirely in order.

'And you have no witness for the soliciting charge,' Goodfellowe intervened.

'But we do have a suspicious substance, sir. And the constable's bloody nose.'

'That was accident,' Jya-Yu protested, but the inspector ignored her, continuing to address Goodfellowe.

'I'm not going to charge the lady at the present time but we'll release her on bail to return at a time when our lab analysis of the substance is completed. Probably in about six weeks' time. When we know what it is, then we'll know what to do.'

'And in the meantime?'

'If you'll let me offer you a word of advice, I should concentrate on running the country, sir. Tears and trouble. That's all a gentleman like you will get from becoming tied up in a case like this. People have such suspicious minds.'

*   *   *

26

Corsa was feeling out of sorts. He hated receptions, even in Downing Street. Three hundred people crushed into a couple of steaming drawing rooms where they sipped cheap wine—Spanish this month, Sainsbury's had a special—and waited for one of the Prime Minister's funny little speeches. Corsa was used to making dramatic entrances, demanding the attention of all present, not shuffling along in an anonymous line, like his father. In a crowd his lack of physical stature made him feel claustrophobic, insignificant. He hated cheap wine, held disdain for casual acquaintance and had no high regard even for the Prime Minister. How could one take a man seriously whose eyebrows resembled two ferrets locked in coitus?

He turned to take out his frustrations on the Minister for Overseas Development, a man of giggles and girth who wore his suit as though beneath its immense folds it hid a chest of drawers with all the drawers open. 'Bunny' Burrowes was also notoriously Catholic and unmarried. And, this evening, he was a target that had moved out into the open. The *Herald* had recently launched a campaign exposing the high infant-mortality levels in Angola caused by an epidemic of flu believed to have been introduced by European nuns. As his features editor had pointed out to Corsa, the death rates in Angola were no higher than in Iraq or Mongolia but, as Corsa had in turn pointed out to the features editor, there was little public sympathy to be generated by Arabs or Orientals 'and black babies have such enormous eyes. So appealing.' Anyway, neither Iraq nor Mongolia had a Royal visit planned for three months' time. So the *Herald* in traditional campaigning mood had promised to build them a

27

hospital. Much fanfare, still more moral outrage, and all by Royal appointment. Great publicity. Sadly for the plans and promises, however, the *Herald*'s campaign had found its readers in a profound state of compassion fatigue. Both heart strings and purse strings remained steadfastly unplucked, and the *Herald*'s appeal was a quarter of a million short—money which Corsa had neither mood nor means to find from his own resources. So, privately and with great politeness, they had asked the Foreign Office whose officials, still more politely, had said no. Yet here, giggling in the middle of the Green Drawing Room, was the Minister in all his voluminous flesh. Corsa felt a challenge coming on.

'My dear Minister, what a pleasure.'

Burrowes scowled at the interruption. Unlike some of his colleagues he did not welcome over-familiarity with the press, being neither photogenic nor particularly prudent in his private life. He replied with no more than a nod of his heavily jowled head and was about to pick up his interrupted conversation about costume with the country's leading male ice skater when, with only perfunctozy apologies, Corsa took his arm and led him off to a quieter corner.

'Not your bloody hospital, Freddy,' Burrowes started, objecting to the heavy hand upon his sleeve. 'I've seen the papers. It won't wash. We don't have the money.'

'Of course you have the money, Bunny. It's simply a matter of priorities. But of course I understand your difficulties.'

'Good,' responded the Minister, his eyes dancing back to the skater and making to leave, but Corsa kept a firm grip on his sleeve.

'I merely wanted to make sure that you had been fully briefed on the opportunities.'

'What opportunities?'

'The opportunity to get some richly deserved credit. For the Government. For the Foreign Office aid programme. And, when it comes down to it, for you.'

The Minister pulled distractedly at each of his pudgy fingers in turn as though checking that the press man hadn't stolen any in the crush.

'Think of the free publicity,' Corsa continued. 'The hospital building is all prefabricated. We could load it onto an RAF transport and fly it in together. You and me. Accompanied by a handpicked selection of reporters and television cameramen, of course. Imagine the reception. The crowds on the runway. Laughing children, weeping doctors, dancing mothers, and as many effusive local dignitaries as their Mercedes can shuttle in. The lot. And you and the Cardinal being greeted like saviours—which is precisely what this hospital project is all about.'

'The Cardinal?' enquired the Minister.

'Yes. I've had a word with his office,' Corsa lied impetuously. 'They say in principle he'd be delighted to help. Thinks it's an excellent idea. Sort of absolution for the nuns. We Catholic boys should stick together, Bunny.'

Burrowes' fingers began dancing across the folds of his damp chin. Even on a good day he was no longer what he could regard as young, and his contemplation of indiscretions both past and proposed had begun to produce in him a growing attachment to his religious roots, and particularly to

29

the understanding and forgiveness those roots might provide. Yes, if the Cardinal was considering giving his personal approval . . .

'And the *Herald* would keep the campaign going. Reports on the children saved, the disasters averted and the good deeds done. Your good deeds, Bunny. Right through the summer.'

Burrowes' jowls wobbled in growing anticipation. Public duty and personal piety all wrapped up in one endless photo opportunity, right through the summer—and the next reshuffle. The Minister's eyes grew moist.

'It's only a drop in the ocean so far as your budget is concerned but it's in a damned good cause. Your cause. An excellent cause, don't you think?' Corsa continued, and the Minister found himself nodding in agreement. He'd get stick from his officials when he went back to the office, but he could squeeze it out of the disaster fund and pray that Bangladesh wouldn't disappear beneath flood water again this year. A gentlemen's agreement forged for God's work. After all, that was a Minister's job, to decide. 'For the greater good,' he burbled enthusiastically. 'And sod the civil servants.'

At last Corsa allowed the Minister to return to his ice skater. Two hundred and fifty thousand. Not a bad return on ten minutes' work and a glass of Sainsbury's Rioja. It was fine sport and the fool hadn't even realized, had been so pathetically grateful. How he despised them, the politicians, the would-be rulers with their airs and arrogances, strutting around this tiny world of Westminster like peacocks with their flight feathers plucked.

He found himself wandering away from the general crush, stepping around the White Drawing

Room in search of more convivial distraction. He examined a Constable landscape of storm clouds and sodden fields, not one of the painter's best. Corsa had better in his own boardroom, although in private he preferred more modern works, the sort of things in which it looked as though reality had been taken apart and put back in an entirely different order. Rather like his accounts. On a table by the window stood four china dolls, porcelain figures of former Prime Ministers—Gladstone, Wellington, Disraeli and Palmerston, giants of the Victorian age but all with private lives and peccadilloes which would in the modern era have brought them low long before their time. 'Publish and be damned!' Wellington had challenged his mistress when confronted with her all-too-explicit diaries. Nowadays she would, and he would too. Be damned, that is. Cut down to size quicker than a forest of mahogany.

'The only good politician . . .?' a voice beside him suggested.

Corsa turned to find another guest, an elegant woman in her early forties, smiling at him mischievously.

'I'm sure we all retain a considerable regard for them. In their proper place,' he offered cautiously, unable to resist the conditional. He knew her, he thought, but couldn't place her.

'That proper place being swinging from a lamp-post by their testicles, according to some of your editorials.' She held out her hand. 'Diane Burston. I don't think we've met.'

'We have, in a way,' Corsa returned, at last recognizing her. 'You've graced the business pages of my newspapers on many an occasion.'

Diane Burston was a phenomenon. A woman who had risen to the highest ranks of the oil industry on merit and on the basis of her extraordinary financial skills. It wasn't enough any more simply to be a good oil man, not in an industry forced to spend so much of its effort trying to climb out of the holes which a previous generation of eager executives and ill-controlled prospectors had dug for it. Rusting oil platforms, misplaced oil terminals, sinking oil tankers, oceans of oil pollution; suddenly the oil companies had become about as popular as anthrax. And in the game of damage limitation a handsome feminine face coupled with an astute financial mind had proved to be powerful assets.

'Grace is scarcely a word which springs to mind when I think of some of your coverage,' she continued, still smiling but with lips which had taken on the suppleness of etched glass. The eyes were like diamond drilling bits. She seemed surrounded by an air of exceptional intensity and turbulence, a battlefield, not a territory to be entered by those of uncertain spirit. 'Your City Editor on the *Herald* is one of the most prejudiced and poorly informed commentators I've ever encountered.'

'Surely an exaggeration.' He was smiling, as he did habitually, with expensively burnished teeth and lips that were a fraction too thick. But the smile never reached his eyes. They remained restless, in constant search of advantage. Di Burston offered none.

'What else can you expect from a man with his background?' she continued.

'You mean the BBC?' Corsa offered, curious as

to where this was leading.

'Before that. Before the BBC.'

Corsa's puzzlement increased. He had no idea where his City Editor's origins lay. The man was simply another of the phalanx of young, aggressive journalists brought in over the last three years to replace the older, perhaps more experienced but endlessly more expensive journalists he'd inherited from his father.

'You're telling me you didn't know that until eight years ago he was a publicity director for Greenpeace?' There was an edge of advantage in her voice. First blood to the girls.

Corsa, unsure of his next line, turned to examine the view from the window. She was inspecting him, and under pressure he became uncomfortably aware of the genetic Corsa tendency for the waist to spread and the hair to retreat. Early stages, in his case, only a couple of pounds and a few strands, but enough to remind himself every time he looked in the mirror that there was so much more still to do, and so little time to do it.

She came to join him, her voice dropping until it had reached a conspiratorial, almost seductive register. 'You call yourself an entrepreneur, a man of free enterprise, yet you throw open your pages to every bunch of tree huggers who can plaster together a press release. Eco-warriors, New Age nonentities, the menopausal middle-class. Anyone who would rather crawl than drive, or choke on coal dust rather than live within a thousand miles of a nuclear power station. They shout, and you give them a front page. The bigger their lie, the better your coverage. It's a war out there. Seems to me you've chosen the wrong side.'

She had drawn near to him now, in the lee of the heavy sash window, close enough that he could smell her. She was playing with him. He didn't object.

'The public has a right to hear both sides,' he offered, grasping at a cliché.

'And businesses like yours and mine have a right to make a living. Do you really think we can all survive by selling air cake and nut burgers?'

'So what are you suggesting should happen?'

'In my case, what I've already decided is going to happen. As from next month I'm pulling all my advertising from your newspapers.' She allowed the news to sink in. 'You know, Mr Corsa, I spend tens of millions of pounds every year on building my company's image. And all I get for it is hate mail—thanks to you and your limp organs.'

'You're taking this very personally,' he replied, his manhood under attack.

'But of course I am,' she breathed softly. 'Just as I took it personally when your City Editor attacked my pay and pension package, even though it's still considerably less than yours. Touch of double standards, do you think?'

Corsa made a mental note to find a new City Editor. The present incumbent was proving all too tiresome. His staff were there to serve their proprietor and paymaster, not to provide an excuse for giving him a public thrashing. He stood in silence, gazing out from the first-floor window across the broad expanse of Horse Guards. The bell above the arch chimed the hour.

'What do you think that would be worth?' she enquired, indicating the great gravelled parade ground which was used once a year to Troop the

34

Colour and for the remainder as a car park for civil servants. 'Move all the bureaucrats and retired admirals out and sell it for development?'

'That's outrageous.'

She shrugged. 'Look at it another way. That's about sixty million pounds.'

Slowly Corsa began to laugh, genuinely and almost with affection. He'd lost every single round of this contest with his elegant new opponent, and somehow he didn't seem to mind. Something was stirring inside, the germ of an idea which unwittingly she had planted and which, although as yet dimly seen, might yet reshape his world. Or at least rebuild his cliff.

'Ms Burston, you leave me breathless. And defenceless. I surrender! But before you put both me and the advertising budget to the sword, do you think we might discuss this further? Over dinner?'

'Are you after my body or my business?'

'Both if I can. Business, if I have to choose.'

'I didn't think newspapers encouraged adultery amongst public figures.'

'One of the few advantages of my lonely job is that, in this dog-eat-dog world, there is a degree of solidarity enjoyed between newspaper proprietors which ensures that our private lives remain, by and large, just that. Private. A sort of mutual non-aggression pact.'

The diamond bits in her eyes had begun to sparkle. 'I think we had better stick to business.'

'That, too, would be my pleasure.'

'At least for the moment . . .'

*   *   *

They had left the police station by the back

entrance. Fewer staring eyes that way. And it brought them out by the ornate cast iron lamp-post, complete with Royal insignia and griffins, to which Goodfellowe had manacled his bike. The lamp-post was still there, directly beneath the busy windows of the police station, but the wheels of the bike were not and neither was the bell nor saddle. The basket had a hole in it the size of a boot. Goodfellowe picked up the remains, cursed, and morosely let them fall once more to the pavement.

Yet again Jya-Yu burst into tears. 'I'm so sorry. My fault.'

'If what you tell me is true, then it patently wasn't your fault. Don't worry. We'll find a way.' He laid a reassuring hand on her shoulder. 'Anyway, where's your uncle? Shouldn't he have come?'

'No, no,' she protested. 'Uncle be busy in shop, on his own now.' She lowered her eyes. 'I do not want to cause trouble for Uncle Zhu.'

'What sort of trouble?'

She would only give a shake of her head.

'Tell me, Jya-Yu, what was in those packets? What was the powder? The police will know soon enough. Was it cocaine?'

'Never. Not cocaine!'

'Then what?'

'Uncle say it was tiger bone.'

'You mean, an aphrodisiac?'

'A gentleman's pick-me-up.'

'That's a controlled substance, isn't it? Was it tiger bone?'

She looked tormented. 'I'm not sure.'

'If it wasn't, you have no problem.'

She shook her head. 'If it is not, and it is known that Uncle is selling tiger bone which is false, it will

36

be even worse. Great loss of face, great loss of business.'

'You're not serious. Tell me it's not true.'

'But of course,' she protested. 'You see, tiger bone is ancient Chinese cure, helps open up gate of life in man. If it makes man feel he is better lover, then he *is* better lover. Like alcohol, but without the, you know, falling-down problem. You would like to try it sometime?'

Goodfellowe managed no more than what he hoped would sound a dignified and noncommittal grunt.

'Simple, Minister Goodfellowe. With such problems, if tiger bone works in man's mind, then it will work for body too.' Her eyes turned to water once more. 'Which is why I cannot allow it to be thought that Uncle Zhu does not sell good powder.'

'You're trying to tell me that the powder may or may not be tiger bone. But even if it isn't, you can't admit it? Because of your uncle's image?' He ran his hand through his hair, ransacking it in frustration.

'You are kind to help, Minister Goodfellowe. I am so sorry to bother you. Now I make sure you get only best tea. Fresh spring tip. From top of bush. No more mix. No more old dust.' Her emotions were unravelling, she was blubbing now and struggling to show her gratitude. Awkwardly she stretched up to kiss his cheek. Goodfellowe's emotions were equally unsettled. A dismembered bike and several missed votes. Seemed his tea supply had scarcely been Guandong Grade One, either.

He would have been laden with considerably more apprehension had he known what was taking place inside the pub on the other side of the road.

The Marquis of Granby was, in the finest traditions of the brewing trade, a watering hole, not dissimilar to the desert wells around which Arabs would tether their camels and retire to the shade in order to contemplate the hidden meanings of life. Since it was frequented by so many off-duty policemen, the Marquis was usually awash with hidden meanings which representatives of the national media were more than happy to divine. No need to put unscrupulous policemen on retainers to keep their press paymasters informed of who and what were passing through the hands of the Custody Sergeant; a few rounds at the bar of the Marquis were usually more than sufficient. Oscar Kutzman was one such desert dweller, a photographer whose duties were to find and photograph distinguished people in less than distinguished circumstances. The job required talent—a sharp eye, an excellent memory for faces, an exceptional lack of scruple, all of which Oscar had in abundance. He was also conscientious in paying for his tip-offs, one of which only last week had led him to the rear door of a Bloomsbury apartment block at precisely the moment a senior Catholic cleric emerged in the embrace of his four-year-old son.

'Oscar, you find my stories that boring?' his guest enquired, aware that Kutzman's attentions had wandered elsewhere.

'A thousand apologies, my dear Inspector,' the photographer responded, fumbling in his bag. 'You recognize that fellow with the Chinese girl?'

'Beneath the lamp-post? Never seen him before.'

'No matter, I've just remembered. I covered his drink-driving case a few months ago at Horseferry Magistrates.'

'Seems safe enough now, with a bike. Or what's left of it.'

'But with a young girl like that? I fancy not—Oh, that's great!' he enthused, grabbing his Nikon and squeezing off several frames as he studied Jya-Yu reaching up to embrace Goodfellowe. Bound to be a bit grainy in the fading evening light, but with a little help from the darkroom and a judicious choice of neg, it could probably be made to look as though she was kissing him full on the lips. An exaggeration, of course, but scarcely a deception, since Oscar had few illusions as to what this public show of affection might mean in a private context. Not a story, not yet, maybe never, but he'd been around long enough to believe in rainy days when, without warning, the great compost heap of life bursts into flower and onto the front page. This was definitely one for the compost heap.

As the couple disappeared down the street, he turned to his colleague and smiled. 'You know, we may just have paid for your next brandy, Inspector.'

For the second time that evening, Goodfellowe had brushed against the world of Freddy Corsa.

CHAPTER TWO

Corsa kept the scribe waiting, wanting from the start to establish the line of authority. Not that there was ever going to be any doubt on the point, but the gesture nevertheless had to be made. Like genuflecting in a church.

The lift by which the journalist had ascended was glass-fronted, in keeping with the contemporary internal design of the converted warehouse, allowing sight of the first three floors of the building in which were housed the offices of the Granite Foundation, the charitable trust created by Papa and, as in all such matters, transformed by his son. The Foundation owned the building and leased the top two penthouse floors to Corsa at a rent so nominal that it would undoubtedly have been regarded as an abuse had the details been known by the Charity Commission, which they weren't. But, Corsa argued, he gave the Foundation the benefit of his financial acumen and public relations expertise which were of inestimable value. Anyway, all the trustees were placemen, hand-picked 'for their proven commitment to good causes,' as Corsa put it, although the only cause most of them had served had been Corsa himself. Still, it ensured that board meetings ran efficiently and without acrimony.

The penthouse, which was used by Corsa as his London home and for which travellers in the lift required a computer access code, was a stunning modernist creation in steel and glass, shod with a suitable acreage of blond wood. It offered breath-snatching views along the river to where the new headquarters of Granite Newspapers nestled in the shadow of Canary Wharf, while its internal privacy and climate were secured by an adept use of computer-controlled sailcloth shades which surrounded the atrium on three sides. As much as Corsa insisted on being regarded as part of the press establishment, in private his tastes were eclectic, nonconformist, some might say even inconsistent. But never his purpose.

The journalist, when he was ushered onto the terracotta terrace overlooking the river, found

40

Corsa surrounded by fig trees and seated on a planter's chair, talking by telephone with his son's headmaster.

'Headmaster, Freddy Junior tells me you're looking to replace your cricket pavilion. I'd like to help. The Granite Foundation is very keen on worthwhile educational projects, I'm sure they would want to look at it very closely.'

He waved for the journalist to take a seat. Tea was already set out on the table beside them. He indicated that the journalist should pour.

'One point, Headmaster. If they are going to provide the bulk of the funds, I'm sure they would like to think that their name might find its way onto the pavilion. Not quite as important as the Sainsbury Wing at the National Gallery, perhaps, but the principle's the same.'

On the river below a pleasure boat commandeered for a school outing to Greenwich sounded its klaxon and the children waved energetically. Corsa waved back.

'Glad you agree. But, now you raise the subject, I'm not sure that something like the Granite Pavilion has quite the right personal touch. Bit too . . . solid for Sussex, wouldn't you say? Maybe we'd better just call it the Corsa Pavilion.' He winked at his guest, allowing him in on the game. 'But there is one other point we need to discuss, if the subject is cricket. To be blunt, I can't see how the school can have a Corsa Cricket Pavilion if it doesn't have a Corsa in the cricket team.'

A silence fell as the headmaster was allowed to ponder the point.

'Does it matter if his average was only eight last year?' Corsa continued. 'Those runs are worth five

41

thousand pounds apiece if you get your new pavilion. It could be up in time for the annual game with Eton. So maybe it will cost you the match for the next two years, but it'll save the team.' He paused, then a glint of satisfaction crossed Corsa's well-tanned face. 'I felt sure you would feel that way about it, Headmaster. Pleasure talking to you.'

He replaced the phone and turned to his guest. 'Don't think I'm a soft touch—it's not as painful as it sounds. Someone is sure to argue that as generous as my offer is, others should be asked to help raise some of the money. To foster team spirit. So I'll end up offering matching sums, pound for pound. Get away with twenty grand, less than two years' school fees.' He declined to remind the visitor that in any event the money would not be coming from his own pocket but from the Foundation.

'So, Mr Gooley, you want to become the *Herald*'s new City Editor.'

The young man slurped his tea in surprise. 'I hadn't realized there was a vacancy.'

'There isn't. Not yet at least, But imagine for a moment that there were. Why should you replace him?'

Gooley, put off-balance, wrestled awkwardly with his thoughts.

'Why should it be you?' Corsa repeated. 'Or is that too difficult a question?'

'It's an unfair question.'

'Yes, but I'm sure you'll manage.'

Gooley returned his cup to the table, clearing the decks. He was a young man whose playing field of emotions stretched between enterprise and ambition, and the ground in between was exceptionally well trodden. He was not the sort of

42

man to pass by an opportunity without launching himself at it with both kneecaps. It won him few friends, although the *Herald*'s City Editor might have counted himself amongst them, yet Gooley was still of an age where friends were little more than an audience.

'OK. I'm a good journalist. I know the City, the institutions, how to gut a balance sheet.'

'So do a hundred others.'

'But far more important, I know men. City men. What drives them.'

'Which is?'

'Hunger.'

'For fame?'

'No, not in the City. Fame is for the gentlemen farther up the river at Westminster. That's why they die poor and disappointed and in their own beds. In the City the hunger is for wealth. Money. Acquisition. And why so many of them die in other people's beds. They're warmer.'

Corsa was amused. 'You sound as if you've made quite a study of this. Something of an academic, are you?'

It was the journalist's turn to show amusement. 'With my accent? You think I got that at university? No, Mr Corsa, I'm Oldham, not Oxford. Rugby league and Tandoori takeaway, that's me, and I'll waste your money on the finest claret only if it gets me a story. There's nothing academic about me, I didn't need books to understand the way the City men think. All I needed was a mirror.'

'So we're all avaricious, are we?'

'Single-minded. Know what we want.'

'And what do you want?'

Gooley looked carefully around the penthouse.

His eyes were not adjusted to appreciate the refinement, the glow of Lalique, the elegant discomfort of the Mackintosh chairs. He was simply lost in the size of it all. 'I'll bet you've got a hundred silk ties in your wardrobe.'

'A hundred and fifty.' Corsa exaggerated, but the younger man's eyes remained direct, disarmingly uncomplicated.

'I want this, or something like this,' he breathed. 'I want to be part of it all. That's why I want the opportunity to be your City Editor.'

Corsa's appreciation of the man grew. 'But along with the opportunities also go responsibilities. To me. I'm very much a hands-on proprietor. The City is my world, too, and I don't like being taken by surprise.'

'Fair enough.'

'I'm talking a two-way relationship. I tell you what I know; you return the confidence. I want to feel it's a team effort.' Corsa was an excellent player of this particular game, flattering his journalists and editors into subservience, leaving their professional integrity intact while ensuring they did precisely what he intended. 'It's not that I want any inside information, you understand, but I need to know you've got your finger on the pulse. That the stories you print are well founded and not simply dreamed up over lunch. Understood?'

'Sharing inside information with you would be highly unethical'—Gooley paused for no more than the beating of a wing—'if you were to use it. I feel sure our relationship would be based on a deep and mutual trust. If I were your City Editor.'

'Good. Very good.' Corsa mused, then made up his mind. The present incumbent could go chew nut

44

buns. 'Very well, Jim, in the spirit of mutual trust let me give you something. News which you will be the first to hear. Not for printing yet, but I want you to think about it. You know that the Granite Group is the best damn company in the newspaper field, but the others are always snapping at us. And when these new European regulations come in there's going to be one hell of a dog fight. So we are going to be as lean and as fit and as mean as possible.'

Corsa made chopping motions with his hand. Gooley nodded.

'It means that our friend the current City Editor isn't going to be the only one asked to fall upon his pen. I'll be announcing more economies, more streamlining.'

'You mean more sackings at mill.' The journalist leaned forward in his seat, alert. 'How many?'

Corsa hesitated. 'Suddenly I feel as though I'm being interrogated.'

'You are. That's my job. How many?'

'Another five per cent.'

Gooley whistled gently. Another five per cent on top of the corporate ransacking Corsa had already undertaken ... He began to shift uncomfortably as though discovering he was squatting on a distress flare, and straightened his tie defensively. Then he drew a deep breath and returned Corsa's stare. 'That's great news. The Granite Group getting itself ready for the challenges of the new millennium. Committed to driving through reform. Focused strategy. Shareholder values ...'

'You are going to do ... very well, Jim,' Corsa enthused, but the eyes were still sharp, restless. 'You realize, of course, that some of the competition will undoubtedly try to twist the news

45

to make it sound like a measure of desperation. Cutbacks caused by overexpansion, imposed by bankers, that sort of unimaginative crap.'

'Which is why we need to get in there first, set the pace, get people thinking straight. Not have some jaundiced hack from *The Times* getting it all wrong and queering the pitch.'

'Very prescient. There's a deal riding on this.'

'How much of a deal?'

Corsa knew he had found the right man. 'A twenty thousand bonus if after the announcement the shares go up rather than down.'

'Does that mean I've got the job?'

'One final question. You're not a vegetarian by any sad chance?'

*   *   *

'Surely it doesn't all come down to money?'

The question seemed almost to startle the older woman, causing her to pause on her tour of inspection in order to give the matter a considered response. 'It's not just the money, Mrs Ashburton, it's the principle of the thing. What sort of father puts his daughter in that sort of position? Especially a father who's supposed to set an example.'

'I feel Sam should be our main concern.'

Miss Flora Rennie, headmistress and custodian of values both moral and material at the Werringham School for Girls, resumed her walk around Top Field with Jenny Ashburton, her arts and crafts teacher. Mrs Ashburton had just come off the hockey field and had a perceptible dampness of the brow. Typical, Miss Rennie thought. Well intentioned but commits just a little too far. A flawed sense of perspective.

46

'My concerns have to be wider than one individual girl. There are others to be considered. As headmistress I am responsible for making sure that the buildings are refurbished and the equipment replaced—and that I'm able to honour your salary cheques. I can't do that if Mr Goodfellowe doesn't honour his cheques.'

'I hadn't realized.'

'This is the fourth term in a row that his term fees have been late,' the headmistress added in a confidential tone frequently adopted in the drawing rooms of her native Edinburgh. 'Last term's fees are still outstanding, let alone this. Goodness knows what he does with his money. And Samantha can be so disruptive. So badly dressed.'

'Do you know what she does, Headmistress? While all the other girls are buying magazines and CDs and new clothes? Sam buys her clothes at The Discount Store, then comes back and cuts out the labels in secret. So no one will know. And in the holidays while most of the other girls dash off to the ski slopes or a sandy beach, she takes a job waiting on table in a local pizzeria.'

It had begun to rain, a gentle drizzle which was excellent for youthful English character but not for greying hair. The headmistress sought shelter beneath the branches of a magnificently gnarled oak. 'You seem to know a great deal about the girl.'

'She's the most talented artist we have in the school. She uses her art to express herself in a way she can't elsewhere. An emotional outlet. I think it's a form of therapy, for all her other problems.'

'I can't have her problems affecting the other girls. Or her father's problems, come to that. Do they get on—Samantha and her father?'

'I think it's difficult. He's away so much of the time. And no mother . . .'

'Yes, I suppose we should have known what we were letting ourselves in for when she arrived.' She frowned in the direction of a group of girls who chirruped 'Good afternoon, Headmistress,' and ran off giggling.

'Sam's very talented,' Mrs Ashburton insisted, trying to steer the conversation onto more positive grounds. 'And also very well intentioned. I know she gets into scrapes with some of the other girls, but that's no more than frustration. Look at her other side. The charity fashion show, for example. It was her idea and she's doing most of the organization. Beneath those dark eyes there's a huge heart.'

'It's those dark eyes that will get her into trouble, mark my words. I get reports of the sort of boys she sees in her town time.' Miss Rennie pulled her cardigan defensively about her bosom. 'We are responsible for bringing our young ladies into contact with the finer values in life, not the sort of boys whose concept of culture is to spend their evenings bragging through their beer about under-age conquests.' Her voice carried the hint of November wind blowing through the girders of the Forth Bridge.

'She's sixteen,' the arts mistress responded in mitigation. 'Anyway, I think she's very much her own woman. Not easily led.'

Too committed, Miss Rennie reflected once more upon her colleague. A pity. Well intentioned, a gifted teacher. But too committed. It didn't do, not with young girls, who required above all a tight rein. The headmistress sighed; she had already spent more than enough of her day worrying about one problem child, she had other responsibilities to attend to. The hot-water system had broken down yet again; it might require replacing, at whatever cost. 'The fees must be paid,' the headmistress responded, 'I owe it to the other girls. Otherwise— well, perhaps Mr Goodfellowe's neglect will relieve us of any further responsibility in this matter.' And with that she strode purposefully in the direction of the boiler room.

*   *   *

Late-night votes. Endless hours of tedium during which the parliamentary bars remained open while parliamentary minds grew ever more fixedly shut. Get through the business, don't delay, don't digress. Just march and vote. Then, at last, it was over and the exhausted representatives of the people could be released into the custody of the community. Goodfellowe, without wheels, had been forced to join the queue of numbed men and women who waited for taxis, and it was well after one before he clambered up the narrow stone stairs to reach his studio flat overlooking Gerrard Street. The place was pleasant enough, as small flats go, nestling in the eaves of the old Regency house with a mezzanine platform for his bed and a pine-clad ceiling that stretched up into the loft space. Once, a lifetime ago, he had lived in Holland Park. In those days he'd been able to afford a little style and a lot of stucco, now all he had was his parliamentary allowance for second homes which had to cover everything: rent, heating, taxes, insurance, the lot. Not that the heating bills were heavy, not with the meat kitchen on the floor below, where they hung the *char-sui* and duck on long rows of curing racks,

49

forcing the warmth and their sweet-sour aroma upwards. It would make summer a struggle. But the location was convenient and he needed the distraction of something different, somewhere that bustled well into the night and helped fill all those sleepless hours. Chinatown never slept, not until dawn.

They had regarded him with some suspicion when he moved in, the *gweilo* who had come to intrude upon the different families and clans that made up the Chinese community, but he'd made a point in his first week of going to see Madame Tang at her coffee shop and introducing himself, and slowly the word had got round. Minister Goodfellowe, a man who moved in circles of power, a man of contacts, a neighbour who might one day be useful. The Chinese understood that. They insisted on giving him a title and he had never been able to convince them that he was no longer a public figure of any eminence although, in truth, he hadn't tried too hard. It still hurt.

He had just kicked off his shoes and begun brewing a pot of light green tea when there came a persistent buzzing from the intercom. 'Minister Goodfellowe! Minister Goodfellowe!' He was tired like a lashed horse but almost welcomed the intrusion, his emotions still restless, his bed as always cold. The buzzer sounded again. He looked around for his shoes then decided he couldn't be bothered, relishing the cool stone stairs as he padded down two flights in his socks.

He opened the tall door to find Jya-Yu and Uncle Zhu standing on the step, silhouetted against the green neon of the Jade Palace across the street. Uncle Zhu was wearing a suit, carefully buttoned,

50

and his hair was slicked down against his scalp. Jya-Yu was smiling nervously. 'Sorry, very late. We wait until we see your light.'

'Waiting all night? What for? Not more trouble?' he asked, exhaustion leaving his words sharp with accusation.

Immediately he felt a louse as he noticed she was holding a plate on which were six assorted Chinese honey buns. 'Cakes from cousin's bakery. For you, Minister Goodfellowe. For thanks.' She held the plate forward.

A noise whose origins lay somewhere deep within Uncle Zhu's throat began. To Goodfellowe it was utterly incomprehensible but the Chinaman was also holding something, offering it up. Goodfellowe found himself being presented with a construction of chrome and cables and rubber which, on inspection, transformed itself into a lightweight collapsible bike.

Uncle Zhu's head was bobbing effusively.

'Also for thanks, Minister Goodfellowe,' Jya-Yu chirped.

'This is ... so unexpected. Most kind,' Goodfellowe responded, his tired judgement juggling with the implications. He was growing accustomed to the mercantile Chinese mind. 'But how much will this cost?'

'No cost. For thanks. To replace old one.'

The bike was surprisingly lightweight, he could hold it in one hand. 'It would be very useful,' he conceded, 'but I can't accept something so valuable. It could get me into trouble.'

He tried to offer back the bike, but Uncle Zhu refused and began an animated exchange with his niece.

'Uncle Zhu says he get bike in payment from poor customer. Uncle Zhu not ride bike. You take it, no problem.'

'I think I would like such a bike,' Goodfellowe responded, turning the neatly folded package over in appreciation, 'but I couldn't accept it as a gift.' He took a deep breath. 'How much does your uncle think it's worth.' He dug into his pocket and came out clutching a solitary twenty-pound note.

Uncle Zhu's brow darkened. Goodfellowe realized he had committed a mortal offence by offering him money. 'You must understand,' he stammered, 'a politician can get into great trouble for accepting gifts. People have such suspicious minds. Dammit, they'll even do away with Christmas next.' He looked wistfully at the machine. It would be—would have been—the perfect answer, yet it seemed he must lose the wheels just as he had caused Uncle Zhu to lose face.

Suddenly Jya-Yu brightened. 'Better way,' she exclaimed, 'You not take the bike, Minister Goodfellowe. You borrow it instead. Long term. And if Uncle Zhu ever need it, he take it back.' Her face lit in mischief. 'But you understand, his legs very short. I don't think he can reach pedals. So you take care of it until Uncle Zhu's legs grow.'

They both laughed, while the Chinaman stood immobile and uncomprehending. Goodfellowe, his objections overwhelmed by her advice and perhaps just a hint of avarice, gave what he hoped was a dignified bow and accepted the bicycle and the plate. Zhu smiled in relief and immediately turned away, Jya-Yu scurrying after him.

'Just as long as it didn't fall off the back of a lorry,' Goodfellowe admonished as they retreated.

'Oh, no, Minister Goodfellowe. It not even touch the ground. Look, no dents.'

And they were gone, leaving Goodfellowe clutching six sticky buns and a collapsible bike.

*   *   *

'You look like a train-spotter.' Mickey Ross, Goodfellowe's secretary at the House of Commons, was nothing if not direct. She was also mid-twenties, vivacious, Jewish, formidably competent and possessor of a biting wit delivered with a lingering trace of Estuary English which marked her out as being not quite like the rest.

On this occasion no one could argue that she was being less than objective. She had walked in to find Goodfellowe standing in his parliamentary office, his trousers still confined within bicycle clips, his shoes hurled to the far side of the room and a raw toe poking through a new hole in his sock.

'New shoes. A waste of money,' he muttered.

'The old ones were practically walking on their own,' she scolded.

'Anyway,' he riposted, 'aren't you wearing the same clothes as yesterday? Didn't you get home last night?'

'I got waylaid,' she mumbled, losing herself within the pile of morning post she was carrying.

'With Justin?'

'No. Not with Justin,' she replied, sounding as if her fiancé's name had suddenly become a complicated foreign language.

'Mickey,' he lectured, 'I thought you said you have principles.'

It was a mistake, he should have known better. She only knew one means of defence, which was

53

onslaught.

'I do have my principles and I had my principles last night, too. It's just that I lost them.'

'Where?'

She pouted. 'In the hotel lift on the way up to his room. I left them in a bag. A very small bag. Don't worry. I found them again this morning on the way down.' And with that she dumped the mountain of morning mail on his desk. It overflowed like an exploding volcano onto the floor, and he bent down to retrieve it with a groan. 'And Beryl has just called,' she added, with bite. 'The reception on Friday week starts at seven prompt and I'm to remind you once more that it's one of the biggest fund-raising bashes of the year.'

His groans grew more passionate. Beryl Hailstone was the chair-monster of his local party in Marshwood. A woman of similar age to Goodfellowe, she had once made a pass at him, had been rejected in instinctive and unthinking horror, and had never forgiven.

It seemed unlikely that this was to be Goodfellowe's day, for on top of the pile of correspondence he had retrieved from the floor was a letter from his bank manager. The letters from his bank were getting shorter and more peremptory in the months since the old manager had been forced to make way for a new, younger model. The personal touch and understanding had gone, and in its place Goodfellowe had found only codes of financial conduct set by computer and implemented by automatons who sounded on the telephone as though they should be selling fruit from a barrow in Brewer Street.

'Sorry,' Mickey offered, her concern genuine.

54

She was always the first to know. She was the one who sorted out the rental for the fax machine and computer, booked his train tickets, picked up his dry cleaning, took care of so many corners of his private life and knew often before he did when the autumn of his accounting had turned to harshest winter. Like now.

He shivered. 'Do you find you can never sleep?'

'Sadly not. Men simply don't have the stamina.' She paused, noticing the shadows of exhaustion beneath his eyes. 'But some-thing's troubling you, Tom.'

'I had another set-to with Sammy.' His tone was quiet, stripped of all pretension.

'What was it this time?'

'The usual. She wanted money for some charitable fashion show she's putting on at school. I said something . . . well, she caught me at the wrong moment, I suppose. So she stormed off without any money, I was left without any invitation and I don't even know when I'm going to see her again. My own daughter. Added to that I got a bollocking last night from the Chief Whip for missing several votes. He was particularly foul. I think I've decided I hate the entire bloody world. Or is it simply that they hate me?'

With a sense of bitter purpose he drew back his desk drawer. Reaching within, his fingers closed around a feather-flighted dart. He measured the weight in his hand, smoothing its feathers, stroking it as though like a weapon of mercy it might relieve him of all his cares. Then he hurled it in the direction of a notice board on the opposite wall on which was hung a collage of images already peppered with holes. A photograph of Beryl

Hailstone. And one of the Chief Whip. The letter of introduction from his new bank manager. His Liberal opponent's manifesto from the last election. A photocopy of an uncomplimentary piece by a *Guardian* sketchwriter. And other pieces. The bill for his final car service just before he sold it. A final demand. The label from a bad bottle of Australian Shiraz which had promised undertones of blackcurrant but instead had suggested beetles. Items from his life brought together by only one strand of logic, the fact that he loathed them.

The dart missed completely and stuck fast in the panelling above. He'd failed again.

'Bugger it. I can't even be miserable any more.'

Mickey began to laugh, playing with his self-pity, challenging him to turn his frustration on her, to find an outlet and let it pass. Clouds of anger flooded across his eyes, warning of the approaching storm.

'You're a witch.'

'You're right. And I shall probably burn. But in the meantime,' she said, sitting primly at the chair in front of his desk and taking out her notepad, 'let's see if we can't cast a spell on a few others. Like the bank manager,' she announced, ticking him off a list. 'He's young, bound to be pathetically impressionable. Invite him to lunch on the Terrace. For the price of a plate of subsidized sausage and a half-decent bottle of wine you'll be able to tie up your overdraft for months. You can invite me too. I'll be sweet to him, and you know I'm irresistible.'

'You are incorrigible.' He meant it as an ill-tempered accusation. 'How do you have the nerve to slink out of hotels looking guilty?'

'I don't. What's the point in slinking out looking

guilty when you can stride out and let everyone know you've had a good time?' Ignoring his scowl, she returned to her list. 'Darling Beryl will be quite content if you're on time and wearing trousers and are nice to the right guests. I'll type you out a list.'

'If God is merciful I shall die first.'

'So long as you're wearing trousers, that's fine.' She put the notepad aside. 'Then there's Sam.'

He sucked in a lungful of air and released it, his body shaking, as if he were trying to expel all the twisted emotion within and start afresh. 'I'm a father, a replacement mother, a social worker to seventy thousand constituents and common bankrupt, all at the same time. No wonder I make such a mess of everything.'

'You're not bankrupt yet.' She was determined not to give his self-pity office space. 'And none of it is Sam's fault.'

'You think I don't know that?'

'Of course you do. But does she?'

'I take the point. I hadn't realized you threw in your services as an agony aunt, too.'

'I'm Jewish and I'm still breathing. What do you expect?'

'I long ago learned to stop expecting anything,' he said, meaning it.

'Look, you're supposed to be the grown-up one. So you haven't got an invitation to the fashion show. You think she's going to issue one in gold-block lettering and send a chauffeur-driven car? Go. Surprise her. If you can't find the right words, at least show her that she's more important than your bank manager or bloody Beryl or any number of your complaining constituents. Just be there for her.'

A chink of light appeared through the storm clouds. 'OK,' he nodded. 'Put it in the diary, will you.'

'I already have.'

'For pity's sake, won't you let me win one round?'

'For your sake, not if I can help it.'

He stood up abruptly. 'That's it. I've had enough. I'm going to leave you to handle all the post today on your own. I'm going off to broaden my mind.'

'Where, in case Downing Street or the Vatican should ask?'

'You can tell them I'm going for a therapeutic Chinese massage. With one of Jya-Yu's prolific tribe of cousins, Dr Lin. She's set me up with some free sessions.'

'This isn't something menopausal, is it?'

'If it is,' he said, searching for his shoes, 'I intend to enjoy it.'

He was halfway through the door when he turned with an after-thought. 'Tell me, what would you do if you discovered that Justin had—how can I put it delicately?—spent the night in a hotel room?'

She stretched out a leg, casually examining her tights, as though deeply unconcerned. 'I'd have him for sausage stuffing, little bits and all.'

'Do I detect the odious whiff of double standards?'

'Not a bit. A man doesn't get filleted for what he's done, but for getting caught. I'd remember that, if I were you, while you're having your Chinese massage.'

*   *   *

Corsa's relationship with women benefited from two principal advantages—three, if one remembered his ability as a press proprietor to keep the dogs at bay. The first was his sense of physical control—the green-black eyes, the hand movements, the careful tailoring, even the deliberate way he walked, not hurrying as some shorter men might. Others waited for him. His second advantage was a wife who had known even before they had married that she would have to share him, and not solely with the Granite. But besides the Granite, she comforted herself, there could be no other mistress of importance. And there never had been. Sex for Corsa was simply another aspect of power, to be exercised and indulged over as broad a landscape as possible, particularly with wives of important men, the sort of St James's club men who could neither hide their disdain nor satisfy their brides. An empire of English cuckolds, as outdated as the ugly oil paintings that hung in their drawing rooms. The saving grace in Corsa as far as most women were concerned was that they knew exactly what they were going to get—a physical intensity which he would lavish on them in the most elegant of surroundings, for a while, so long as business did not intervene. 'A hand on my chest and an eye on his watch,' as one of his lady acquaintances had remarked, but not in complaint. The eyes hovered restlessly, trembling, like the tip of a hawk's wing, but the smile at the corner of his mouth was constant and unwavering. So was the passion. Irresistible, for some. Then, with an insouciant wave of farewell, it would be over.

Diane Burston, however, was a different matter. Since he had met her at Downing Street his mind had been tossing on an ocean. Every wave lifted his spirits, allowing him a tantalizing glimpse of what might be the way ahead, a way to survive. Then he would be cast down, the vision dashed, and he would be surrounded by hideous, violent seas that threatened to overwhelm him and smash him on the rocks. The bankers had been more difficult than he'd expected, solicitous as ever but posing more questions and requesting more paper, which on this occasion it seemed they were intent on reading. They had begun to feel the pressure, too, and like all bankers were keen on passing that burden onwards. He'd found himself struggling, even at one stage leaning in argument on their long relationship and friendship. That's when he knew he was in deep water, for friendship didn't travel far down Lombard Street.

And he had found his thoughts straying all the more frequently to the oil executive. Not to her body, as delightfully preserved and presented as it was, but to who she was, and what she was. As the seas grew steadily rougher they threw him higher still and for fleeting moments he was finding a clearer sight of salvation, and such was Corsa's natural self-confidence that only rarely did he allow himself to think that he might not reach it, however distant and difficult the goal might seem. Yet he knew it would not be possible without Diane Burston, and others like her.

He'd arranged supper at Le Caprice, and Mayfair at that time of night was choked. He was driving himself—the chauffeur already knew more than enough without needing to know where Corsa might be spending the night—and he'd been cruising for ten minutes. He'd found not a single free parking space around the streets and already two clamping teams were patrolling, falling like flies upon a feast. The NCP right next to the restaurant had space but parting with money was tantamount to admitting defeat. Parking in London was war, and Corsa refused simply to quit the battlefield. Maybe it was meanness, perhaps it was the growing tension or the meeting with the bankers that reminded him that every penny might yet count— he put it down to his Neapolitan instinct, which abhorred being told what he could or could not do, and drove round one last time.

He'd passed the ancient mini-Honda three times already. A bright yellow anti-nuclear sticker shone out from the back window, and there was a sign warning of babies on board. It was also so outrageously parked that it took up space which could have accommodated two large saloons. Selfish bitch. And it was getting late. Time to put up or push off. *Fa fan culo*. This time he did not pass by, but eased his car up against the rear bumper of the Honda until he felt the gentlest of rocking motions to indicate they were in contact. Several tons touching tin. Then he gave it a little more gas, scarcely more than a kiss of encouragement. He was surprised how easily the Honda shifted, almost four feet. It bounced along the kerb, scraping the wheel trim, but a woman driver would scarcely notice the difference. And space had been created, he was in. A minor victory. And an omen, he hoped.

The restaurant was crowded—tonight's highlights were a celebrating playwright, the moment's slickest fashion photographer, a leading libel lawyer whose hennaed hair was betrayed beneath the overhead lights. They all paused as Diane Burston walked in, men and women alike, wondering who she was meeting, where she bought her clothes, envying the maître d' as she let her coat slip from her shoulders and into his hands. She bore that quality in a woman which goes beyond beauty and suggests control, a reversal of the primeval rule that men hunted and women waited helpless within the cave for the hunter's return, the type of woman for whom a man's first reaction is a buckling at the knees rather than any stirring of loins.

'Good evening, Mr Corsa. Hope I haven't kept you waiting.' Which she had, deliberately. He didn't mind, not with the eyes of every man in the restaurant upon him.

They busied themselves with the functions of ordering. She cast her eyes over the menu for no more than a few seconds but knew precisely what she wanted. He had planned for champagne but everything about her suggested this was a woman of substance rather than froth; he ordered a vintage Montrachet.

'I was intrigued by your invitation, Mr Corsa . . .'

'Freddy. Please. And I wanted first and foremost to apologize. I've read again some of the coverage the *Herald* has given you. I didn't care for it. I'm sorry.'

'A letter of regret would have been sufficient.'

'No it wouldn't. I mean what I say. The *Herald* was wrong.'

'That's kind of you to say so. Sadly, of course, the damage has already been done.'

The waiter had finished laying out fresh cutlery, fish for her, *côte de boeuf* for him. Corsa picked up the steak knife, placing his thumb to the blade in the half-light as though checking its capacity to do damage.

'I've got rid of the City Editor.'

'Goodness,' she replied, 'what you men will do in pursuit of an advertising contract.'

'Oh, no. Don't misunderstand. This has nothing to do with your cancelled advertising. I'm in pursuit of something much bigger. And to avoid any confusion, as much as I appreciate your coming here this evening in a manner which is more than capable of starting a Cabinet crisis, I am not talking about trying to get into your bed.'

'Then I have failed,' she mocked. 'When I talk business with men who don't want to get into my bed I find I've lost half my advantage. Men are such little boys at heart. They seem incapable of concentrating on both coitus and contracts at the same time.'

'I didn't say I don't want to get into your bed. But that's not the point of this evening's discussion. And I'm a very grown-up boy.'

They paused as the waiter arrived with sparkling water. The fresh ice cracked and spat in the glass.

'You told me when we met at Downing Street that your corporate image is everything.'

'True.'

'Then why don't you start taking it seriously?'

She refused to rise to his bait. 'I spend tens of millions of pounds on it, as you know. Some I used to spend with you.'

'On advertising, yes, but it's an art form that has had its day. You've got to grow far more sophisticated. At least as sophisticated as your enemies.'

'Enemies?'

'You go into battle every day with eco-warriors

63

who are trying to kill you. One oil spill, one rusting drilling platform being towed around the North Sea in search of a burial place, a baby seal which dies on a beach from unknown causes—any event like that, so long as it happens in front of a camera, and all the millions you spend on your image as a warm and caring oil company become about as effective as confetti in a Force Nine gale.'

'Much the same can be said when newspapers like yours scurrilously and inaccurately accuse me of greed for getting a pay increase.' She intended to wound but with Corsa it had no more effect than a soup spoon lobbed at a charging rhino.

'Precisely! But have you ever asked yourself why you get such a hard time in the media? You've got to remember that even if journalists aren't bone idle they're all up against tight deadlines. We need news in a hurry. So the pressure groups lay a feast before us—videos, apocalyptic quotes, regular updates, even free propaganda T-shirts to wear in the garden at weekends. If we want a picture, they lay on one of their helicopters to get us the best shot.' The bottom half of his face had grown animated, yet the eyes remained hard as coal. 'D'you know the last thing they do before they chain themselves to trees or cut holes in the fence around a nuclear power station? They check to make sure that the batteries on their mobile phones are fully charged.'

'But those bloody people make it up as they go along. They lie.'

Her lips had tightened, he was getting to her. He raised a patronizing eyebrow. It was his turn to mock.

'They lie!' she repeated. 'Doesn't that matter to the press?' Her nostrils flared in protest, then slowly subsided. 'Forgive me. I'm not usually naive.'

He leaned forward tenaciously, both hands gripping the table. 'You told me yourself that it's a war out there. And how do you fight it? Maybe you call a meeting of some planning committee, prepare a holding statement, discuss what, if anything, you dare to say. By which time it's already too late. As far as the media are concerned you give us nothing but yesterday's sardines wrapped in slices of stale bread.'

She paused, running her finger around the rim of her wine glass, listening to the mournful note.

'Forget about advertising,' he insisted. 'It's hard news you need to worry about. Play the enemy at their own game. Get your retaliation in first. Screw 'em!'

The wine waiter had returned with the Burgundy. Grand Cru. Exceptional. From a chateau that nestled against the rising hills outside Puligny which the waiter knew and much loved. He handled the bottle with almost phallic respect, presenting it formally, running his fingers gently down its shaft, demanding both their attention and admiration. Then he produced a corkscrew, sheathed it around the long neck and twisted and turned and screwed until the arms of the corkscrew seemed to rise gently above its head in a gesture of feminine surrender. The cork came out with a sigh of silk sheets. It was a wonderful performance, a gesture so rich in overtones that Corsa shivered in appreciation, as he did with all good business. She'd noticed too.

She raised her glass. 'I'll drink to that.' She stared directly at him across glasses filled with fine, honeyed liquid. 'It sounds, Freddy, as though you

65

want to lend me your front page.'

'Oh, no,' he smiled, 'not lend. I've something much better in mind for you.'

* * *

Goodfellowe had fallen for Werringham School as soon as he had driven into the grounds on his first visit—and well before he had discovered the cost. By that time it had been too late, his heart was committed, and the expense was simply another part of life that his thought processes struggled desperately to cordon off and ignore. The school was set in thirty acres nestling in the cupped hand of the Somerset uplands as they pushed towards the River Exe. That first time, as he had driven along the school drive—when he still had a licence to drive—there had been azalea and maple and pleached limes. Buzzards rested in the huge cypress trees before gliding gracefully up on the thermals that gathered in the bowl of the hills. If it couldn't be home for Sam, it was as close as she was likely to get in any institution. Warm and protecting. But it could never be home.

The day of the fashion show he arrived unannounced after a slow train journey from Waterloo. He had hoped to remain inconspicuous, the reminder about term fees still burning in his pocket, but no sooner had he reached the porch of the old sandstone manor house which formed the centre of Werringham than he was intercepted by a regional television crew. 'Bright girl, your daughter,' the female interviewer smiled as they stood him in front of the camera. 'Badgered us into sending a crew. Made us feel that if we refused we'd be responsible for famine throughout the whole of central Africa. Didn't tell us you were coming, though.'

And he had said a few words about the school and the girls and the example that the young could give us all. Then he had run straight into Miss Rennie.

'An unexpected pleasure, Mr Goodfellowe,' she acknowledged, looking him sternly in the eye. She had the sort of Presbyterian stare which seemed to go straight through to his bank balance. 'I hope you'll have a chance to linger after the fashion show. I would welcome the chance of a quiet conversation.'

'I'm afraid I must be back in Westminster for seven. A vote.'

'A pity. We need to talk. It's not ideal but ... perhaps we could sit together during the show. The opportunity for a few words, at least.'

There had been no question of a refusal and, much out of sorts, Goodfellowe had gone in search of Samantha. But it was not to be. Parents were not welcomed in changing rooms where twenty teenage girls were in a state of considerable excitement and undress. Instead he spent a few minutes strolling around corridors which smelt of lunch and wood polish, remembering his own school days. The memories stirred once more, making him grow angry, stubborn. Even after all these years he could still feel the arrows of teenage torment, buried in him up to their feathers. The humiliation of being forced to pack, to leave in the middle of term through no fault of his own, yet in disgrace. The taunts of his fellow schoolboys who didn't understand, and his wretched inability to respond because he didn't understand either. He didn't

67

understand why his father had let him down, had let them all down, and why the name of Goodfellowe had become something which excited only derision. That had been the reason he'd gone into public life, to restore the name of Goodfellowe. And that was also why he could never let Samantha down in the same way, no matter what the cost.

He squeezed in beside Miss Rennie onto one of the familiar coccyx-crushing chairs which breed in the storage rooms of every place of learning. She was sitting ramrod straight, as though on guard. A no-nonsense pose. He decided not to flannel.

'Miss Rennie,' he muttered, 'thank you for your patience, but I think you'd like to know that I'm seeing my bank manager next week. I feel sure the problem with the fees will be resolved then.'

'That is kind,' she nodded thoughtfully, staring ahead. 'Kind. It's been worrying.'

'There's no need for you to worry, Headmistress.'

'Oh, but I do, Mr Goodfellowe, I don't wish to be impertinent, but—well, this isn't the first time. I've often wondered why you don't do what I understand many other politicians do and take on a consultancy, perhaps, some outside interest which would help you with the school fees. Relieve the pressure.'

He sighed. 'Perhaps you're right. I do have one consultancy as it happens, with the CPF .'

Miss Rennie raised an eyebrow.

'The Caravan Park Owners' Federation.'

The eyebrow, a tiny tangle of heather, rose still further.

'But I've always thought,' he continued, 'that— how can I put it without sounding too pompous?— the job of an MP is in the House of Commons and his constituency. Not around boardrooms and lobby groups.'

'But term after term, Mr Goodfellowe. And we all share in your pain, truly we do.'

He doubted that, but decided this was not the time to argue the point. 'I'll think about it. I promise. But I must remind you. Not a word to Samantha. I don't want her to worry.'

'Mr Goodfellowe, I shall breathe not a word but it would surprise me if she didn't have some grasp of the situation.' He could see the genuine concern in her grey eyes. 'Samantha is a very talented and resourceful girl. We would be sorry to see her go . . .'

'I trust there's no question of that, Headmistress. As I said, next week . . .'

'It's not entirely a matter of money, Mr Goodfellowe, but what is best for Samantha. To be honest, in spite of the excellent work of which she is capable and her initiative in organizing the fashion show, she doesn't seem happy here at Werringham. Surely you must have noticed?'

'Well, I . . . hadn't noticed, to be honest. She's going through a phase, of course. But most teenagers do.'

'She's a lonely girl, Mr Goodfellowe, with few friends.'

'Oh,' he responded, deflated. 'I suppose it doesn't always help having a politician as a father. She must get ribbed about that. My fault.'

'It's more than that. She doesn't want to fit in. I've never been sure she ever wanted to come to Werringham.'

'It's true that she was very happy at her old school. But after her mother . . . well, I'm in London all through the week. It had to be boarding school. There was no other choice.'

'I'm not unsympathetic, you understand, but I must bear in mind what is best for Samantha. She has considerable ability, of that there's no doubt, and her artistic skills are exemplary, but at times she seems to be easily distracted. Even stubborn. She flatly refuses to participate with the other girls at team sports. Goes off on her own during her town time—I suspect going to places I would regard as altogether undesirable. And with older boys.'

'What are you suggesting about Sammy?' Lurid pictures were beginning to float across the parental mind.

'Nothing. I am merely expressing concerns. Samantha is unhappy. And, I fear, not altogether the best of examples to the other girls. I have them to consider, too.'

The conversation had been blown into poorly charted waters. Suddenly he found himself wishing for a return to the more familiar if equally hazardous ground of his personal finances but, before he could respond, a splash of Live Aid music had showered upon them and, through a fog of dry ice, the fashion show had begun. Down a catwalk built from the centre of the stage emerged a parade which combined exuberance, propaganda, Viyella and vivid colours, hats, sequins, satin, yards of youthful thigh and a measure of naive taste.

Then there was Sammy.

He could not stifle a sharp intake of breath. The clothes themselves, designed by Samantha and made up by other more skilled seamstresses, consisted of carefully flared trousers which began three inches below her navel and had laces down the thigh. Her shoes had huge heels which made his blistered feet weep in sympathy. Three inches above the navel began a crop-top which outlined a figure that had become undeniably soft and feminine. At that moment and for the first time he realized that his little girl, so innocent in school uniform and shapeless jeans and jumpers, was growing up all too fast. It made her unfamiliar; he was suddenly afraid he was losing her. A large waistcoat of patchwork velvet finished off the clothes. Above, around her neck, was a gap where her mother's locket might have been.

So far, none of this was exceptional apart from the effervescence and simple sense which had gone into the effect. What caused further intakes of breath from all around—not just from himself but most noticeably from Miss Rennie—were the deeply personal accessories. The spikes of brilliant orange where before had been soft auburn hair. Purple lips. The bared left shoulder from which sprouted the tattoo of a rose in bloom. And another gap, between halter and hipsters, where a gilded chain encircled her hips and threaded up to an all too obvious gold ring that had been pierced straight through the flesh of her navel.

The cameras were beside her now, following her confident strides up and down the catwalk. She appeared heedless of the stir of unease from parents in the audience, perhaps even relishing it. Yet in the farther recesses of the hall something else stirred. Approval and applause began to break through like spring daffodils, cautiously at first, then more abundantly and with greater confidence until they had spread inexorably through the carefully planted rows of chairs and were swirling

71

around the foot of the stage. The cameras turned on the audience, which began to respond, elders matching the enthusiasm of their offspring.

But not Goodfellowe. He remained immune to the infection sweeping through the hall. This was his little girl, barely out of braces and bobby socks. Or was it? She seemed strangely unfamiliar, unknown to him. 'What on earth do you call that . . . that . . .' —words failed—'grunge?'

'You're out of date, Mr Goodfellowe. That's definitely post-grunge,' Miss Rennie offered without a trace of humour, but joining in the applause as the cameras panned towards her. It was the only way. Apparent enthusiasm. The honour of the school was at stake.

*   *   *

Cameras appeared to be everywhere that week.

It was Friday, mid-afternoon, and Goodfellowe was driving—more correctly being driven—back to Marshwood. One of the few blessings of being stripped of his licence was that the Member for the neighbouring constituency, Lionel Lillicrap, was a colleague of long standing and had been more than willing to help with lifts. In fact, Lionel was the only blessing which arose from that sorry episode—apart from the fact that he could drink without damnation for at least another eight months.

Goodfellowe and Lillicrap had entered the House together, twelve years earlier, sharing in the early days both ambition and a Commons office, yet it had been Goodfellowe on whose brow the laurels of early promotion had fallen. Indeed, he had been the coming man. He was granted grudging respect by his civil servants and, more grudgingly still, by his colleagues, and it was agreed by consensus that Goodfellowe had far to go. Cabinet Ministers engaged in backstairs battle in order to secure his services as their Number Two, regarding him as a rock in the stormy legislative night. They reserved for Goodfellowe the highest parliamentary accolade, that he was 'a safe pair of hands'. As he hacked his path through the Ministerial jungle his diary had struggled to fit in days in Davos and weekends in Washington. An invitation to sit around the brown-baize Cabinet table seemed an inevitable next step.

It had been the trip of a lifetime and as companion on that trip he had taken Lillicrap as his PPS. Rising Ministers are allowed Parliamentary Private Secretaries, ambitious men and women who are willing to engage in the most menial of tasks around the House on behalf of their masters, pouring drinks, running errands, taking in dirty parliamentary laundry, carrying their Minister's papers in the hope that one day they will be able to carry such papers in their own right. One foot on the ladder, yet with the other still stuck in the cloying mud of the backbenches. If it had been innately irksome for Lillicrap to watch his contemporary speed ahead of him, at least he was grateful for the opportunity to follow, and he took reassurance from the fact that he was fully five years younger than Goodfellowe—he had time on his side.

And time within the Palace of Westminster has an uncanny ability to produce the perverse. Goodfellowe's resignation in order to attend to his pressing family problems generated considerable sympathy, but political careers are built on today's

73

ambition rather than yesterday's sorrow. The rising star had turned to burnt-out meteorite and cold, cracked rock. Now Lillicrap was in the ascendant, a Government Whip—'a rack master,' as Goodfellowe had once observed, 'with access to all the instruments of parliamentary torture.' 'Not at all,' Lillicrap had countered with a smile, 'merely a parliamentary social worker, a shoulder for troubled colleagues to cry on.'

And Lillicrap had honoured the claim. It was he who had helped with the loan to keep Goodfellowe's battered head above water, and also with the CPF consultancy through which he intended to pay it off. A Whip's work, but also the service of a colleague and friend.

'What are the chances of finding another consultancy, Lionel, d'you suppose?' Goodfellowe enquired. They had just passed the tiny aerodrome at Fyfield on the A303 and were about to enter the stretch of single-lane carriageway that gets choked on a Friday afternoon unless you manage, as they had, to make an early start.

'Thought you'd been a bit quiet. Broody. Want another, do you? But I thought you hated having to accept the last one?'

'Needs must. I'm still in the middle of a war zone and getting shot at from all sides. You're right, I dislike the idea intensely. But I have Sammy to think of. Anyway,' he added, attempting to make light of it, 'I may have to buy myself a new bike.'

'What happened to Old Beryl?' Goodfellowe had once complained of how the saddle of his bike constantly bit into him. Lillicrap had promptly named the beast after the other main rectal discomfort in Goodfellowe's life.

74

'Got demolished. Outside Charing Cross police station. It'll play hell with the crime figures.'

'Something for which I hope you'll be apologizing personally to the Home Secretary. But in any event I suppose we'll have to help. Can't have you failing to get to the House. Missing any more votes.'

'Ouch.'

'Sorry. Chief Whip's told me to rub it in a little. A lot, actually.' Lillicrap was juggling the steering wheel with his knees while opening a bag of Liquorice Allsorts at sixty.

'Thank him for me.'

'If you want our help with another consultancy, that practically puts you on the payroll, old chum.'

'I wouldn't sell my soul for a palace, Lionel, yet you expect me to sell it for a caravan park?' Goodfellowe sounded prickly. He declined the proffered Berty Bassett.

'Look, there's a way out of all this. Something which would help both you and me, get you back into everyone's good books. You know we've got the new Press Bill coming down from the Lords any day. It's Heritage Department fodder so I'm the lucky Whip in charge of it. I want you on the Standing Committee. Helping me out.'

'You mean doing your donkey work.' Goodfellowe hoped he didn't sound churlish. Being pushed around, however tactfully, by his former PPS would take a little getting used to. Their relationship had been turned on its head and he had his pride. In any event, slogging away on the Standing Committee, examining the entrails of the Press Bill inch by mucky inch, failed to fill him with any enthusiasm.

'It's not likely to be too much work: the Bill's got to go through by the summer recess. Of course, there are any number of more tedious committees you might be put on if the Chief gets his way.'

Goodfellowe groaned.

'Come on, Tom. Help me out. And help yourself, too.'

They were on Salisbury Plain and through the window Stonehenge was beginning to turn to ochre-blue shadow in the late afternoon mist. Goodfellowe always found the simple Welsh-hewn megaliths a sight to rouse his spirits, a symbol of hope that pushed the urban clutter and confusion of London far from his mind. Four thousand years ago they'd dragged those huge slabs across hundreds of miles of hostile countryside with nothing but their hands, ordinary men with exceptional dreams who wanted to change their world, to build a monument that would stand and survive as a beacon of hope not only in their dark Neolithic age but in times that were to come. Which presumably was why the faceless men who decide such matters were planning to bury this majestic stretch of the A303 inside a tunnel, pouring the British motorist and his money down a sightless black hole while reserving the inspiration for the exclusive enjoyment of Japanese tourists.

'Bollocks.'

Lillicrap, still pondering his Standing Committee, took Goodfellowe's conclusion as acceptance of his request. 'That's great. It'll be fun working together again. Tell you what, I'm going shooting in Scotland again this summer. Glorious Twelfth and all that. Come if you'd like. Do some damage to the grouse and the malt. We could

76

celebrate our hard work together. Slaughter and swill. Bring Sam, too.'

'I'm not much of a shot, Lionel . . .'

'No matter. There's miles of good fishing or even walking.'

'Truth is, I think it may be a little beyond me. Even with a new consultancy.'

Lillicrap grinned reassuringly. 'Don't worry too much about that. Look, I've been shooting on the same estate ever since I got into Parliament. They owe me a few favours. I can get you a very good deal. Believe me, the money will be no problem.'

'We'll see.' Money was always a problem, but that concern paled into insignificance next to Sammy. She would go ballistic if he announced they'd be spending their summer turning Perth-shire into an alfresco abattoir. She would be more likely to arrive with a picket line than a party frock.

Lillicrap popped another handful of licorice and put his foot down to clear a milk tanker which was struggling along the single carriageway. The Range Rover didn't even complain, eating up the distance—as well it might at almost fifty pence a mile, courtesy of the Members' mileage allowance. A hundred pounds travelling to, and a hundred pounds travelling fro, every time Lillicrap visited his constituency. Goodfellowe had known some MPs to travel three and four up with each of them putting in a claim. Pity was they didn't offer a bike allowance. Maybe he'd suggest one, on health grounds.

It was a few miles beyond Stonehenge that they came across the accident at the roundabout. A B-reg Fiat filled with students on their way to a frolic in Exeter had entered the roundabout too fast and had failed to make the final corner, clipping the kerb and leaping straight into the trunk of an ancient ash. The bonnet was up and crumpled, the misshapen windscreen had evil smears of something dark and dribbling on the inside. Blue steam wafted from the engine compartment. Two of the doors had been forced open by the impact and from one a young man was trying to crawl, dragging himself by a single arm, the other lying awkward and useless by his side. Already three drivers had found excuses to pass the scene, slowing only to spy. The driver of a veal lorry approaching from the other direction had shown more concern and had slowed but was in difficulties finding a safe place to park.

Goodfellowe indicated the grass verge, scarred and chewed by the Fiat's desperate tyre tracks, and Lillicrap gently eased the Range Rover over the kerb, flicking on his hazard lights as he did so. 'Call the rescue services,' Goodfellowe instructed, leaping out.

The smashed car had four occupants. One was sitting on the verge, head buried in his hands, another two lay unconscious in the front seat while the fourth was still trying to claw his way from the back, his only good hand reaching out imploringly as he saw Goodfellowe approach. Steam—or was it smoke?—continued to pour from the engine. The ignition was still on, whining, sparking electric blue and yellow in warning. Something acrid burnt in the back of Goodfellowe's throat as he approached. He reached across and had to battle with the twisted key stuck in the ignition before the system fell silent. He had also succeeded in smearing blood from the collapsed steering wheel across the sleeve of his jacket. Beside him, the driver appeared to be

78

in a bad way, his facial injuries weeping horribly. Better not touch him, best to wait until the emergency services arrived. The driver of the cattle truck was wrenching at the far door, trying to get to the other front-seat passenger, who was beginning to stir. Goodfellowe turned his attention to the pleas from the back. The student's right collar bone and probably his arm were fractured. He had dragged himself halfway out of the door but could go no further, every effort twisting his face with pain. He raised pleading eyes to Goodfellowe.

'Help me.'

Goodfellowe dropped to his knees to give him some support and as soon as he had reached around the student's chest the boy seemed to give way, falling into his protector's arms. Slowly, with considerable difficulty, Goodfellowe eased him out of the car and onto the grass.

'They're coming!' Lillicrap called from the Range Rover. He threw across a car rug.

The boy was shivering, his teeth chattering with shock, yet a sudden energy seemed to take hold of him. With his good hand he clutched urgently at Goodfellowe, drawing him closer. 'Are you p-p-police?' he whispered, stammering. There was blood in his eye, Goodfellowe wiped it away with the boy's own ripped shirt-sleeve.

'No. They're on their way.' He meant it to sound reassuring but the boy seemed only to grow more agitated.

'Please. A favour. In my shirt pocket.' His crooked arm tried to inch towards the pocket, but the pain made him seize. 'Please.' He was sobbing.

Goodfellowe's fingers probed inside the pocket and emerged clutching a small plastic bag of what

79

looked a little like green tobacco.

'Grass. Only enough for a couple of smokes. Bin it for me? Before the police get here?'

Goodfellowe hesitated.

'If they find it on me . . . Please.'

The student made another desperate attempt to reach the bag himself but the pain was too much. He sank back, teeth cracking, a look of despair glazing over his bloodied eyes.

Goodfellowe held the drug in the palm of his hand. He had grown old with the ethical certainties which were regularly laid out for inspection at Westminster, but there was another world outside the palace precincts where the moral insights of politicians had a habit of vaporizing on contact with reality. So the drug was illegal. But it was soft. The boy, knowing it was illegal, had taken the risk. Just like Jya-Yu. And like Jya-Yu, he had lost. Punishment was due, but wasn't this accident punishment enough? Yet for Goodfellowe to conceal the drug would also be wrong. And yet, and yet . . . the boy was only Sammy's age.

Hell, before he'd become one of the country's great moral authorities Goodfellowe had tried the stuff himself. At university. A Sixties' child, like all the rest. He shoved the bag in his pocket.

It was at this point that Goodfellowe looked around to see if anyone had spotted the exchange. He noticed Lillicrap still standing well back under the protective cover of the Range Rover.

'Give me a hand,' Goodfellowe asked, trying to shift the lad. Lillicrap ventured over with reluctance, stepping toe-first through the churned grass as though practising ballet steps.

'Better wait for the emergency services, perhaps.'

He sounded distracted. 'I'll get my fire extinguisher, just in case,' he offered, and made to return to the Range Rover.

'Come on, Lionel, just help me make him a little more comfortable.'

The image of the self-assured Whip was beginning to slip. 'Look, Tom, perhaps it's better if we left this to others. We've no medical experience. Might do more harm than good.' He lowered his voice, looking at Goodfellowe's soiled hands. 'Have you thought of AIDS ?'

'Bugger AIDS. These boys need help.'

'And it's coming.' Already they could hear the sirens in the distance, trying to force passage through the tangle of traffic which had spread in every direction. 'We've both got engagements to get to—and look at the state of your trousers.'

For the first time Goodfellowe became aware that he was kneeling in mud. 'I'm staying until the ambulance gets here.'

It was a good ten minutes before the rescue services arrived and the student had agreed to let go of his hand. As Goodfellowe wiped his own damp brow and straightened up he realized Lillicrap was right. He looked a mess and felt worse. He needed something absurd to lift his spirits.

He found it at the edge of the roundabout. Lillicrap, now in his shirtsleeves and clutching his stained car rug like a battle trophy, had completely lost his coyness and was giving an animated interview to a passing local television crew. Goodfellowe laughed until the tears poured down his cheeks.

Much later, when the laughter had been forgotten and they had struggled for more than two hours to fight their way through the ensuing jams, Goodfellowe arrived long after time for his constituency function—to be met by Miss Hailstone. She was always an extraordinary sight. Her lips gave the impression of being cut from cheap wellingtons. They were the colour of bright red plastic and squeaked absurdly as they moved. Her hair had grown prematurely orange and was swept back in a style that defied both gravity and fashion, and which, combined with an extravagant bust, created the impression of a man o' war casting around in search of fresh winds. She was under full sail as she headed directly for Goodfellowe.

'Mr Goodfellowe . . .' —she was always excessively formal when firing salvoes—'I thought I'd made it sufficiently clear how important this evening was so that even you couldn't misunderstand. Don't you want to get re-elected? You really might have made the effort. Some of our most important supporters have already left and—good grief, man. Just look at you!'

For a moment she stood speechless, taking in his appearance. His suit resembled something housewives find on Monday mornings buried at the bottom of the laundry basket.

Goodfellowe smiled wryly. 'Evening, Beryl. How's the HRT?'

*　　　*　　　*

Corsa threw another log on the fire. It didn't spit. Swiss hearths weren't allowed to misbehave. In any event, it was only for effect; the late afternoon sun hovered so full and red that even high in the mountains above Gryon they could still enjoy drinks outside on the balcony.

They had all come. Some had flown in via Geneva, others through Lausanne. The skiing season was about to finish yet there had been a foot of fresh snow which lent a crystalline quality to the air, making the drive around the tip of Lac Léman and into the mountains of Valais nothing less than spectacular. Corsa had chosen a provident spot for his Swiss hideaway. The attractions of the breathtaking panorama across the Rhône Valley to the mountains of France beyond were exceeded only by its status as a tax-free headquarters for the international operations of the Granite Foundation. It seemed little more than pedantry to point out that no employee of the Foundation had ever set foot inside.

Yet it had been no easy task to gather together the five men and one woman, Di Burston, who had made the journey. Weekends in idyllic locations were neither unusual nor irresistible to the industrial leaders who at this moment were fraternizing on his balcony; it was business rather than beauty that had drawn them here. A transformation of their corporate prospects, he had promised them, like some doorstep insurance salesman. He'd refused to take no for an answer, and his boots were considerably bigger than most.

They'd been there scarcely an hour but already the informality of snow-draped Alps and invigorating air had relaxed them. The executive chairman whose company produced 400,000 cars a year had also produced his latest mistress, whom he was allowing to 'synergize', as he referred to it, with the others. She'd once asked him what the word meant. 'Comes after synagogue but before syphilis,' he'd explained. 'Keep it that way.' By contrast the

European head of a tobacco multinational was there with his wife—'in my business we're not allowed to misbehave even in private,' he'd complained, but they were clearly a devoted pair and already at ease. So was the CEO of the world's second-largest nuclear-reprocessing operation, who looked a little like Trotsky with glowing eyes and a moustache like a bramble which appeared to have taken root across his face. Released from the inhibitions of home, he had already propositioned the butler, who had refused, and he was now working his way broadmindedly towards Diane. She, as always, was stunning, standing centre stage in a Karl Lagerfeld tracksuit and explaining to the big-hitter from the UK chemicals industry how he might improve his backhand slice. Meanwhile to one side, cautious and seemingly diffident, stood a Japanese gentleman who everyone referred to simply as Mr Hagi. Hagi had one of those indistinguishable Oriental faces which to Europeans seem neither formed nor finished, with no striking feature to pick him out of a crowd. Yet he had found little difficulty in attracting attention after pouring a billion dollars into the virtual-reality ranch he had created in a cow pasture a few miles from Brussels and its cross-Channel rail link. He drank only tea.

The sun had begun to slip, the final embers of day burning themselves out on mountain peaks as the shade temperature plunged several degrees. They retreated inside to the flickering hearth and the raw wood walls which acted as a backcloth to several fine pieces of art from the collection of the Corsa Foundation. The Japanese admired two slender Tang statues almost a metre high, remarking on how difficult it was to smuggle such large artefacts out of China without getting them damaged. Corsa promised to give him the name of his restorer on the Portobello Road.

A meal had been prepared which somehow managed to cater for all their dietary whims, even Mr Hagi, who seemed to enjoy little other than raw fish. He feasted on gravadlax. But no business was discussed, not during the meal.

'A little like Poirot, isn't it?' the chemical king enquired, glancing around the dinner table. 'When do you put on the funny accent and tell us who's done the foul deed?'

'According to much of your press coverage, you're all as guilty as sin,' Corsa replied. 'That's why you're here.'

And with the minimum of fuss the table had been cleared, the fire replenished, drinks laid out and the staff dismissed. Wife and mistress were guided in the direction of the Jacuzzi.

'My pitch is simple,' Corsa began when all was quiet. There were no papers. 'You have two things in common. You are exceptional business leaders, corporate warriors of the first class. Yet you are all being slowly bled to death because you don't control the most important weapon in today's corporate warfare—your images.' He waved a hand in the direction of the Japanese. 'No, Mr Hagi, that doesn't apply to you—yet. But I hope to show you that it will.'

Corsa handed each one a thin sealed envelope. 'For later,' he instructed with deliberate mystery.

'You see, the media control your images. Yet none of you control the media. We, the media, are the king-makers. And the destroyers, if need be. It's quite simple. We say the currency is about to weaken, so the following day there's panic selling in the financial markets. And the currency becomes weak. We print a story which states that two friends are rivals for political honours and, by the weekend, they've become those rivals. And if we suggest a husband's close relationship with an actress is the subject of his wife's close scrutiny, then you can bet that by the time the milk has splashed over his morning cornflakes that's exactly what she's doing.'

'You admit you print it even if it isn't true?' the car manufacturer interrupted.

'You miss the point. If we print it, it becomes true.'

'To you truth is simply a commodity?'

'Look, in your industry you send off researchers to find out what your customers want. If they want their cars green with sun roofs and chromium headlamps, then you manufacture cars that are green with sun roofs and chromium headlamps. If you run a television station or a newspaper you do exactly the same. Find out what the customers will buy.'

'And manufacture it.'

Corsa let Nuclear's remark stand to attention in front of them for a moment.

'We don't take hostages in the circulation war. If the great British public want to read that Martin Bormann is living as a bisexual vicar in Bognor Regis, or Five-A-Side Fiona does it with half the Chelsea team after every big match, they've got a right to it the same as any other customer.'

'But that's just the tabloids,' Chemicals interjected.

Corsa beamed. 'Think business! Not gutter press

86

and respectable rag, but simply business.'

They looked nonplussed.

'The tabloids encourage everyone to have sex at least nineteen times a week. If we don't we're all left to feel inadequate. Yet if we do, those very same tabloids splash our names all over the front page with illustrated highlights inside. Meanwhile the learned broadsheets make their living editorializing about the nation's fall into moral turpitude. And who owns the respectable press? The same guys who own the gutter press. They all lie end to end and indulge in practices that would cause blushes even in Bangkok.'

The Japanese spoke next, slowly but distinctly. 'You make it sound as if you are not a newspaper man at all, Mr Corsa.'

'I'm not. At least, not like the rest. I understand my business better than any of them.'

'In what way?'

'Because I understand image, and because I control it. Hitler and Goering couldn't destroy Winston Churchill, but I could have. Destroyed his reputation, his power, his place in history. The destiny of great people—and great companies—lies in the hands of the media. If the media say your new products are great, you're a success. Yet every time they print a sensational front-page story about how you, all of you personally,'—he pointed accusingly around the table—'about how you're killing innocent kids through radiation leaks or tobacco smoke or drugs like thalidomide . . .' His audience began to shift uneasily. 'You spend hundreds of millions of pounds a year between you on advertising and corporate communications and lobbying to manufacture your images, your corporate truths. And practically every penny is wasted. Blown away by a single front-page exclusive branding you as no better than corporate child-killers.'

'So what precisely is it you're suggesting we do? Stop wasting our millions advertising in your newspapers?' It was Diane Burston, the first time she had spoken.

'Go direct. Buy the media. Buy the front pages, not just a couple of columns inside. Then use them. To sell your own industries—and, even more effectively, to bury your competition.'

'That's one hell of a sales pitch. Buy into an industry just when everyone else is selling.' Tobacco's tone indicated he was not taking the matter entirely seriously.

'That's the point. The Press Bill will force the biggest players to sell some of their titles. I'm suggesting we buy and take their place. Control your own fortunes. Buy the news coverage you want.'

'But no one is going to be allowed more than twenty per cent . . .' Tobacco objected.

'No one. No *one*. But a private consortium made up of six or seven players, with the lines of ownership buried behind shell companies and investment trusts which no doubt you all have located in very private homes like Liechtenstein and Luxembourg . . .'

'Or Switzerland.'

'Precisely. Together we can control as much as we want without the authorities ever catching on. Newspaper shares are cheap anyway, and I'm offering you a means of increasing their value to you many times over. How much would it be worth to have free advertising? To poison the waters for your competitors?'

'To hang the bloody pressure groups out to dry,' Nuclear interjected with an edge of bitterness. He was catching on.

'Dig away at their private lives, their finances,' Corsa added. 'They're practically all deviants. And,' his lips parted encouragingly, 'the public has a right to know.'

Diane started laughing and the exchange began in earnest. 'Someone would see through the scheme, bound to.' —'Did they see through Maxwell?'—'Safety in numbers. And in trusts.' —'A consortium. A very private club. With our own club magazine.' —'Might get the bloody Government off our backs.' —'Great.' —'The majesty of the press. Think about it. Always fancied being a king.' —'Or queen.' —'Oh, to stuff Greenpeace.' —'And we'd still have the value of the newspaper shares.'

Tobacco, however, remained concerned. 'But that's it. I know nothing about newspapers, nor do any of us.'

'Except me,' their host interrupted forcefully. 'And I want what you should want: to be part of the mightiest media group in the country. I know the business, I can make it work for you.'

'But can we trust you, Mr Corsa?'

'Trust me? What has trust got to do with it? Don't trust me, control me! I'm willing to back my judgement in the most practical fashion, by allowing the consortium to start its work by buying a substantial stake in the Granite Group. Take hold of the reins. That's my commitment. My business where my mouth is.'

Corsa's frank enthusiasm was beginning to prove

infectious until, cutting through the general hubbub that ensued, came a pounding from the far end of the table. The slap of Hagi's hand summoned them to silence.

'But what of me?' the Japanese demanded, his voice quivering in offence. 'Why am I here? My business is entertainment. Fun farms. Not death factories. I have no image problems. No . . .'—he struggled furiously with the consonants—'pressure groups.'

'Mr Hagi, there are pressures in every field. Even in fun farms.'

'What pressures?'

'OK. Let me ask you all to look inside the envelopes in front of you.'

They took up the envelopes, opening them with distinctive styles. Some tore at them like alligators playing with prey, others pecked like cranebills. Hagi approached his with such caution that for a moment Corsa thought he intended to reuse it.

From each fell share receipts. Ten thousand pounds' worth.

'I purchased these shares this morning. In your names. And you will see that they are shares in what Mr Hagi modestly calls his fun farm.' He inclined his head in the direction of the Japanese. 'By this time tomorrow they will be worth considerably more.'

'What!' Hagi's voice and eyes were incandescent. 'You screw around with my company!'

'Not screwing around with your company, Mr Hagi. Screwing around with your opposition.'

Corsa crossed to a fax machine that had been sitting unobtrusively in the corner of the room and pressed a button. It began to warble.

'Your main opposition—your only true competition, Mr Hagi—is the Wonderworld complex just outside Paris. Been having a particularly rough time, and they are in the process of major financial renegotiations with their banks. Big discussions about future attendance levels. Am I right?'

'Correct.'

Corsa took the paper from the fax machine and laid it on the table. 'I thought you might like to see tomorrow's front page.'

The paper bore a miniaturized version of the *Herald* , with a splash headline.

'Child Sex Ring Targets Wonderworld.'

'Sadly for your competition, my intrepid journalists have found evidence of paedophile activity at Wonderworld.'

'It is true?'

'Mr Hagi, several million children under the age of sixteen go through Wonderworld every year. Of course it attracts perverts. Just like every fun park in the world. But I have the feeling it won't be attracting so many families, nor many bankers. Not after this.'

'You manufacture story?'

Corsa smiled. 'Manufacture? Such an ugly word. I prefer to see it more as a fishing expedition for the truth. Some newspapers like to fly-fish. I find it easier simply to chuck in a couple of sticks of dynamite.'

'Boom,' Di Burston offered, softly and very sensuously.

'This will blow them apart,' Hagi insisted.

'And you will be there to pick up the pieces. You see, gentlemen, image is everything.'

CHAPTER THREE

Goodfellowe decided he might have been a trifle impetuous with Sammy. The ginger spikes had proved to be no more than a wash-'n'-go frolic for the fashion show; the tattoo had also been nothing more than a temporary adornment, and even though the hole in the navel was all too lasting and left him feeling queasy, he'd been unable to articulate his objections with anything other than pompous flannel. His parables about how officers in World War I had been dragged to muddy deaths by their lanyards made him appear vaguely senile, while the fashion show—Sammy's fashion show— had been a startling success, to which he had contributed exactly sod-all. Time to climb down from his mountain top and share a little humble pie.

Except humble pie was not on the menu at The Kremlin, Westminster's newest restaurant, which stood no more than a brisk umbrella walk from the House of Commons. This was to be a time for reconciliation, an opportunity for him to recognize Sam's blossoming maturity and—if he must—to acknowledge that fathers had to grow up, too. It would be worth the damage to his fragile finances. Anyway, he'd been carrying a considerable burden of guilt and The Kremlin seemed an appropriate place to offload it, although he'd have preferred it if they'd managed to recognize him when he arrived and made a little fuss for Sammy's benefit. Instead he got the table by the noisy kitchen door.

'You've never taken me anywhere like this before. I wasn't expecting it. You'll have to explain the menu.'

Sammy's observation embarrassed him. It wasn't

so much the implication of meanness but her recognition that lunch was somehow part of the rite of accession, of passage from puberty to adulthood. To independence from him.

'Be good to do it more often. It's so difficult with you away and, you know, my job. We never seem to have enough time for each other.'

'You're always so busy.'

'Suppose I am. Do you think I'd be better if I had any other job?'

She examined him with all the brutal honesty of a teenager, then shook her head. 'No. Except we'd have more money.'

'Money's not everything.'

'That must be why we don't have any of it.'

He had hoped lunch would be relaxing, like a warm mineral bath. Instead she seemed intent on throwing in buckets of ice cubes.

'I'm sorry about the fashion show. About not being able to help. I thought you were splendid. Your clothes were . . . splendid.'

'Daddy, what do you know about clothes?'

'What do you mean?'

'Look at yourself. That jacket's a disgrace.' More ice cubes showered down.

'Yes, I had an accident. Tried to have it dry-cleaned, doesn't seem to have worked.'

'The button's coming off!'

He looked down and began to fiddle, only to find the thread unravelling and the button falling into his hand. Diffidently he popped it into his pocket.

'How's school?' he asked, trying to find conversation.

She merely shrugged.

'The headmistress said you'd found some friends

in town, outside the school.' He didn't entirely know how to handle this so he bundled on. 'In fact she's a little worried they might not be the best sort of influence on you.'

'She's a snob. Anyway, she's only really worried because one of the girls in our group got drunk last term,'

'You drink?'

'You told me you did when you were sixteen.'

The temptation to produce more parental flannel was almost overwhelming. 'But how do you buy drinks? You're under age. And you can't afford it.'

'We know a group of boys who are older. Nineteen, twenty maybe. They buy the drinks.'

'You go drinking with . . . older boys.' He seemed barely able to get the words out as visions of teenage decadence and the back seat of his first Hillman Minx crowded his mind.

She laughed at his discomfort, sparkling like a spring dawn. 'Oh, Daddy, you're such a dinosaur. Don't worry, I'm not going to disgrace you. I don't do drugs, and I'm no silly slapper.'

'Slapper?'

'How would you like me to put it? A girl who lets her guard and everything else down for a miserable rum and coke.'

His eyes had become like oysters, swimming in confusion. His little girl . . .

'I'm not like that,' she said sweetly. 'In my case it would take at least two rum and cokes.'

She was laughing at him again, but not cruelly, merely teasing for his inability to be anything other than a father. As she continued to splash the bath water at him he was rescued by a woman who appeared at his elbow. She apologized for the situation of the table. 'We're very fully booked. I'll make sure you have a much better table next time, Mr Goodfellowe. So what can I get for you?'

Sammy frowned at. the menu. 'Have you got anything which isn't dripping in blood?'

'Would you prefer cremated meat or simply something vegetarian?'

'I'm a veggie.'

'Are you?' her father asked, startled.

'If nothing on the menu appeals, will you leave it with me?' the woman offered. 'Chef does something with a stir-fry and home-made noodles which ought to get this place a Michelin star.'

'Sounds fine. Come on, Daddy, let's make it for two. Spirit of adventure.'

'I'll have the lamb. Medium rare. And a half-bottle of something red and Californian.' He felt in need of a drink.

The woman finished taking the order and apologized once more about the table. 'We'll do better for your next visit, I promise. It's been a pleasure meeting you, Mr Goodfellowe.' And with that she had disappeared.

'She fancies you, Daddy.'

'Don't be preposterous.'

'Daddy, we girls can tell.'

He glanced after the woman but she had already gone. What was her name? He couldn't even recall what she looked like. Preposterous.

'How long have you been a veggie, anyway?'

''Bout six months.'

'Truly? I didn't know.' He paused. 'Quite a lot I don't seem to know about my daughter, one way and another. Seems we've a lot of catching up to do. Look, it's Easter in a couple of weeks. Let's make some time together then, Sammy.'

'I hate being called Sammy. It's Sam.' Her jaw tensed into a premeditated position. 'And I've got other plans for Easter. Julie Rifkind's parents have invited me to their place in France.'

'But . . .' He searched for an argument. 'The cost.'

'No cost. They're driving. It's all free.'

'Your job at the pizzeria. They're expecting you.'

'Stuff the pizzeria. I want some fun.'

'But . . .'

'It's a chance to practise my French,'

'I'd hoped we could be together this Easter.'

'Are you going to take me to the South of France?'

'I thought . . . we could go and visit your mother. Together. You haven't been for so long. I hoped we might get her to give you the locket herself.' It was moral and material blackmail, a father's duty.

'Mummy won't have the slightest idea whether I'm there or not. And the locket's not my style anyway. I've changed my mind.'

Goodfellowe shuddered. The locket had become a symbol of the competing demands made upon him by wife and daughter, it had been tormenting him for days. Now she had thrown it away in a single offhand phrase. His world was spinning; he thought it might topple off its axis. The last piece of the universe which had once been his family was beginning to disintegrate.

It had been so different, five years ago. Then he had been a successful politician, surrounded by Ministerial red boxes and a devoted family. Elinor. Sammy. And poor Stevie. He'd thought it almost idyllic, yet as he had scratched away at his soul throughout the endless nights since then he had come to realize how much he had taken for granted. The charge up the political slope with a wife at his side and children on his shoulders. Their unquestioning support. And particularly their immovable presence.

Then it had all disappeared, all except for Sam. They had been holidaying and he'd promised to take Stevie swimming. But Ministerial boxes take no account of holidays or promises made to energetic thirteen-year-olds, and he'd been buried in papers at the time he should have been with Stevie. Elinor had remonstrated, they'd argued, and she had been forced to take Stevie swimming in his place. Perhaps it would have made no difference if he had been there, perhaps Stevie would have been too adventurous and the riptide would have dragged him under in any event, but what does a man do when his only son goes out to play and never comes back? What can he do, except blame himself? Just as in turn Elinor blamed herself. She had seemed to recover physically from the ordeal, but on the anniversary of Stevie's death she had taken herself off to her room and had never again participated in a world which had taken Stevie away. Involutional melancholia, the doctors called it. First they had tried to cajole and persuade her back to normality, then stuffed her with pills, even though there was nothing physically wrong with her. She was simply inconsolably wretched, worthless, hating herself and all aspects of life without Stevie, and that included hating her husband. She had moved from bedroom to back room, then to stays in hospital, finally to the psychiatric nursing home, the best that Goodfellowe could afford—better even.

Yet the size of the bills did nothing to diminish his own torment. The guilt of a father who should have been there, saving his child, not stroking his red box and its ambitions.

He had been left with only Sam. Now even she would not be there for him.

'I particularly wanted to spend this Easter with you. For us both to visit your mother. She deserves it.'

'And I deserve France.'

'That may be just a fraction selfish, young lady.'

That was too much for her. 'Selfish? Is it any more selfish than sending me away to school? Shuffling the responsibility onto others?'

'It's a very fine school. It costs . . . hell, it doesn't matter what it costs. What else could I do?'

'Show you loved me.'

'But I do.'

'All I wanted was a bit of time, Daddy. Can't you see? I had no mother, no brother. I needed a father, not a boarding school. But you never had time for me.'

'Sammy . . .'

She ploughed right through him. 'I'd get more time with you if I were one of your whining constituents. You make time for everyone else in this world but me. So now I'm making time for myself, doing what I want to do. For once. I'm going to France. Whether you like it or not.'

The meal was arriving and they paused to save general embarrassment. It was true, he reflected. He'd given up his Ministerial office to sort out his personal life, yet he had only immersed himself in other work to dull the pain, to exhaust himself so that he could somehow sleep at night in the frozen

98

wastes of his bed. How could a single parent living half the year in Westminster take care of a teenager? She had to go away to school. Yet had he in truth also sent Sam away because she reminded him of all the things he'd lost?

They began their meal in silence.

'It's not been easy for me,' he started again. 'I've tried to do my best for you. Perhaps you don't realize the sacrifices I've had to make.'

'Oh, I do, Daddy.' Her eyes were beginning to rim with tears. 'Every time I want to take piano or horse-riding lessons, and you say no. Every time I have to borrow a pair of shoes even to appear in a fashion show. Every time I spend my holidays working in the pizza parlour wondering what my friends are up to in Florida or the Far East. I think I understand your sacrifices very well indeed.'

'Look, I can't afford to take you off on trips.'

'Then why, for Christ's sake, are you trying to stop me taking myself?'

Her voice had risen, his voice too, others were noticing. He began to be grateful they weren't sitting in the centre of the restaurant after all. She knew about wounds, how to be on the receiving end; now she'd learnt how to inflict them. If this was growing up, he didn't care for it.

'Watch your language,' he growled.

She was sobbing, silently.

'You want some pudding?'

She shook her head, wiped her eye, wouldn't look at him. 'I want to go.'

He was going to argue with her but could think of not a thing to say. He waved for the bill.

Its arrival gave him more pain. His whole week's allowance gone in one disastrous hour. Enough to

99

have bought her two pairs of shoes. Then the woman was at his elbow once more. A telephone call for Mr Goodfellowe. He followed her to the small bar, where she apologized. She had deceived him. There was no telephone call but, a private word, there was a problem with the credit card. The terminal was rejecting it. Rejecting him. Even the machinery was joining in.

He seemed to have lost the will to fight back, even to concoct a pathetic excuse. It was over the limit again. He paid by cheque and left with his cheeks burning. He desperately wanted to get out of this place and leave all its memories behind.

As he collected their coats he fumbled in his pocket for a coin, thrusting it at the cloakroom girl.

Only later did he realize he had given her his button.

*　　　*　　　*

With heavy head—the Californian Cabernet had driven deep, especially without cheese—and with still heavier heart, Goodfellowe found a place on the green leather benches behind his Front Bench. During his days at the Dispatch Box he had been in the very midst of the battle, at the point of the Opposition's bayonet charge, so close he could almost smell the fried onion. Now he was drawn back from the front line, a soldier no longer expected to lead but simply to obey, to do the right thing, whatever and whenever his generals required. Cannon fodder. Yesterday's Man in an arena which had time only for the moment. It was galling enough to a man with pride, let alone opinion, and the many fine moments when he had led his own oratorical charge against the Opposition had been cast into the pit of history. Now he rarely spoke, content to growl and grumble from a sedentary position— 'sitting on my principles,' as he described it to Mickey.

The Opposition had called the debate, on environmental policy, and their benches were crowded. While the Environment Secretary prepared to marshal the Government's defences at the Dispatch Box, Opposition Members affected an appearance of nonchalance, waiting for the moment to turn from indifference to ridicule. Gangling legs were thrust forward, boots first, as though ready to trample on whatever argument was put before them. Boots placed well in front of brain. Some were even propped up on the Clerks' Table in a manner which would have caused outrage in any other club, but the sporting of soles along the Front Bench was an ancient privilege whose origins stretched back into the mists of time, probably to Eton.

Goodfellowe rubbed his blister, slowly hardening inside its leather shell. You could tell a lot about a politician from his shoes, he reflected. The youthful sound-bite rebel whose shoes were usually covered in mud, not from service in the parliamentary trenches but from lingering around the lawns of College Green where the television cameras were to be found. The fashionable militant, usually an academic, wearing his Caterpillar boots with pride as though he stood ever ready to join the hunger march from Jarrow, even though Caterpillars cost £130 a pair. There was the patent leather of the man who spent too much time shopping for his shoes and his politics in Brussels, and the rural brogue which spoke of countryside and old-fashioned courtesy, a Member to be relied upon, a man who regarded the serving of his constituents and the thrashing of hunt saboteurs as a public duty. Nearby one could find soft Italian loafers, the mark of the made-by-Armani man, all professional style with soft Italian suits that covered little but soft Italian principles. And brown suede shoes, brothel creepers, like conjoined eyebrows the mark of a man intended for the gallows, or perhaps for lunch at the Groucho Club. But mostly the footwear was simply a little too old and frayed, the polish of earlier days faded by wear. They were dull, some downright scruffy, the sign of men in constant distraction who were too busy saving the souls of others to worry about their own.

The shoes along the Front Benches told their own story of the day. The debate had been called by the Opposition to coincide with the publication of a report from The Earth Firm, a prominent pressure group, whose conclusions were damning in their indictment of the Government's failure to meet its stated environmental commitments. Line after line of Government election promise had been analysed, and page after page of detailed denunciation had been handed down, an effective piece of pressure group propaganda that had conjured lurid headlines. During the morning not a single volunteer could be found from the Government Front Bench to be dragged to Broadcasting House for the ritual radio flogging, but the Opposition rhetoric had been savage, comparing Ministers to 'vultures picking their way through the remains of their manifesto to see if anything still survives.' Elderly spinsters fled in terror from their breakfast tables. Those of sterner constitution anticipated the afternoon and the delights of witnessing a Minister being keelhauled before the House.

All the components for the humiliation had been brought together. The report. The emotive issue. The accusation. The flight from evidence to exaggeration with images of infants being poisoned and withered in the womb. And the time of punishment had arrived. The Opposition spokesman rose with fire in his breast, his colleagues tapping their shoes on the green carpet in expectation. He made much of the report, and then some more, charging the Government with craven pandering to pressure. 'They have become slaves to the vested interests,' he thundered. Opposition MPs cleared their throats and stamped their soles in approval.

Only one thing was missing. At such close range, bayonet to bayonet, it is usually difficult for condemned politicians not to show some response to their impending fate. A certain sallowness of cheek. Maybe a smile that is made of frost and looks ready to shatter. A flicker in the eyes that betrays, if not remorse, then anguish. But not this Minister, not today. She sat diminutive behind the Dispatch Box, squeezed between the men, adjusting the pleats of her dress, whispering to a neighbour, rummaging absentmindedly in her handbag, even enjoying some of the Opposition's gallows humour. And all the while she smiled serenely, as though listening to a church sermon.

It wasn't natural. Something was wrong. The Opposition spokesman began to lose his stride. All along the Opposition Front Bench the shoes began twitching in discomfort, as though every member of the Opposition team had dressed in a hurry and put on a pair too small for them. They fidgeted. Scratched. Then it was her turn.

'It is often said, Madam Speaker, that a politician should never be caught in public with either his morals or his mistress, since in the end he will need to betray both of them. This afternoon has been a splendid example of such masculine folly.' From behind her came roars of support. At the moment none of her backbenchers had the slightest idea what she meant, but it was enough that she had come out fighting.

'The Opposition has taken for its bible this ... report.' She held it up for the inspection of the House as though expecting someone to make a bid, before flinging it down upon the Dispatch Box. 'And we shall judge it by the morals and many mistresses which may be revealed.'

More anticipation, more shoe-shuffling. Then she held in her hands a copy of the *Evening Herald* , displaying it with pride. Members strained forward to catch its contents.

'Since the Opposition is so notoriously short-sighted, I shall read it for them. The headline says: **"Eco-Chief A Cheat .**" '

She read out the relevant details, savouring them, repeating many of the best, banging her pointed finger against the Dispatch Box for emphasis. Opposition feet stopped fidgeting, stopped moving at all. Rigor mortis had set in.

'And so it seems, Madam Speaker, that the author of the report in which the Opposition places so much trust is not the paragon of truth and virtue we had been led to expect. It seems he has been living with two different women, neither of whom is his long-abandoned wife. He has been claiming two lots of dole money, in spite of the fact that he draws a considerable level of expenses from The Earth Firm to fund his duties as a professional agitator. In addition, he also draws disability benefit, although his sad and obviously enervating disability doesn't apparently prevent him spending most of his time chained to trees.'

She waved her copy of the *Herald*. It was the turn of the Government benches to stamp their feet, like Zulus appearing over the ridge.

'It never ceases to amaze me how these professional protesters have the strength to get on their bikes and cycle around the country in search of any discomfort other than a proper job.'

More cries from the warriors behind. She fixed her opponent across her half-moon glasses.

'The Honourable Gentleman should take care. He seems to be climbing into beds which are already too crowded.'

Game, Set, Debate. The parliamentary sketchwriters had rarely had such rich pickings. 'Opposition Lost Up Amazon,' one was already scribbling. 'Bedtime for Bozo,' hacked another.

From his perch up in the Visitors' Gallery, Corsa turned to his companions with a face flushed with contentment. Beside him Cars and Nuclear sat silently. Both were lost in serious thought.

*   *   *

She took her finger from her mouth. 'Success hasn't changed me,' she said. 'I feel no different now I'm earning four million from when I was only earning two.'

'Shuddup.'

The finger went back in, but only for a while. 'My mother always told me that men who offer you champagne after five usually end up trying to drink it from your navel.'

'Will you be quiet and concentrate?'

The finger hovered indecisively. 'Mind you, that really is a wonderful vintage you've . . .' And the rest was lost in a tremulous moan which began to soar like the song of a nightingale through the night sky, rising almost beyond reach before it came slowly to rest and finally died.

They lay silently on the bed for several minutes, looking down the river to the bonfire of ambitions which was the City, ablaze with electric flames that reflected from the dark and turbid waters of the Thames.

She crooked her neck. 'Blast. You've ruined my nail.'

She held up her finger. The nail was bitten clean through.

Corsa took it as a compliment. 'I'll buy you a weekend at a health farm so they can repair it for you.'

'A weekend? You could buy the entire bloody farm using nothing but the small change from the money you're asking for.'

He rolled back from her, examining. 'Somehow, of all people, I never expected you to mix business and pleasure.'

'I'm not.'

'What the hell was the last half-hour?'

'You exaggerate. Eighteen minutes.'

'So that was the voice of complaint I was just listening to?'

She pulled the sheet protectively around her

106

body and examined the bitten nail once more. 'I'm here for two reasons, Freddy. The first is because I met an actress in my aerobics class a few weeks ago—can't remember her name. Don't suppose you can either. But she knows you well enough.' She rolled over so that she was facing him, running a finger up the line of his navel, slowly, all the way to his lips. Her voice smouldered like sulphur. 'She told me you made her feel useful. I thought to myself, anyone who could make that foolish young girl feel of any use whatsoever must have a talent.'

'Was it . . . Anthea?'

'No. Can't remember, but definitely not Anthea.'

'And the second reason?'

'Because this afternoon I and the other members of the consortium agreed to your absurd plan. If the newspaper titles come up, we'll help you buy them.'

'And Granite?'

'Not alone, not on its own, but as part of the package. When the others are available, we'll take a chunk of Granite as well.'

His whole body shivered. His breathing quickened as though being transported once again into ecstasy, except this was much, much better. She had brought him everything. The money to save Granite, to paper over all his shortcuts and save his fraudulent hide. But even more, to make him the biggest player on the field. The game was on, and he had just rewritten all the rules. The bonfires of the City seemed to burn with a renewed brightness; he hoped his bankers were sitting right in the middle of the flames.

She tried to hide her smile as she watched his passions flare once more. 'It's all business, you see. I'm here in your bed simply to reassure myself that—how can I put it?' Her finger retraced the path down from his lips, more slowly. 'To make sure you could deliver on your promises.'

'And your verdict?'

'Anthea—whoever—was a silly girl. Too easily convinced.' He could feel her broken nail digging into him. 'I'm a natural sceptic, Freddy. I'd like to come to a more mature conclusion. So do you think you could run that past me again? Do that to me just one more time?'

He withdrew the sheet that she had wrapped tightly around her. 'With that amount of money, my love, I could do it to the whole world.'

*   *   *

Goodfellowe had been sitting for the first five minutes of the morning examining the usual stack of daily drudgery that Mickey had left on his desk. Which way up to start, he wondered? Top to bottom, maybe dealing with the important matters first? But that would only make progress seem ineffably slow. Or from the bottom up, getting through the first three inches of dross at a pace and glowing in the illusion that he was doing his job? The phone butted through his contemplation of duty.

'I've got a lady from The Kremlin on the line,' Mickey announced cheerily. 'Won't tell me what it's about. Says it's personal.'

Memories of torn credit-card vouchers buzzed around his head like angry wasps. 'Did you tell her I was in?' he demanded.

'Did I tell Justin that last night's overtime was worked out at the Hippodrome?'

He paused. What would the caller be after? No,

it couldn't be money. Not yet. Not even his cheques bounced that quickly. Caught between the whirlpool of his curiosity and the rock represented by his constituents' correspondence, he decided to swim for it. Mickey put her through.

'Mr Goodfellowe, this is Elizabeth de Vries.'

He recognized the voice. Now he thought about it, the tones were delightfully modulated and just a little breathy. Almost like an actress. And the theatrical name. But a touch too experienced still to be waiting on table, he thought.

'I'm sorry about the credit card,' he started in, 'some silly computer blunder . . .'

'No, it has nothing to do with that. It's . . . I hope you'll forgive me, I may be about to make a fool of myself, but you left a tip with the cloakroom attendant.'

'Yes.'

'Which turned out to be your suit button.'

Mercy, was there no end to the humiliation?

'It's just that I know how difficult suit buttons are to replace, and I thought it was worth calling to let you know where to find it.'

'That is . . . a generous thought,' he muttered, wincing.

'If you're coming in for lunch or dinner soon . . .'

Anguish. 'My diary's rather full at the moment.'

'Never mind. You seemed to enjoy your glass of wine and we're having a wine-tasting in a couple of days. Perhaps you could spare half an hour?'

'What sort of wine?'

'Does it matter?'

'Does, actually.' At last Goodfellowe had discovered an opportunity to fight back. 'You see, as

109

a backbencher I get precious little chance to indulge my principles, so when the opportunity arises I tend to get very stubborn. Cling to them like a drowning man.' A good analogy, he thought. How often he had felt he was being swept along by irresistible currents and disappearing slowly from sight. 'In my humble view the Common Agricultural Policy as directed by our masters in Brussels is little short of a Criminal Rip-off Agricultural Policy. So I sulk, stamp my foot. And I won't drink any of its wine. Silly, I know, but we politicians have to find some way of exercising our consciences, otherwise they get rather rusty.'

Her laughter was like a brisk shower. He felt refreshed.

'You're in luck, Mr Goodfellowe. I often think my wine supplier did special duty for the KGB. Has the best vodka in town, and seems to have discovered where all the good Eastern European vintages are being hoarded. Georgian, Bulgarian, Hungarian, even a little Czech. Would that meet with your principles?'

'Superbly.'

'Well, bring your principles along and we'll see if we can reunite them with your button.'

He sighed. 'Sadly, and after much patient resistance, I'm afraid that suit is no longer for this world. With or without its button. My daughter was most insistent on the matter.'

'We women can be such bullies.'

'Somehow they tend to run my life for me. Only fair, I suppose, while I rush around the backbenches saving the world from extinction.'

More infectious laughter. 'So, Mr Goodfellowe, we girls at The Kremlin shall expect you here at the wine-tasting. And no excuses.'

'Can I have the name of the manager or owner? I'd like to thank him.'

'Shame on you. And still more shame.'

'What do you mean?'

'What happened to those principles of yours? The rust seems to have rotted them right through.'

'I don't understand. I was only asking after . . .'

'Mr Goodfellowe,' she chided gently, he thought in a slightly Irish brogue, 'I am the owner.'

*   *   *

The motorcycle being ridden by the Chancellor of the Exchequer had wandered off line. With a desperate flick of the machine he tried to negotiate it back onto the firm pavement but the tyres were already scrabbling in the rubble of the roadside, their grip gone. He panicked, his limbs froze and he failed to release the throttle. Fool. Into oblivion at full speed—thus he had lived his entire life. Hopelessly out of control, he was drawn towards the crash barrier at the side of the long left-hand turn into Glen Helen, striking it with a fearsome blow which sent the machine spinning wildly into the stone wall on the other side of the road. Beside him the Transport Secretary let forth a whoop of triumph, celebrating by putting his own bike into an outrageous wheelie.

At about the same desperate moment the Opposition's Spokesman for Defence Affairs had finally got the hang of the joystick and put in a complete three-hundred-and-sixty-degree barrel roll in his attempt to lock onto the enemy F-14s that were scavenging through the clouds ahead of him.

Another flick of the controls, a bead of sweat, then a sighting dead ahead. At last the target indicator blinked hungrily. Contact! He fired the tracer, his thumb squeezed tight until the nail went white, and the first Tomcat went spinning out of sight. Then a second. Easy! It was as he was lining up on the third that a wire brush of warning scraped up his spine. Damn. They had locked onto him, too. He had no time for fear, only regret. Their first missile blew out his starboard engine and then the cockpit screen in front of him shattered. The machine began a slow turning dive, like a duck shot from the sky, and for a moment he was held upside down, his glasses slipping. Then a searing orange-red flash surrounded him as he exploded.

Game over.

The basement of Hamley's, the best-stocked toyshop in the world, reverberated with the sounds of fun—the roars of motor-mania, the noise of failure and despair, the blast of air hockey tables, all but drowned beneath milk-curdling screams of interplanetary aliens being cut to ribbons with lasers as flashing signs warned of 'strong animated violence'.

'Just like the House!' exulted the Opposition Defence Spokesman as he climbed out of the 360-G-LOC Master Blaster cockpit, brushing down his suit as though it were full of shards. 'Except in this place you get a chance to come back from the dead.'

'Give me Questions any time,' the Chancellor threw at him, easing himself off his TT superbike, still glassy-eyed with excitement as he reached for another sip of champagne. 'You need to be no older than fourteen for this lot.'

'As he said, just like the bloody House,' the

112

Transport Secretary agreed, as parliamentary friend and foe set off in search of more Sega sensation.

The party was being thrown to mark the retirement of Rupert Cramp, the Westminster lobby's most senior correspondent, and the ardent teenagers who normally set up camp in Hamley's basement had been replaced by an equally ardent but entirely less agile contingent of statesmen, editors, scholars, wits, pundits and politicians, all of whom seemed to have left their middle-age reserve in the cloakroom and were now intent on fulfilling some of their wildest dreams. Mostly these focused on the machines, although a growing number were turning their attentions to the tastefully clad hostesses as alcohol began to dull the dexterity if not the drive. In the midst of the crowd 'Duke' Frobisher, Westminster's most barbed sketchwriter, stood locked in battle with the Creature from the Swamp; an entire cohort of politicians from all parties cheered to a man as their tormentor became impaled upon the creature's tusks and, accompanied by suitably gruesome stereophonic sound effect, slowly sank beneath the mire.

Goodfellowe was enjoying the revelry—and the champagne, which was green and dry and plucked from vines six thousand miles away from France on the floor of the Napa Valley. He hadn't been invited but Lillicrap had and insisted that Goodfellowe accompany him, practically dragging him by the arm from the Smoking Room. Goodfellowe used to get invited to such gatherings as a matter of course; nowadays his only consolation was in the amount of postage he saved on the replies. Yesterday's Man. He couldn't deny it hurt, like running his soul up against a cheese grater, leaving little scraps of self-esteem behind, not just because of the loss of attentions and courtesies but because he was now stripped of power, the opportunity to make a difference. And if he couldn't make a difference, what was he doing in Parliament?

He dismissed such naive self-indulgence from his mind as Lillicrap guided him over to a table where, through a plateful of lobster tails and quails' eggs, a woman was expounding on the wickedness of discrimination between the sexes. 'You have to agree, don't you?' she turned on the newcomers.

'I'm a Whip,' Lillicrap objected, recognizing a powder-room Puritan and waving his hands in the manner of a referee stopping play. 'We're not allowed opinions.'

The woman cast eyes of inquisition at Goodfellowe.

'I'm sure it's a case well worth dwelling upon,' he mumbled through a mouthful of fish roe.

'Dwelling-schmelling!' the woman accused, seeking succour in her glass. 'You male politicians are about as much use as ringlets on a rabbi. Useless decoration.'

'And I do hope you're enjoying the party,' Goodfellowe added, irked, but his coolness only appeared to encourage her.

'Fancy phrases, fine promises—anything so long as it wins you votes and doesn't involve you in actually doing anything.'

Goodfellowe considered ignoring her. It would have been the most tactful alternative, but Goodfellowe's schooling had been badly fragmented and he always assumed he'd missed the relevant lesson on tact. Instead he decided to tell her what he thought.

114

'That is silly.'

'Silly?' Her voice rose an octave, summoning her wits to battle. 'Tell me, what do you politicians do in that place?'

'We try to help.'

'Help who? Not people like me you don't.'

'I'm a politician, not a consultant psychiatrist.'

Her finger, crimson of nail and encrusted in gold, was jabbing at his heart. 'You're a public servant. We pay you to do what we tell you, not to be offensive.'

'No. You put me there to do what I promised you I would do. No more. You've bought my time in that palace of entertainments, not my mind.'

'You're sent there to do what we tell you.'

'No. Otherwise you might as well simply sit in front of the television screen and decide every issue by pushing buttons. Trial by Teletext. Sentence by Sky. Do away with Government and let Gallup take over.'

She threw back her head in contempt. 'That's nothing more than an argument for arrogance. Ignoring the people.'

'And that, since you insist on pressing the point in the middle of what was otherwise an entirely social occasion, is an argument for indulging yourself every time you wake up with a migraine or discover your husband's just employed a secretary twenty years younger than you are.' He paused. 'Or maybe thirty.'

'Are you deliberately trying to be impertinent? Is this how you treat women?'

'When I came to sit and enjoy my drink I thought you were trying to tell us there shouldn't be any difference. Or have I persuaded you otherwise?'

'God, you men are so bloody arrogant. And you'll never get my vote again.'

'A fact which I suspect will come as a considerable relief to us both. Now, since other people have come here to enjoy themselves I suggest that one of us leaves. Which is it to be?'

'Damn pity,' Lillicrap intervened. 'We were all enjoying that.' Others around the table agreed, chortling their encouragement. The woman suddenly realized she had become a spectacle, grabbed her handbag and without another word left.

'Sorry,' Goodfellowe apologized. 'Just occasionally I get fed up being the world's punchbag.'

'Don't apologize when you clearly don't mean a word of it.'

A guest was extending his hand. Lillicrap effected the introductions. They shook.

'A pleasure to meet you, Mr Corsa.'

'Freddy, please. We'd all been trying to find some way of getting rid of the old crow. Should've known we'd need a shotgun.'

And they whiled away many minutes enjoying the banter and the spectacle of grown Ministers making deliberate fools of themselves until Corsa glanced at his watch.

'Come on. Allow me to blast apart your good standing on the machines just once before we go,' Corsa encouraged. 'What's it to be? You choose. Super Vixens?'

'Might be good practice for my constituency AGM,' Goodfellowe pondered. 'Better still, let's try Alien Interlopers. Particularly if one's wearing scarlet lipstick . . .'

So they had sought out the machine, hustled the controls and spent several contented minutes dismembering toad-like holo-grams which were pursuing an astronaut.

'Tell me—I'd appreciate your opinion. We're thinking of taking on Wes Phibbs as a columnist. I know he's fashionable, an item on all the chat shows, but is he a good idea?'

Goodfellowe hit another alien and edged himself ahead on the scoreboard. 'Well, his parents were born in Trinidad and he's impeccably politically correct, so perhaps that's a good recommendation for a modern opinion-former. Doesn't stop him being a shit.'

Corsa sighed in disappointment. 'That's the lump in the custard: he's so damned predictable. No freshness. What I'm looking for is someone who can do the sort of job you just did—getting past the sticky labels to the heart of a thing. Not covering it in second-hand sarcasm.'

Green alien gore had momentarily washed across the screen, obliterating the view, which returned to show a final alien about to pounce upon the unfortunate NASA spaceman. With a stream of tracer Corsa cut the creature in two.

'Congratulations,' Goodfellowe offered. 'The press wins. As always.'

'And insists on having the final word,' Corsa mused, using one last burst to obliterate the astronaut, too. 'No prisoners.' He turned purposefully to his partner, 'I don't suppose you would care to become a columnist.'

'I'm a politician.'

'Which puts you in touch with matters of the moment. You've the experience of a Minister, and an approach that is highly individual. Some would say bloody cantankerous. Sounds about right. For a columnist.'

'You don't know that I can write. *I* don't know that I can write,' Goodfellowe argued, feeling flattered and clearly turning the matter over in his mind.

'If the writing needs a little polishing, I have a menagerie of journalists who can write. Trouble is, all too few of them can think. That's the job spec.'

It was growing late, they began to drift upstairs to the exit.

'Why me?'

'Why not?'

'Oh, Mother.'

Goodfellowe's curiosity dissolved in distress. They had emerged to discover Regent Street awash in a sudden cloudburst.

'I came by bike,' Goodfellowe explained ruefully. 'Collapsible. Bit like the Government's majority.' He gazed at the malevolent skies. 'By the time I make it back to Westminster I shall have come to resemble the Alien Interloper rather more closely.'

'I suppose it's up to the *Herald* to rescue the Government yet again,' Corsa insisted, hailing his chauffeur. 'Just shove your wheels in the boot. Plenty of room. Consider it a bribe.'

Like a magic carpet the Rolls-Royce appeared before them, the bicycle was ceremoniously settled behind and Goodfellowe found himself travelling back to the House in splendour. They were accompanied by an early butterfly which had been beaten into confusion by the rain and had sought refuge inside the car. It perched on the back seat, drying its wings.

'Look, Tom, consider my offer. It would give you a great platform to air your views, and we'd pay you well. Say fifteen hundred a time? Entirely informal, whenever you felt the muse strike. But if you wanted I could guarantee a spot once a month. Doesn't even need to be political. We could ask you to do a few travel pieces —you know, our intrepid columnist reports from the slopes of Saas-Fee, or why not bugger off to the beaches of Bali? The more exotic the location, the more our readers like it. We pick up all the bills. And take someone if you want, your daughter, a friend, whoever. It's all the same to us, makes no real difference to the cost. What do you think?'

Twelve times fifteen hundred equalled ... Goodfellowe found that his breathing had become very shallow. Perhaps he wasn't in the back of a Rolls, perhaps this was simply another exotic mind machine parked in Hamley's basement and Bali was nothing but a riot of virtual reality. But Sega-world was always sunny, never dripping with rain.

'Do you believe in Fate?' Goodfellowe asked. 'Things being drawn together?'

'Don't think I do. Fate, fortune, luck—you make it yourself.'

'Most of the religions of the Orient believe in Fate, often through the conjunction of stars and planets or the intervention of any number of gods.'

'So?'

'I have the feeling that Fate might have brought us together this evening, Freddy.'

'Who knows? Does that mean you'll think about the offer?'

Nearly twenty thousand a year? Free holidays with Sam? An end to his nightmares, just for voicing his views? 'Yes, I'll think about it. Very carefully.'

They had drawn up beside Westminster Hall. Goodfellowe climbed out, marvelling still at the change of fortune that had suddenly appeared in his life. This was really how the other half lived, tossing around tens of thousands as if they scarcely mattered, because they didn't. The chauffeur, who was wearing a far better suit than Goodfellowe, helped him extract his bicycle from the boot. He felt like throwing it away, hurling it back into that old world of problems and pressures which now was all but gone. He could be his own man. Independence!

'Goodbye, Tom.'

They shook hands.

'Thank you, Freddy.'

Goodfellowe watched as his new saviour drove away. Corsa looked round in the back seat to return the wave, offering almost a formal salute and a smile. The press man also noticed the butterfly, exercising its wings. He crushed it in one hand.

* * *

Mickey had left his letters for signing and his messages in two orderly piles on his desk. Although she was young she had never let him down and he signed the letters without a second glance and, indeed, in many cases without a first glance. Impossible any other way. He received on average some two hundred letters every week, forty every working day and on days like this substantially more. Most were farmed out to government departments or ombudsmen or The Benefits Agency—yes, particularly The Benefits Agency—or a local authority office for reply. Mickey would provide a covering letter for him to sign, which

120

might be his only contact with the problem. The letter he was signing now was in reply to a protest that the lawns in the local park were not being mowed as diligently as once they were. What did she expect him to do, cut the bloody thing himself? He scribbled his signature impatiently. The next reply was to a regular complainant in which he explained that since she could still walk half a mile to her local betting shop he had no intention of supporting her application for disability benefit. Disability benefit? If it covered having to put up with pains in the backside he'd be a millionaire.

Sixty-three letters were signed. Sixty-three constituents would know by the weekend that their Member of Parliament had personally scrutinized their problems and called the appropriate agency to account. Practically none would be left better off, an entire Swedish mountainside would have been stripped of its leaf cover, more methane produced than by a thousand over-stretched cattle, and democracy would have been done. Politics had become a spectator sport. Meanwhile Macedonia burned, Tanzania starved, China was imploding and Brussels regrettably wasn't. He needed a drink.

'Hello, Tom. I'm glad you could make it. But you're a little early.' Elizabeth de Vries was radiant in the subdued lighting of The Kremlin. 'It'll give us a chance to enjoy a glass ahead of the crowd.'

He smiled in apology, wondering to himself why he'd rushed. Not just the wine, welcome as it was. Perhaps it was the unfinished business of the lunch with Sam, or simply the unique red-draped atmosphere. The basement restaurant glittered. Mirrors hung in heavy gilded frames and candlelight flickered across the polished Muscovite

121

memorabilia—a bust of Lenin, a varnished chunk of the Berlin Wall, a plumed headpiece of the Imperial Guard. There was even a drilled-out and decommissioned AK-47 assault rifle set like an exclamation mark alongside a dark and brooding Orthodox triptych of immense depth—all remnants of an inspired trip Elizabeth had begun only hours after the Wall had come down. She had set off with her new divorce papers and a vintage but stubborn Ford Transit from which she had lived and shopped and almost starved for five weeks, returning with a concept for a new restaurant which eventually had come to life behind the oppressive grey brick walls of a basement in Marsham Street. Two earlier establishments on the site had appeared and fled in rapid succession, customers deterred from entering by the inauspicious exterior. Elizabeth de Vries, with a cheap lease and rich marketing skill, had turned its forbidding aspect to allure, flooding the place with vodka and high spirits and determined in its first two months of operation to ensure that everyone left laughing.

'I failed,' she admitted to Goodfellowe as they relaxed over a glass of Balkan Zilavka. 'You didn't enjoy your lunch here.'

'You noticed.'

'Wouldn't be doing my job if I didn't.'

'My young daughter—well, not so young. You have children?'

'No. I can't.'

'I'm sorry.'

'You're not allowed to be sorry in The Kremlin, Tom. I don't permit it.' Her eyes were the colour of Seville marmalade, round and impish—very direct, he thought, particularly for a woman—and she had raspberry-plum highlights in her dark hair which matched perfectly with the surroundings. He wondered how on his first visit he could have been so blind, for without doubt this was her world. She and The Kremlin were one, sparkling, tasteful, a hint of dark mystery and a generous helping of fun.

The fun had continued throughout the wine-tasting. Sweet Tokays from the laval dust of Hungary, a Czech Sauvignon with more acid than enterprise, a powerful Georgian Naparevli red with which they had cursed the bones of Stalin, and finally dessert wines full of peaches from the Crimea to toast the memory of the Light Brigade. He'd forgotten that he'd already had a session at Hamley's; by the time he had finished he thought he could hear the tramp of Stalin's commissars drawing up behind.

'You didn't finish your last lunch. Stay for dinner?'

For a moment he was torn, taunted by a mixture of conflicting appetites and confused by hopes of financial independence as a top columnist, but he had learnt never to live off promises and he hadn't yet written a word. 'No thanks. Work to be done.'

'But I insist,' she said, taking his arm. 'You're not going to tell me you'd prefer to eat at another restaurant?' She gesticulated theatrically like an abandoned maiden cursing the gods, then burst into laughter. 'Please, Tom, be my guest, keep me company—on one condition, that you accept my apology for the inevitable interruptions I'll get during the evening. We waitresses are a pretty frenetic bunch of girls.'

'You're mocking me.'

'Only a little.'

'It's politicians who usually have to apologize, always dashing away in mid-course for votes. But this evening they've let us off the leash.'

'Good. You'll stay.'

By the time he was ready to leave, Goodfellowe was thoroughly relaxed and a little drunk. With the encouragement of a fine wine whose origins the following day he could not even recall they had celebrated his new career of sand and snow, and indulged only a little his sadness at losing office. Over a final glass he had explained a few of his difficulties with Sam, and with yet another she had reassured him that teenage girls are genetically constructed to find cause, any cause, for retaliation against their parents. Her care and consideration exceeded by a perceptible distance the bounds of mere hospitality and for a moment he thought she might regard him as some sort of damaged dog, a charity case, but by then he was too numb to mind.

'I think I may have to leave my bike behind,' he suggested as she saw him to the door.

'Having a man's bike chained overnight to a girl's railings could do terrible things for her reputation,' Elizabeth teased. 'Let's fetch it inside. The bike can stay. You can't.'

Their farewells were exchanged in laughter and he made his way back home in an imprecise manner that came not solely through exhaustion but also exhilaration. He felt warmer, more relaxed and comforted than at any time he would normally allow himself to remember. He climbed the stone stairs, too tired to make himself any tea or fold his clothes, too elated to care, and threw himself into bed.

The cold sheets struck him like an arctic bath. He knew Elizabeth had genuinely enjoyed his company,

Sam had suggested as much. And with a flash of ice-green clarity he realized how much he had delighted in hers. It wasn't the wine or the money or the meal that had left him feeling elated, it was Elizabeth. Capital E.

He wanted more. But he couldn't have it, wasn't allowed. He was married. As he slipped between the sleepless sheets, he hated himself for it.

*   *   *

Sam's surroundings that evening had been considerably less elegant. The old Wooton Minster Methodist Hall had undergone many refurbishments during its hundred-and-thirty-year existence but the works had all been relatively superficial; when the chill autumn winds blew the door continued to rattle, the draughts still searched out the corners and ghosts continued to moan softly in the rafters, just as they had in grandma's time. Yet it was clean and cheap and such things still mattered to the local organizations that used the hall, particularly to the Art Club, many of whose members were pensioners with a keen eye for value. They brought their own tea and coffee and biscuits and set the room to their own requirements, arranging the chairs to form a broad circle at the warmest end of the room. In the middle of the circle they placed a chair for the model over which was draped an old red crushed velvet blanket. The Club regularly attracted fifteen or so enthusiastic artists who were never late. Neither was Sam.

Art had become a powerful motivator in Sam's life. She possessed an ability to see below the surface of things, particularly of people, and capture their spirit on paper in a manner which

125

defied the conventional limits of two dimensions. Her art gave her a very special dimension. At every turn in her life, with her father, at her school, she found only restrictions, rules that seemed intended to control her and deny her self-esteem and independence to the point where often she felt no better than an anonymous package placed upon the remorseless conveyor belt of teenage life. Yet through her art she found one outlet no one was able to control, which allowed her to express herself, to release the emotions which often she couldn't even articulate but which somehow she was able to reveal most vividly on paper. It was more than a skill, it was also a safety valve, a means of raging against the night and of conjuring up the loves and sweetness for which she had no other outlet. Jenny Ashburton, her art teacher, had been quick to recognize both the talent and the torment. 'You can't draw if you don't feel, Sam. Don't be afraid of your emotions, the only thing you have to fear is hiding them.'

So Sam had drawn, beyond the abilities of any other pupil and beyond the resources of the school's formal art classes. With the encouragement of Mrs Ashburton, she had joined the local Art Club as its youngest and most enthusiastic member, finding adult friendships as well as drawing experiences she could not get within the walls of Werringham. Experiences like Thursday-evening life classes.

Sam joined in the good-humoured bustle as the members grabbed their own pitches, setting up their easels and donkeys in their favoured positions, erecting the small spotlight which would look down upon the model's chair and plugging in the fan heater, then setting out the crayons and colours.

They had no instructor, couldn't afford one, yet they found more than adequate compensation in the shared enthusiasm for their endeavours and the fact that here for the next two hours they would be able to escape the demands and monotony of the lives they left outside the door.

They were ready. Except for one small detail. The model hadn't arrived.

Mrs Manley-Peys, the organizing secretary, looked at her watch. 'She's a new one,' she announced; 'perhaps she's having trouble finding the hall.'

'She only has to ask someone,' Mr Frunz commented. 'It's the only hall for miles.'

'Give her another five minutes,' Miss Jardine offered optimistically.

So they had given her five minutes. Then another five. Slowly, as they waited, the atmosphere began to drain away, the sense of fun and adventure turning to mild irritability. She wasn't going to turn up.

Mrs Manley-Peys drew back thin, irritated lips. 'Such a pity. Can't seem to rely on anybody nowadays. Thank goodness we didn't pay her in advance.' She pondered over the biscuit tin in which their evening subs had been placed. 'I suppose we'd better give everyone their money back.'

Expressions of disappointment came from all sides. They wanted the evening and the adventure of drawing, not their meagre subs returned.

'Mrs Manley-Peys, how much do we pay the model?' Sam enquired.

'Quite generously, I think, in the circumstances. I know it can get a little draughty at times, but most of the models seem to truly enjoy it. Find it relaxing, almost therapeutic.'

'Yes, but—how much?'

'Twenty. Ten pounds for each hour. This is such a disappointment,' she continued. 'One or two evenings like this and you find club members beginning to drift away. Do you think she's had a breakdown or something?'

But Sam was no longer listening. Ten pounds an hour was almost four times as much as she was paid for sweating the evenings away at her local pizzeria. Twenty represented an entire weekend's income. It was a world of confusing values. And she had the trip to France coming up for which she knew her father would give her no pocket money.

'We've still got to pay for the hall,' Mr Frunz was complaining, examining the biscuit tin. 'A complete waste.'

'No it's not,' Sam interrupted.

'You want us to draw thin air, young lady?'

'No need, Mr Frunz, you can draw me. I'll be the model tonight.'

CHAPTER FOUR

The Easter recess spent at his home in Marshwood had been unnaturally quiet for Goodfellowe. No Sam. That meant no quarrels and brooding silences, to be sure, but also no opportunity to indulge in quiet moments of parental pride which made the pain worthwhile. He even lacked the customary contact with Beryl, something for which he shed no tears, but it caused him to wonder if she were up to something. She usually was.

He rattled irrelevantly around the empty family

128

home, during the day taking advantage of the clement weather to hack his way through the wildlife park that once had been his country garden—a pointless exercise, but it was good for the soul—and during the long evenings attempting to drown the emptiness by rereading favourite novels and turning the stereo volume up so that the windows rattled. It didn't work, Mahler, Mozart, not even Mani-low. As the light began to fade so did his mood of stoicism, soon to be undermined by alcohol. Self-pity began to take hold. Nights stretched before him like an empty desert where sleep was as elusive as rain, and he began to fear their arrival, knowing that being left on his own in the company of his emotions was dangerous. On Easter Day itself he found himself in Sammy's room trying to make contact, to find some anchor for his feelings. He sat on the end of her bed with its familiar coverlet, surrounded by the posters of dolphins and pop stars that littered the walls and the cuddly toys crowding along the shelves, imagining he was telling her a bedtime story. He even started reading the first few lines of *Black Beauty*, out loud, before he choked. *Black Beauty* was six—no, eight years ago, a time of innocence. Before their world fell apart. The radio alarm stood blinking in rebuke on the bedside table; it hadn't been reset in months, not since the last power cut. Sammy wasn't here. He wasn't making contact, only trawling through times past and lost like some hapless archaeologist. Tears fell—he'd rediscovered the need for crying—until they gathered on the tip of his chin and, drop by gentle drop, spattered across the pages of her book.

He returned to London two days early, drawn not

only by the welcome distraction of Gerrard Street's all-night noise but also, he had to admit privately, by the opportunity of seeing Elizabeth again. He was angry about Elizabeth. There was no place in his life for another woman, but nevertheless one had arrived. At a time when he was desperate to bring a semblance of order to his existence he'd succeeded only in adding a further element of confusion. It didn't help that he was drinking too much, although he was still sufficiently clear-sighted to realize that his circumstances made him an ideal candidate for election as a parliamentary drunk. It couldn't be long, he knew, before he would watch the pity that he still found in some colleagues' eyes turn to derision and contempt. He was too proud for that. Something had to be done.

He rose on the morning that Parliament was due to reconvene with a tongue as tough as a lizard and tasting as though it had been basted in bat oil. Two bottles of cheap Aussie Shiraz could do that and still leave enough to drive that hammer inside his skull. Bloody idiot. He knew he needed help. And perhaps a little punishment. Time to sort himself out, to beat his life back into shape.

The concept both of punishment and of beating his life back into shape made him think of Dr Lin. The doctor was a practitioner of the art of Tui-Na or deep manipulation, less a massage than a medicinal assault upon the bones and internal organs of the body which, on the one previous occasion Goodfellowe had tried it, left him aware that there were several parts of his anatomy with which he had simply lost touch. Lin had found the slumbering muscles and systems of the Goodfellowe physique and woken them in a manner which left them complaining for days, yet which Goodfellowe had found eminently reassuring. They were still there ... Goodfellowe had reached that point of maturity which passed as middle age in anyone else's dictionary, where seeds of doubt about his physical competence had begun to germinate—his stamina, his speed, his waistline, even his virility, he questioned them all. He hadn't been to bed with a woman for four years and voices began to insinuate that even if the opportunity arose, little else might. Such self-doubt is demeaning, corrosive in a man, but the gremlins had been confronted and put to stinging flight by Dr Lin's beaming pork-pie face and the meat-cleaving hands that had worked their way from the tips of each individual toe to the very top of his scalp, prodding, bending, guiding, re-educating. And, once the dull ache had dispersed, it had proved undoubtedly reinvigorating. He needed more. Forty minutes later he was lying on the good doctor's treatment couch, stripped to his underpants, regarding the doctor with trepidation.

'Good morning, Minister,' Jya-Yu's cheery voice rang out. Lin spoke not a word of English and Jya-Yu acted as his interpreter in the treatment room. 'Doctor say you tense today. Need good stretching.'

The rack again. Goodfellowe winced as he was seized by the leg which proceeded to perform an arc in the air over his shoulder.

'Doctor ask if you feel pain. If you do, he be very gentle with you.'

Goodfellowe did not respond. He deserved a little punishment. It didn't stop the guilt, but it certainly distracted from it. Anyway, his underpants were slipping and for the moment he was more

131

concerned with rescuing his dignity before Jya-Yu.

'Doctor say your liver very hot. You drink too much.' It was a statement of fact, not a criticism. The Chinese, Goodfellowe was discovering, were remarkably uncensorious. Was that why there were so few Chinese editors? 'And your shoes too tight. Make bad bowels.'

'How can he tell I'm constipated simply by twiddling my toes? And how does he hope to cure it by tying knots in my legs?'

'Chinese medicine does not deal with single parts of body,' Jya-Yu explained as a bone cracked in his hip, 'but at whole system. Look at things all round about, not just little bit at a time.'

Dr Lin's enormous hands were rushing up and down his backbone like a terrier in search of rabbits. The doctor was beginning to perspire with his exertions, turning his small white cap a fraction every few minutes to wipe his brow.

'For example,' continued Jya-Yu, 'Doctor have strange lady in last week. She complain that she live in house full of greenfly, and greenfly were burrowing under her skin, giving her terrible itching.'

'Sounds a little peculiar,' Goodfellowe muttered through tightly clenched teeth. The terrier seemed to have found an entire warren of rabbits hiding beneath his deltoids and was determined to dig every last one of them out.

'She say she go to three Western doctors, all of who say same thing. She need psychiatrist. Mental case. But Doctor Lin ask her if anyone else live in same house and have same problems with greenfly. She say no. So doctor say it cannot be greenfly. Then he start asking other questions. You know

132

what he find?'

Goodfellowe gasped, rendered hoarse by reason of the armlock which the doctor had placed around his neck.

'She your age,' Jya-Yu continued, 'have women problems. Hormone changes. Menopause. Make her skin very itch-itch-itch. Not mental at all. She need only a few pills and Bob is your honoured uncle. You see, very important to look at things all round about.' Her performance over, she gave a little bow.

In spite of himself, Goodfellowe laughed. He was beginning to feel better now, more relaxed. The head was clear, the Yin had made contact with his Yang, his chest seemed to have filled out to twice its normal size and both oxygen and optimism were forcing their way back through the system. He felt sure the burning sensation cascading down his legs would disappear eventually.

'Doctor say you very fit. For your age.'

Lin slapped him cheerfully; it hurt. He decided to take it as a compliment. Looking at things all round about, the good doctor had pronounced him fit to do battle. He felt better, standing straight, re-enthused. A warrior in St Michael's underwear.

Outside the surgery the real world was lying in wait for him. As he spilled out onto the street he was greeted by a newspaper billboard. 'Granite Expansion Plan' it proclaimed. The *Evening Herald* was filled with coverage of Freddy Corsa's latest corporate pronouncements, overflowing with phrases such as 'dramatic new strategy for growth', 'challenging environment ushered in on the back of the Press Bill' and 'extensive new financial support in the pipeline.' There was reference to new

133

investment partners, although Goodfellowe noted that no names were mentioned. The edition also contained a profile of Freddy Corsa which, even by the normal standards of proprietor hagiography, was unusually effusive, emphasizing his strong family and charitable commitments even as he moved to fulfil his ambition to place Granite amongst the largest companies in its sector, while the *Herald's* diarist nominated him as one of the country's most exciting young entrepreneurs. The Stop Press carried the announcement that the Granite share price had risen in response, on the basis of which the new City Editor had, entirely without announcement, ordered himself a new sports car.

Less prominent, indeed entombed in the detail of an inside financial page, was the statement that in order to prepare for this great leap forward Granite was undertaking yet another review of its internal systems and manning levels—'to ensure the company is in the leanest and fittest possible shape for the opportunities ahead.' Gain through pain.

Goodfellowe read it all. The explanations. The analysis. The veneration of Freddy Corsa. His new friend. A man on the move.

In spite of his odiously pinching shoes, Goodfellowe found a new spring in his step. Lin's muscle medicine had worked and he could feel the sun on his back warming his spirits. It was time for a new beginning, time to find a new way ahead. Perhaps the many fragments of his life could be made to fit together after all. As he kicked at pigeons in Trafalgar Square he took several decisions. He resolved to telephone Sam in France for no other reason than to let her know he hoped she was having a wonderful time. He would book dinner tonight at The Kremlin—but only half a bottle. And he would drop a note to Freddy Corsa to offer warmest congratulations—and his own services as Fleet Street's newest occasional columnist.

Tom Goodfellowe, he decided, and with only the slightest limp, was back in business.

*   *   *

For many, the House of Commons is a jungle inhabited by Great Beasts, and even occasionally by a Great She Elephant. This jungle is one of the noisiest places on the planet. The Great Beasts spend much of their time crashing through the undergrowth, guarding their territory jealously and ensuring that the other animals are aware of their presence by releasing terrifying roars in an attempt to induce fear and submissiveness. Confrontations are frequent, accompanied by theatrical and skilfully choreographed displays of aggression, but while all this activity might result in the trampling of a few small trees and shrubs only rarely does it draw blood. A sham. However, it's a great show for tourists.

In the jungle there are few Great Beasts. Most of the animals are less formidable, mere ground squirrels who find safety in burrows, popping up only briefly to see what all the noise is about before disappearing once more, or chattering marmosets who gather in the treetops to gossip and throw the occasional nut of protest at the back of a passing Great Beast. The nut-throwing rarely has the slightest effect, in spite of the fact that from a treetop a marmoset can sometimes see much

135

farther than any Great Beast.

The treetops of the parliamentary jungle are to be found in the formal rooms which divide off the Committee Corridor, a long and richly panelled passage that runs along the riverside flank of the Palace of Westminster. While the Great Beasts fight out their battles on the floor of the Chamber, it is up in Standing Committee that much of the real work of Parliament is performed, scrutinizing new legislation and examining every line of a Bill for any inadvertent intent or casual prejudice that may have been woven into the text by the parliamentary draftsmen. From the Committee Corridor the view can be much clearer, less obscured by the clouds of dust which rise from the strainings of Great Beasts below. Committees can offer reasoned advice, encourage second thoughts, even suggest new ideas—although more often than not the Great Beasts are making too much noise to hear.

It was from this vantage point, shortly after Parliament had resumed from its Easter recess, that Goodfellowe found himself amongst twenty-four other Members in Committee Room 10, a substantial room of Pugin wall coverings and towering ceilings, where he had been summoned by Lillicrap to do his duty in the passage of the Press (Diversity of Ownership) Bill. The Committee Room was laid out on three sides with chairs and desks; the Chairman and his officers at the head, Government forces on his right, Opposition to the left, and the public scattered to the rear of the room. Goodfellowe sat in the last of three rows of seats allocated to the Government while Lillicrap, in the manner of an eager collie, sat guarding his flock from his position on the front row. The work of the Standing Committee, any Standing Committee, though often intriguing, is rarely enthralling and although to the distant eye Goodfellowe appeared to be busily engaged in studying Committee papers, in fact like many of the other Members present he was surrounded by constituency correspondence. There seemed little in the detail of Clause 2 Subsection 8 to engage him, so he occupied the time between votes in tasks such as signing letters and trying to fathom how he would cope with an engagements diary that resembled Bombay railway station in the monsoon season. Rush, crush, cancellations, unexpected alterations, a schedule bordering on chaos, but where did it all get him? There seemed to be precious few departures. And looming ahead were preparations for the next election, whenever that might come, which meant interminable evenings closeted with Beryl. For a moment he considered throwing himself on the tracks.

His eyes wandered to the huge oil canvas which hung on the half-panelled wall on the opposite side of the room. It depicted a scene from the Napoleonic Wars, a great naval engagement of flame and ferocity in which Nelson was locked in combat with a French battleship. The Frenchie always reminded Goodfellowe of Beryl. She was dismasted, her rigging torn like cobwebs and her gunwales reduced to matchwood, but still there was defiance, still her cannon blazed, even as she was going down she refused to give up. And one of the pieces always seemed to be pointing directly at him. He had noticed that wherever he sat in that room, one of the Frenchie guns was always aimed in his direction. The muzzle followed him around like eyes on a Picasso. As Beryl would, every day throughout the next election.

He was concluding that he would need not only a blind eye but also a deaf ear if he were to survive a campaign with Beryl when his attention was distracted by a member of the Opposition who was standing to pursue a Point of Order. Betty Ewing was complaining in persistent manner and broad Birmingham tones that her amendment had not been called in spite of the fact that it raised matters of fundamental importance to the Bill.

'I appreciate you won't give reasons for not selecting my amendment,' she protested to the Chairman, 'but can I encourage you to reconsider? We're told by Europe that we've got to change the ownership rules for British newspapers, but it's like playing games with mirrors. Who owns the newspapers anyway? In fact, how do we know this isn't simply a great European prank to ensure that British newspapers end up in the hands of foreign owners.'

'They already are,' one of her colleagues interjected drily, while the Committee Chairman, Frank Breedon, a curmudgeon and particularly so after lunch, drummed his fingers impatiently.

'The point I'm trying to make, Mr Breedon, is simply this. There is no logic in changing the rules of ownership if there is no way of knowing who the owners are. Shareholder lists are practically incomprehensible. They tell you that the Tom Dick & Harry Investment Trust own shares, but who in turn owns Tom and Dick and Harry? This Bill will be meaningless without an amendment requiring a far more rigorous identification of anyone with a beneficial interest in the ownership of a newspaper.

So that we know precisely who they are. Spelled out, on a central register. We can't allow foreign owners to hide behind all sorts of incomprehensible corporate structures.'

Several Members were on their feet trying to intervene and the Minister, too, was rising.

'Order! Order!' the Chairman barked. His voice was habitually loud, an attempt to compensate for his deafness and what was more than a measure of ineptitude. 'I've had a Point of Order from Mrs Ewing. Let's deal with that first.' He nodded in the direction of the Minister.

'Further to that point of order, Mr Breedon, can I assure the Committee that such fears are unwarranted? There are rules of disclosure required by the Stock Exchange which guard against covert ownership . . .'—he ignored the snorts of derision and experience from across the floor—'and anyone who wilfully evaded them would be liable to prosecution.'

'How can they be prosecuted if we don't know who they are?' Betty Ewing threw at him. 'They could run rings around the regulations. We need a central register.'

'What the Honourable Lady proposes is simply not practical,' the Minister continued. He paused to moisten lips desiccated by a lifetime of reading out civil service briefs. 'If those shares are owned by a pension fund, for example, are we supposed to make changes to a register every time someone leaves his job or dies? We might be registering literally thousands of such changes every day. No, it wouldn't work. Couldn't work.'

Amidst chatter on all sides another Opposition Member had risen to pursue the matter. 'I don't often play the Puritan, Mr Chairman, but if we don't know who the owners are this whole Bill is rendered utterly and completely and stupidly pointless. Like so much else of what comes out of Brussels.' He smiled as even Government members responded loudly to his last point.

'It would greatly assist the Committee if members would come to order. And if Puritanism wasn't intermingled quite so freely with points of political principle,' Breedon interjected, offering a little joke under pressure. It didn't succeed. As the Chairman turned to consult on a point of procedure with his officials, crossfire erupted beyond the reach of his deaf ear.

'We need a central register,' Betty Ewing persisted.

'It's another Brussels bungle,' added her colleague.

'We can't bury the Bill in bureaucracy,' the Minister complained, gesticulating across the floor to the Opposition. 'Why should we impose heavier burdens on newspapers than on other industries?'

'Because newspapers are different.'

The collective attention of the Committee Room was suddenly drawn to a new player in the game. The Minister turned to look in surprise and not altogether with warmth at Goodfellowe who, from his seat in the back row, shifted uncomfortably. He hadn't intended to intervene, his attentions had been elsewhere, on the gun barrel, on the constituency correspondence. Anyway, Government backbenchers weren't supposed to rush forward to prop up Opposition Members engaged in duels with Ministers. But there it was. It had slipped out, almost unintentionally, rather in

140

the manner that a dish might fall out from behind a partially closed cupboard door. Lillicrap, the master of closed cupboards, looked on in concern.

'They are different,' Goodfellowe repeated, feeling forced to justify himself. 'We have always set newspapers apart from other industries. That's why they don't pay VAT, for instance.'

'And why they get handed so many knighthoods and peerages,' someone from the Opposition quipped.

'Government grovel,' another added. 'You'd think there was an election coming.'

'Did anyone mention Maxwell?' a third enquired.

The Minister turned to mouth a silent but unmistakable oath at Goodfellowe. Like a gun muzzle exploding.

'Order! Order!' Chairman Breedon demanded gruffly, his attentions now back with them and aware he had lost control. He was in tetchy mood, needing to reassert his authority, and his irritation focused on Goodfellowe. 'Frankly it's surprising and exceedingly annoying that someone of the Honourable Gentleman's experience should try to turn this Committee into a school playground.'

Goodfellowe began to protest—he'd stated no more than a point of fact—but Breedon was having none of it. 'Making disruptive comments from the back row may have been excusable in the Honourable Gentleman's classroom but no one is going to get away with it in mine.'

Goodfellowe began to rise to his feet. 'Further to the Honourable Lady's Point of Order ...'

'No, sir!' Breedon's hand slapped down on his table, sending his steel grey forelock and various items of paper fluttering. 'I have made my ruling.

141

The amendment is unacceptable. The Honourable Gentleman's intervention is unacceptable. That is the end of the matter.'

Goodfellowe was left astonished by the outburst. What on earth had he done to merit such treatment? His intervention was admittedly ill-considered, unorthodox perhaps, but scarcely objectionable. The passions being roused by this Bill seemed to require more explanation than that provided simply by the Chairman's post-prandial discomforts. He looked to Lillicrap seated at the end of the front row, beseeching him for support. Lillicrap shrugged his shoulders and turned away.

*   *   *

They were seated at the best table in The Kremlin, next to the Tsar's piano, which still bore the scars of its liberation from the Winter Palace in the form of angry bullet holes. Goodfellowe's mood was similarly apocalyptic. What had been intended as an occasion to mark Mickey's twenty-fifth birthday— 'Take me out to dinner, somewhere very public. I'll wear a disgraceful dress. The men will all drool and the women will be wondering what it is you've got. That way we'll both enjoy it.' —had instead turned into something of a post-mortem on the afternoon's proceedings in Standing Committee. Goodfellowe seemed to have a mind for little else in spite of Mickey's very evident attractions.

'He just went for me. Out of the blue. Bizarre. Does he dislike me so much?'

'It was probably nothing personal, Tom, you simply happened to be handy, a convenient target. Breedon is a parliamentary eunuch, one of those Members who never had the chance to make it big.

142

He's resented never being a Minister and probably thinks you're an ungrateful bloody fool for having given it all up. Now he's become chairman of some committee and he wants to show he's the biggest swinger in town. He's going through one of those phases.'

'What do you mean "one of those phases"?'

'You know, those phases you men go through. Always having to prove their masculinity. Doing push-ups and going to the gym so you're fit enough to chase bimboes. As if the bimboes you lot chase are ever likely to run away.'

'I do not chase bimboes,' he corrected her, a trifle stiffly.

'Why not, Tom?'

'What?'

'Why not?' The question was in earnest. 'You can't cut yourself off from half of humanity simply because you've had some terrible luck.'

Anyone else he might have told to mind their own bloody business, but not Mickey. 'It's not a thing I care to think much about,' he responded defensively.

'Look, I'm the agony aunt, remember? And of course you think about it. That's why you take so much interest in my sex life, because it helps compensate for your own. It's also why you've been staring into your custard all evening, rather than at me. It's not that you don't like this rather fetching little dress which just about manages to cling to me, it's that you like it all too much. Every other man in the restaurant is staring at me, but you won't allow yourself to.'

'Mickey,' he protested. 'You're my secretary. And, if it comes to that, my friend.'

'I know, Tom. But in truth I'm not talking about me. I'm talking about someone else, another friend, a partner. You deserve it. And I think you need it.'

'Not possible.' He shook his head, then shook it again more slowly. 'There's a part of me I have to lock away.'

'You lock it away and all it does is kick at the door trying to get out. It does you no good, Tom. You've taken enough kicks as it is.'

'I am married, Mickey. That means a great deal to me.'

'Good for you, Tom. I mean that. I know the sacrifices you make for your wife. I get the bills, remember? But you sacrifice too much of yourself, and one day you'll find there's nothing left to give. And don't forget I've been brought up by a Jewish mother. I've got an hereditary doctorate in guilt.'

She was pushing it, really pushing it and maybe too far. But someone had to, for his own good, and who else was there? He was studying his plate with the fiercest intensity. Slowly his head rose, his eyes filled with anguish, and more than a little fear.

'This is a hell of a long way from Frank Bloody Breedon.'

'Oh, he's no problem,' she responded gaily, aware that a change of mood was called for. 'He hates you all on a Tuesday and Thursday afternoon because the Standing Committee forces him to rush his lunch.'

'Acid indigestion.'

'Good grief, no. Her name's Victoria.'

'You mean . . .?'

'That's right. He's going through "one of those phases". Taken to the gym and everything. Sends his secretary out for little presents—toiletries,

144

scarves, jewellery. Nothing too expensive. And not the sort of thing you do for the wife.'

'But how do you know?'

'Because you men are bone idle when it comes to lechery and lust. Victoria is a researcher, one of the American students we get over here for a year's work experience. So on Tuesday Brother Breedon gives his secretary twenty quid and sends her out for "some little token" as he describes it, a birthday present for a niece. He seems to have acquired a lot of nieces recently. Anyway, she comes back with a set of ear-rings which by Wednesday afternoon are dangling from Victoria's little lobes. Even you should be able to figure that one out.'

Goodfellowe leaned back in his chair as though trying to distance himself from something deeply unpalatable. He looked at Mickey in astonishment, as if seeing something for the first time. Then, his expression still incredulous, he started to shake with laughter. It struck him with such force that he had to stifle it behind a starched napkin. 'You are good for the soul, you know that?' he gasped, wiping bleary eyes.

'I reach the parts other bimboes cannot reach, you mean.'

'I suppose so.' His face shone with gratitude. 'So, Breedon thinks—and I quote you accurately, I hope, Miss Ross—that I'm an ungrateful bloody fool. He'll be a complete misanthrope after every lunch. And this is the man I've got to spend every Tuesday and Thursday with for the next three months. Great. You've cheered me up no end.'

'What are birthday parties for?'

Suddenly someone else had appeared at their side. It was Elizabeth. 'I want you to know that

145

when Mickey booked the table for you, Tom, she also asked for an enormous cake out of which would leap a scantily clad super-jock, but I told her The Kremlin wasn't that sort of place. Although maybe it should be.' A hand fell gently on Goodfellowe's shoulder as she inspected the table to ensure that all was as she had prescribed. 'Perhaps your Mr Breedon would eat here even more frequently if it were.'

'Save me, I'm not going to keep bumping into him here as well, am I?' Goodfellowe muttered.

'He keeps some very interesting company at lunch, does Mr Breedon.'

'So I've been hearing.'

'Don't have such a closed mind, Tom. Why, only last week he was deep in discussion at this very table with one of the big Moggies.'

'Moggies?'

'Media Owners' Group. The fat cats of the media world.'

'Fascinating. What were they discussing?'

'My dear Tom, this place is like a confessional. Couldn't repeat what I heard. It would be breaking all sorts of professional confidences.' She was sounding deliberately coquettish. She bent low, whispering. 'Although it's astonishing what you do hear. You'd be surprised how many ungrateful bloody fools treat you like the wallpaper, never notice you're there.'

Mickey giggled. Goodfellowe flushed, but was not to be distracted from his purpose.

'I've always wondered if this place might be a front for the KGB. Would it be a gross violation of professional ethics to know which of the Old Toms was taking my beloved Chairman out to lunch?'

146

Elizabeth puckered. When teasing men, which she did often, she had a habit of pursing her lips as if directing a kiss, then twisting her lips to one side as though to deprive them of their expected pleasure. She was teasing now, but Goodfellowe was too in earnest to notice.

'Do you think the KGB might be interested in coming in as a partner? I've got a set of their handcuffs somewhere.'

'Elizabeth!'

'You win. It was Freddy Corsa.'

'Damn.' Goodfellowe uttered the word softly, as though he were slowly deflating, leaving him with insufficient breath for more forceful expression.

'Of course!' Mickey exclaimed. 'Just before Christmas. In Las Vegas. Breedon was the *Herald's* celebrity correspondent at the heavyweight fight. You know, eight hundred words and all expenses paid? Justin stayed up all night to watch it, said it was a real dog, that I give him a better fight than he saw then. Three rounds of patacake with more clinching than you'd get in the showers at Wormwood Scrubs. Anyway, he mentioned Breedon's article, said he was surprised he was a fight fan.' A smile of unadulterated mischief spread across her face. 'Come to think of it, that was the week Victoria wasn't around either. Said she was going back home.'

'I wonder what a first-class week for two in Las Vegas costs,' Goodfellowe mused. 'With or without the fight tickets.'

'You think the *Herald* paid for Victoria too?'

He recalled his own conversation with Corsa. 'I have a sneaking suspicion they might.'

'That's not against the rules, is it?' Elizabeth

asked.

'Probably not. But maybe it should be.'

Elizabeth adopted a conspiratorial tone. 'And I wouldn't suppose for a moment that your Mr Breedon was having lunch in order to plan any further arduous travels he might undertake on behalf of the *Herald*. Do you? At least, not unless you're an awful old cynic, Tom Goodfellowe.' And with another pucker Elizabeth left to tend to her other guests.

'You know she fancies you,' Mickey stated, sounding almost bored.

'Stop going on about that,' he snapped.

'Wasn't aware I'd mentioned it before.'

But Goodfellowe was elsewhere. At lunch with Breedon and Corsa. At Hamley's. In Las Vegas. And in Committee Room 10. He was suddenly aware that all was not as it once had seemed.

* * *

'You certainly know how to show a girl a good time for her birthday treat,' Mickey remarked, running a hand through her tousled hair.

He chose not to hear. They had returned from The Kremlin to the House of Commons, she with her skirts swirling and he with a look of great intent, switching on lights and raising the eyebrows of the duty policemen as they went. Now she was seated at her computer while he raced a finger through the bound edition of the Register of Members' Interests, an annual publication designed, in the inevitably somewhat pompous wording of the reporting committee, 'to provide information of any pecuniary interest or other material benefit which a Member receives which might reasonably be

148

thought by others to influence his or her actions, speeches or vote in Parliament, or actions taken in his or her capacity as a Member of Parliament.' The Register was supposed to show who was doing what with whom in the belief that, so long as it was done in public, it must be decent. But, in many Members' minds, it also had to be relevant.

'It's not bloody here.'

'What ain't?' When she was tired, the gloss occasionally fell from Mickey's accent, and it was past eleven.

'Look. Here's Breedon's entry. No mention of journalism or writing. Sweet nothing about Las Vegas.'

'Maybe he forgot. Maybe it was a one-off. Maybe he doesn't regard his interest in boxing as having anything to do with his being a politician.'

'What? You think he was sent all the way to Las Vegas because of his sex appeal and intimate relationship with the Marquess of Queensberry? '

'He presumably thinks so.'

'And what of Pennymore?' Goodfellowe had turned at random to another page of the Register which featured a high-profile colleague. 'He's writing all the time, even scribbles the occasional theatre and film review, yet the only reference here is to "occasional journalism". And he reckons he earns less than ten thousand a year from all that?'

'We can soon see.'

'How? '

'Would you accept that no self-respecting Member of the House is likely to sell his soul for less than a pound a word?'

He remembered that Corsa was offering more. 'A reasonable working assumption.'

149

'Then if we find the words, we've found your answer.' Immediately she began tapping away at her keyboard. 'We can log onto the newspaper libraries and see what they have on the esteemed Member. Let's try the *Telegraph* first, shall we?' And in a little while she had on her screen three articles that the prolific Pennymore had penned over the last year. 'That's three thousand, now let's have a look at the *Herald*. Then the *Mail*.' And so they had begun a search through Fleet Street's finest, identifying articles, calculating both wordage and poundage and coming to a figure considerably in excess of ten thousand.

'Is he on the fiddle?' Mickey enquired.

Goodfellowe shook his head. 'Perhaps not. He appears to be a bit of a tart, puts himself about, doesn't seem to have a regular contract with anyone. So "occasional journalism" is probably technically correct. Maybe he doesn't earn more than ten thousand from any single source. And I suspect he would argue that his television and theatre reviews have bugger all to do with politics so don't need recording in the Register.'

'So he's another one with so much sex appeal he feels he has a public duty to share it.'

'But his Register entry is so hugely misleading. And he's on the Press Bill Standing Committee. But then, so am I. And Freddy Corsa has asked me to write for him, too.'

'Bit of a coincidence.'

'Strange world. If we were taking as much money from any other industry there would be cries of corruption and outrage. Led by the newspapers, of course. But so long as we keep scribbling articles they seem to have an excuse for shovelling as much

150

money at us as they like.'

'Dirty bath water.'

They were silent for a while, contemplating the road they had suddenly started to venture down.

'Maybe we should pull the plug on it,' Goodfellowe muttered. 'Is all this press money meant to cover our votes as well as our articles? I want to find out.' Goodfellowe continued to stare at the screen intently. Suddenly he became aware that he was leaning very closely over Mickey's shoulder, his hot breath falling over smooth bare skin and his eyes, when lowered, being afforded a view that was beyond despair, like fruit in the Garden of Eden. Temptation tore at his roots. They were alone on their own island, cut off from the rest of the world, in a place where rules could be and often were remade. Every instinct in his body seemed to have come alive and they were all primordial, growing stronger with each passing beat of her chest. He felt he might do something stupid, something that he would bitterly regret. He could not move back, would not move on, his resolution in turmoil. At that moment, and much to his relief, she yawned.

'But is there any fun in finding out what everyone is up to?' she asked wearily. 'I know it only upsets Justin.'

He drew back, the spell broken. 'It's too late now, but there's work for you in the morning. I want you to go through every member of the Committee, examine their entry in the Register, then play around with your computer thingy and see what you can find.'

'Sounds fun.' She yawned again.

'It may surprise you, Miss Ross, but even Members of Parliament have been known to succumb to temptation.'

'I do hope so,' she smiled, brightening, and switching off the screen.

It was gone midnight as the duty policemen saluted the Member and his young lady companion with tousled hair and careful mascara and a figure which, even with her coat on, demanded their attention. The girl swung her hips as she passed.

Neither man took his eyes off her retreating form. One moistened his lips. 'You know, Baz, think I'll get myself elected.'

'What, all that unpaid overtime?'

'Yeah, you're right. Could wear you out, all those late nights. Could be a real killer,' he smiled wistfully.

*   *   *

The sun had yet to disperse the late spring mist that was clinging to Whitehall like fog on an undeveloped film. It was not yet eleven, an uncommon time for guests to be found in The Kremlin. Yet when Elizabeth walked in bearing the spoils of her trip to the Tachbrook Street market Goodfellowe had already been waiting for some time.

'I invited myself. Sorry,' he offered, and nothing more.

She looked searchingly at him—the sapless cheeks, the rim of sleeplessness around the eyes, the hurriedly knotted tie. Elizabeth said nothing, disappearing into the kitchen with her carrier bags of meat and herbs and reappearing moments later bearing two huge glasses—bowls, almost—of orange-drenched champagne. 'You obviously need it. I've a feeling I may be in need of it, too.

Nazdarovie.'

They raised the glasses and continued to sit silently for a while. He'd rehearsed his thoughts in fine detail throughout the night, yet the lack of sleep had caused their rhythm to disappear and with it his resolution. He needed the drink.

'Is that piano for real?' he asked, searching for somewhere, anywhere, to start.

'What are you, from Trading Standards? You want to know whether my piano is a genuine Tsar Nicholas with authentic Bolshevik bullet holes? The twenty pounds I paid for it in a Ukrainian street market says it is, and I consider it entirely possible that the date of 1932 on the maker's stamp inside is a wicked forgery. But you know me, I'm just a gullible wee girl.'

'Do I know you? Truth is, I know very little about you.'

'A maid of mystery.'

'De Vries. Is that a maiden name, a married name?'

'Neither. But I was scarcely likely to flourish on Planet Westminster with a name like Molly O'Malley, was I now? We came from County Carlow, my parents were great traditionalists. Molly was good enough for Daddy's grandmother, so it was good enough for me. Elizabeth de Vries is a stage name that I use in this little basement theatre. On the other side of the water I'm Molly O'Malley and proud of it.'

'Unusual. Someone in Westminster who seems to know precisely who they are.'

His maudlin observation was interrupted as the door swung open, In came a street cleaner—highway sanitation officer, in the jargon of

153

Westminster City Council's multiple employment codes, complete with luminous overjacket and cigarette wedged behind his ear. His strides, languorous and loose, brought him clumping across the floor to a point where he stood distractedly in front of Elizabeth, clutching his cap and conducting a patient examination of his nails.

'Mornin', Libby.' He ignored Goodfellowe completely.

'Good morning to you, Ted,' she replied, extracting a folded ten-pound note from the pocket on her blouse and handing it across.

Ted replaced his cap with a gesture that might have been a form of awkward salute and, without passing another word, departed.

Goodfellowe sat mesmerized. 'A man of restricted vocabulary,' he muttered, 'but apparently very flexible understanding of the street sweeper's book of rules. Have I just seen a backhander being passed?'

'Backhanders are for cynics,' Elizabeth chided, 'and totally unnecessary in this island of opportunity which you politicians have created, where the streets are not only paved with gold but always swept scrupulously clean. Particularly outside busy restaurants.'

'Tell me that wasn't a backhander.'

Elizabeth gave the point careful, even extravagant consideration before replying. 'This is the way it works. Ted is my turf adviser. He advises me on the turf. Once a week I give him ten pounds to place on a horse he fancies—after all, what do we Irish lasses understand about such things? He's very conscientious, regular as rain. Never offers an ungentlemanly word. And who knows, one day I

154

might even win. In the meantime he and his crew do a wonderful job with those messy black bags on the pavement outside, don't you think?'

'A damned backhander!'

'Get a life, Goodfellowe.' Elizabeth arched an elegant eyebrow. 'You'll be telling me next that the glasses of champagne I give to the traffic wardens are no better than bribes.'

'I am truly shocked.'

'And I'm a soft touch. I've been known to give champagne to almost any waif and stray I find on the doorstep.'

'Ouch.' He felt obliged to laugh at himself. 'You have a way of putting things in perspective.' Then more seriously: 'I think that's why I've come.'

'Your move,' she said softly. Her words seemed to reawaken the lost rhythm of his thoughts.

'I used to imagine I was a good man. Sometimes I used to dream I might one day even be a great man. High office. The highest, perhaps. Leaving my mark upon history. A sort of one-man armada on the high seas, someone who could go anywhere, achieve anything. Make a difference. That mattered to me, Elizabeth, making a difference.'

'Mattered? Past tense?'

'Turned out I wasn't the armada but an old barrel which once they'd emptied they threw overboard. No longer needed on voyage. Now I'm a piece of parliamentary driftwood. If I make any mark on the sand, it's wiped away with the next tide. My shoes pinch, my hair's going grey. And I seem to have made one awful mess of my life.'

'I think you're being too harsh.'

'Look,' he said with feelings on the flood, 'I'm supposed to help run the country yet I can't even

155

manage myself. My private life's a ruin, my financial affairs no more than rubble. Sam—you remember, my daughter?—she's the most important single thing in my life, perhaps the only thing that truly matters any more. Yet in her life I count for nothing. My wife is locked in an institution where she doesn't know if it's night or day, and all this, this'—his voice was beginning to snag on the pain— 'hell on earth is nobody's fault, no one to blame. So why is it I feel so bloody guilty?'

'Because you care, Tom. Perhaps too much.'

'Or is it because I'm irredeemably arrogant and an ungrateful bloody fool? You know, all this mess could be cured, or at least eased, simply by accepting a proposition from Freddy Corsa that I should allow my thoughts on issues of public importance to grace his newspapers. I should be flattered; no one else seems too interested in what I've got to say.'

'And why not? It's an offer which Breedon had no difficulty in accepting. It's the sort of thing politicians have been doing since ... well, since there were politicians.'

'Seems so easy, doesn't it? Travel in company, and in some comfort, with Fleet Street's florin in my pocket. My wife needs it, my daughter needs it, Corsa's proposal is legal, it's entirely within the rules. So I've climbed on board. Written him a note accepting his extraordinarily generous proposition. He's waiting for the first article now. And yet ...'

'You suspect life is one great backhander.'

'It's like rain, Elizabeth. A few drops can make a harvest. Too much and the whole farm gets washed away.'

'And is there a downpour?'

156

'With Corsa? Hell, I don't know. Half of me wants to find out, the other half keeps yelling that I'm an utter idiot because if I do I wave goodbye to the one chance I might have of sorting out my life. What you don't know can't tickle your conscience.'

'So you want to ask my advice as to whether supping with the Devil and pocketing his thirty pieces of silver is the way out of damnation?' She examined her glass coyly. 'After my performance this morning I'm not sure I'm the one to pontificate.'

He touched her hand, lightly, then withdrew it with evident reluctance. 'You've done enough by listening. Anyway, my conscience is a bit like a duck pond; a little muddy, too many weeds, maybe dried up a little since I was a young man. But the ducks eventually come back and flap around. Stir it up. I'll wake up one morning and know inside myself what it is I have to do.'

'Then I'm puzzled. What's the problem?'

'Uncertainty.'

'About Corsa?'

'And about you.'

'Oh, oh. Somehow I thought I'd be needing this drink.'

He cleared his throat with the sound of feathered thunder. 'I want to get to know you better, Elizabeth. Very much better. If you'll let me.'

'I hate to disappoint.'

'But if I do it will be too late to wake up in the morning and discover I was wrong. And it might be. Disastrously wrong. My wife and my marriage are of great importance to me yet I hang onto them by the thinnest of threads. It wouldn't take much to break it.'

'I see.' She sounded sad.

'Part of me now hopes you'll laugh me out of your restaurant and solve the problem for me.' The other part clearly didn't mean it.

Her eyes had melted like Carlow dew. 'Tom, I can't decide such matters for you. I'd like to help, very much. More than perhaps up to this moment I'd realized. But whoever else might be in your bed in the morning, the one person you've got to be able to wake up with is yourself. Only you can decide if there's room there for Freddy Corsa. Or anyone else.'

Goodfellowe found dew in his own eyes. 'Anyway, why on earth would a beautiful woman like you be interested in a piece of overweight baggage like me?'

She puckered. 'Because if I can't be the skinniest one at the party, I'm just not going to go.'

*   *   *

Goodfellowe's desk usually resembled a recycling centre disappearing beneath an overflow of paper. This afternoon, however, it appeared unusually peaceful. Mickey had taken it over. To one side of the desk was a notebook with a number of different coloured highlighters, to the other a borrowed volume of the current *Who's Who*, and in the middle, pinned open by the weight of a wilting potted azalea, was the Register of Members' Interests.

'There's no clear pattern. But maybe that in itself suggests a pattern,' she said, without looking up at Goodfellowe as he came in. 'In some cases it's ail too simple. Here's your Caravan Park Owners' consultancy, amount and source both listed under your name, clear as a sunny day at Clacton.'

'It rained last time I went.'

'But other MPs bowl the ball with a different spin. Take Quentin Cripps. He has a laundry list of company directorships but he doesn't give any figures. His entry says the directorships are remunerated, but doesn't give an amount.'

'Can he do that?'

'I chatted with his secretary. She says the directorships have nothing to do with his being an MP so there's no reason why he should go full frontal. Other Members use descriptions like "corporate consultant" and give practically no details at all, even about the source let alone the amount. In fact, going through the Register I can find surprisingly few sources of income listed above ten thousand. As the pile of gold grows higher, the details seem to get lost in mountain mist.'

'The gods on Mount Olympus shall remain invisible to mortal eye.' He sat down on the edge of the desk. 'But what about the winged messengers of journalism?'

'The mountain mists grow ever thicker. Lots of them list an interest like "occasional journalism" or "income from sundry writing". It's huge, something like a third of all backbenchers have media income of that sort. But you rarely get any precise figures, how much it's worth. Or who is paying them.'

The telephone rang, he picked it up. It was Lillicrap. 'Can't, I'm busy,' Goodfellowe barked and replaced the receiver.

'What about the members of the Standing Committee?' he pressed.

She consulted her watch. 'Aren't you supposed to be there?'

'This is more important. Both to me and the Committee.'

'OK. I've looked at ten members of the Committee so far, in addition to Breedon. Seven of them list some form of income from journalism or writing, but there's not a single detail. No mention of who's paying them or how much. And it's on both sides, Government and Opposition.'

'As you say, a pattern of obscurity.'

'But is it a deliberate pattern? You think they've been fixed?'

He took a long time before replying. 'No,' he said eventually, shaking his head. 'I don't believe it, not of them; many are fine people. Good colleagues. I don't want to believe it.'

'That's not an argument. That's an epitaph.'

'You're right. So let me try a little harder.' He began pacing in front of the desk, measuring his steps as carefully as he measured his thoughts. 'I was approached by Corsa. Offered a deal, money in exchange for work, perfectly legitimate. That didn't corrupt me, at least I didn't feel corrupted. But maybe it was part of the great editing process of power. I would have been encouraged to feel grateful. Obligated. To see the story through his eyes.'

'To see the Press Bill through his eyes.'

'We never got down to that but, yes, I suppose you're right. I would certainly have to listen to the arguments of my employer and benefactor with the greatest of care. Another thing. No one asked me to write for them until I became a member of the Standing Committee. As much of an egotist as I am, even I was surprised at the interest. I'm not exactly the most obvious parliamentary pin-up of the

160

month. So I suspect I was offered the minimum deal.'

'If you don't tell me what it was you'll never sing baritone again.'

'Practically twenty thousand, guaranteed. And lots of free holidays. Could even have taken you along, if I wanted.'

Mickey whistled. 'Of course, personally I'm beyond corruption. But even I have my weaknesses. Barbados. Bermuda. Bognor, in the right company.'

'And if the majority of the Committee share your keen sense of morality . . .'

Goodfellowe's reflections were brought to a sudden end as, without warning, the door burst open. It was Lillicrap, flushed of cheek and with eyes that looked as though they should have been staring from a police poster.

'Tom, you bloody truant. What the hell are you up to? You're supposed to be helping the Committee.'

'I think what I've been doing has been helping the Committee . . .'

'Not if you're here you're not. Dammit, four of our side are away sick or mucking out in their constituencies and I'm about to lose another in ten minutes. When he goes the Opposition will troop out after him. We'll lose our quorum and the rest of the day's business. This is an important Bill, Tom, we can't afford delays, and we can't afford Government backbenchers playing the spoilt child.'

'You want my support, Lionel. Just as last week you so readily gave me yours over Breedon?'

'Grow up, Tom. You weren't put on this Committee to go frolicking with the Opposition. Or to put the phone down on me.'

161

'Lionel, old friend, you're being offensive.'

The rebuke seemed to calm the flustered Whip. He decided to try another tactic. 'Sorry, sorry. Look, this Bill is my responsibility. If I make a mess of this, I'm dead. I won't get another chance. That's why I wanted you on the Committee, Tom, because I knew you'd understand. Please, as a friend, help me. I can't afford to lose a day's business.'

Goodfellowe turned to Mickey. 'He wants me to step outside, for friendship. Bit like Captain Oates.'

'Who?'

'Never mind. Just keep on digging, or filing your nails, or whatever it is you do when I'm not around.' He turned to Lillicrap. 'I'll be there.'

'Ten minutes, Tom. No more. Ten minutes,' Lillicrap warned, assertive once more, and dashed out.

Goodfellowe was there in nine minutes forty. Lillicrap knew the timing was deliberately provocative but couldn't resist a brief look of gratitude, a most un-Whippish indulgence. He still had a lot to learn.

'The Seventh Cavalry has arrived,' Breedon announced. 'We were just about to lose our quorum. The Chair welcomes the Honourable Member.'

Perhaps the remark was meant by way of an olive branch, for settlement of old scores. Goodfellowe took his seat in the back row. He began setting out his papers and signing his constituency correspondence. He kept only half an ear on proceedings for his function as a Government backbencher was clear, rather like that of a log on which the great legislative stones might be laid and then rolled to their final destination. In centuries to

162

come it was possible that people might view the edifice thus constructed with awe. And then again, possibly not. In any event his role would have long been forgotten, buried in the parliamentary mud, but there was always the consolation that without his presence, it might never have happened. Though it never proved much of a consolation. It didn't help him sleep at nights.

Although the seats reserved for Members were no more than sparsely filled, the twenty or so public seats at the end of Committee Room 10 were crowded and there was considerable traffic between the room and the corridor outside, so much so that Goodfellowe began to find it distracting. Well-dressed men and women, mostly young, shuttled back and forth, sometimes only staying to pass notes via the attendant to a member of the Committee, at other times taking a seat for a murmured exchange. The lobbyists were at work. Goodfellowe had heard they'd been ravenous during deliberations in the Lords where the Bill had been first introduced, and had succeeded in changing their Lordships' minds on several important clauses. Evidently their task was now to ensure that minds remained changed. The great editing process of power was underway.

Beneath the muzzles of Beryl's guns, Goodfellowe buried himself once more amongst his papers. The letter in front of him was from a constituent, a dentist who was complaining that his drill gave him migraines yet he was unable to claim compensation for industrial injury. Could this be serious? But only last month a barman had won compensation for his tennis elbow caused, so he claimed, by the repetitive strain of drying glasses. Goodfellowe thought the injury more likely to have been picked up through wringing the hands of litigious lawyers. He had begun to scribble caustically in the margin of the dentist's letter when he was distracted yet again by the opening of the door. At the entrance to the Committee Room stood a young man, no more than thirty but with an expression of the most serious intent, gesticulating to one of the Members occupying the Opposition seats. Signals of mutual acknowledgement were exchanged and the young man handed to the attendant a sheet of paper. Goodfellowc could see the sheet of paper clearly, it was of the palest pink. It made its way along the Opposition bench to where the Member was sitting. And from that pale pink sheet the Member, five minutes later and now on his feet, began to read.

'Mr Breedon, with your permission I would like to speak in support of the amendment which stands in my name on the Order Paper . . .'

Goodfellowe didn't follow the proposed revision and the detailed argument being put in its support, his attention remained focused on the earnest young man who was now sitting in the public seats, nodding with authorial approval as the Member read out every carefully crafted phrase.

The Member had resumed his seat when, without warning even to himself, Goodfellowe found himself standing. 'On a Point of Order, Mr Breedon.'

'Point of Order, Mr Goodfellowe,' the Chairman intoned, accepting the interruption.

'Before this amendment is put to the vote, indeed before any other votes are taken in this Committee, could I draw your attention to the extraordinary degree of interest being shown in the Bill by outside

164

groups? Although I know by convention we never recognize the presence of anyone seated in the public gallery, if we were to do so we would see that most of the seats set out for the public aren't occupied by the public at all, but by paid advocates.' From the public seats came a self-conscious shuffling; several copies of *PR Week* slipped from agitated knees to the floor. 'I don't complain,' Goodfellowe continued, 'such interest is inevitable. This is a major piece of legislation which will result in fundamental changes in who controls our newspapers. It's only right we should hear outside advice and opinion. But there is always a danger, particularly with such considerable commercial concerns at stake as there are in this Bill, that those outside interests grow too— how can I put it diplomatically?—enthusiastic, aggressive, in putting their case.'

Breedon interjected, drumming his fingers and barking loudly. 'Is the Honourable Member trying to make a speech under cover of a Point of Order, or does he actually want the Chair to do something? If so, what?'

Goodfellowe stared fractiously. 'Yes, I do want you to do something, and every other member of this Committee. So often we are accused of being no more than parliamentary pawns who get pushed around the board by powerful outside interests, be they pressure groups, trade unions, big business, or even the professions.

We need to show this is not the case with this Bill. In order to demonstrate we have nothing to hide, I would like to suggest that each Honourable Member of this Committee records for the benefit of the public at large how much money or other

165

benefit he or she has received for articles written for the press over the last two years. Only in this way shall we be able to show that . . .'

Breedon launched himself like a dog deprived of a bone. 'The Honourable Gentleman will proceed with great care,' he instructed. 'Far greater care than he does at present. His point is completely out of order!'

'For Christ's sake, Tom,' Lillicrap sighed, burying his head in his hands. 'Cretin,' a further voice echoed from his left. 'There's the Register,' another added.

'The Register all but avoids the issue of newspapers . . .'

At the mention of the Register, the Chairman's voice rose an octave nearer ignition. 'Is the Honourable Gentleman trying to impugn the integrity of this Committee?'

'Absolutely not. The integrity of the Committee is precisely what I wish to establish.'

'Does the Honourable Gentleman have a shred of evidence for his insinuations?'

'I make no insinuation, only observation.'

'It seems to me he insinuates, he accuses, by raising the issue in the first place.'

'All I seek is transparency, to ensure public confidence . . .'

'Public confidence?' Breedon all but squeaked. 'The Honourable Gentleman is taking a sledgehammer to public confidence by suggesting that the judgement of any member of this Committee might conceivably be influenced by money. Can he give me one example of such influence, just one?'

'My hope is to prove that such influence doesn't

exist.'

'Then the Chair is left all but speechless by the manner in which the Honourable Gentleman goes about trying to gather his proof. Rather like slitting the throat of a witness to ensure there's no chance of them committing perjury.' Breedon's chest inflated as though it might burst, a match for his bulbous eyes. 'Because that's what you're doing, you know, with these wild allegations.'

Parliamentary etiquette had slipped badly as Breedon took the intervention as an assault on his personal authority and, perhaps, integrity. Goodfellowe tried to respond but Breedon was having none of it. 'I think I speak for the entire Committee in deploring the Honourable Gentleman's actions and judgements, which frankly leave open to question his motivation.'

Growls of approval came from all sides. From her position opposite Betty Ewing looked on in sympathy, but she had seen the way the wind was blowing and discretion dictated she should not get caught out in the gale.

Breedon was on his feet, pointing. 'I will not accept this Point of Order. The Honourable Gentleman will resume his seat.'

Goodfellowe looked around. Lillicrap was staring straight at him. The Whip made no sound but the mouthed obscenity was unmistakable.

'The Honourable Gentleman will resume his seat!' Breedon demanded yet again.

Goodfellowe shrugged. 'Or maybe not.' Ostentatiously he gathered up his papers, tucked them under his arm, and walked slowly past Lillicrap. 'I'm going out, don't try and stop me. I may be some time.' With that he went out through the Committee Room door. The quorum was broken, the day's business lost.

Goodfellowe had made no friends, he had certainly kissed goodbye to his career as a columnist before it had even started, but he had discovered a new role. How to be a bloody-minded backbencher. It was a role he thought he rather liked. He had no idea of the terrible consequences that awaited him as a result.

*   *   *

Sam changed in the tiny cloakroom. The floor was cold on her bare feet but she didn't mind. The whole prospect still gave her a thrill, a sense of challenge and discovery, but there was more to it than that. She was good at modelling. She was a natural, could hold almost any pose for as long as most artists wanted, thirty minutes or more. They all wanted her back.

She had found the ability which comes to only a few, that of relaxing and being totally at ease with her body, and it was an ease which communicated itself to others. Her life at school was penned in with restriction and regulation, what she should do, what time she should do it, what she should wear and even the length of her hair. At home it was worse. Don't swear, don't drink, double standards which would never be part of her life, now she was an adult. Yet still they refused to treat her as one. When it came to it, she controlled nothing in her life. Except her body.

She looked at herself in the small, cracked mirror above the wash basin, admiring what she saw reflected. How they would fuss if they knew, just as they had shrieked about her pierced navel. Yet it was her body, hers to do with as she chose, not as they directed, and nobody could change that. She felt at home in her body. It had grown unmistakably feminine, a transformation in her that artists recognized even if the school and her silly father refused to. She noticed the looks of appreciation which some of the younger men gave her before they got down to the serious work of drawing, and she enjoyed it, felt—to be honest, she couldn't describe precisely how she felt. A sense of fulfilment? A sense of danger, perhaps, of discovering herself and of getting her own back on all those who tried so unfairly to control her life. And how she enjoyed it.

The money was great, too.

She stepped out into the room, to where they had set up the lights. They wanted a pose which required her leaning against a wail, stretching, showing off the muscle tone. She felt needed, and very grown up.

The cotton gown fell from her shoulders and the cool air of the hall rushed to meet her body, spilling over it at every point. She thrilled. What a fuss there would be, she smiled to herself, if only they knew.

CHAPTER FIVE

'Tom Goodfellowe, you show all the loyalty of an earl at an orgy.'

He had known the confrontation must come. Where there was an angry Whip, retribution could never lag far behind. Lillicrap had caught up with him later that evening in the 'Aye' lobby, the book-lined hall which runs along the west side of the

House and through which Government Members were trooping to vote. Goodfellowe had hoped to sneak through unnoticed in the crush, but the division lobbies are like military encampments with eyes everywhere. Lillicrap had lain in wait and had brought along Stalybridge for solidarity, another Whip of excessive girth with the grin of an alligator, a man noted for his physical approach to conversation. The pair had intercepted their prey as he had waited in line to register his vote, and now propelled him to the more secluded reaches of one of the great bay windows.

Without preliminaries, Lillicrap launched straight into him. 'We've got little enough time for this Bill as it is without you flouncing out of Committee.'

'I didn't flounce, I walked.'

'What the hell d'you think you're playing at?'

'Lionel, I have a genuine concern. I don't like the smell of this Committee.'

'I don't like the smell of pigsties but they have their uses. Anyroad, we didn't put you on the Committee because of your delicate nostrils or your exotic insecurities. You're a member of the Government Party and we want the Bill, so your job is to hold your nose and play the sodding game.'

Lillicrap's index finger was stabbing repeatedly into his chest, forcing Goodfellowe to retreat. He found the solid edge of a writing desk at his back, no place to go, and Stalybridge was closing in. They had him surrounded.

'Why is Breedon's mind so firmly closed, Lionel, can you answer that? Might it have anything to do with the slightest twinge of guilt caused by his taking expensive trips courtesy of Freddy Corsa?'

170

'You accusing him?'

'No.'

'You accusing Corsa?'

After the slightest hesitation: 'No.'

'Then what's your problem? Breedon has no imagination. He has a mind like a rusted biscuit tin, he's achieved bugger all for the last twenty years and his sex life keeps not only his women awake at nights but half the Whips' Office awake as well. Yet he's a loyal Government supporter. A fine parliamentarian. One of us.'

'And Corsa?'

'Didn't you see what he did for us over that Earth Firm business? Between you and me, old chum, he timed the whole story for our convenience.'

'Is that what we've come to? Government policy dependent on finding some wretched environmentalist with morals as loose as a beer-drinker's bowels. Who cares? Did it make the slightest difference to the principle of the thing?'

At the mention of principle, both Whips gave an automatic and disparaging sigh. 'Have you forgotten what it was like to stand at the Dispatch Box with all guns aimed at you?'

'You're beginning to remind me,' Goodfellowe replied. He could smell Stalybridge's dinner.

'Breedon occasionally writes for newspapers. And occasionally the newspapers pay him for it. Happens to a lot of backbenchers. Seem to remember you've shown an interest in precisely the same thing with Freddy Corsa. Doesn't make you corrupt, Tom.'

'It might do.'

'Then that's your frigging problem. Corsa is a friend of this Government and we don't put friendly

171

media magnates in the dock. Hell, we put them in the House of Lords.'

'We put helpful backbenchers in the House of Lords, too, when they retire,' Stalybridge added. 'At least, some of them.'

'I'm not planning to retire.'

Lillicrap dusted a speck of imaginary dust from Goodfellowe's shoulder. 'In the meantime there's always a knighthood, which many of your colleagues seem to find . . . well, helpful. Particularly if they're looking for an additional consultancy or outside interest to ease their financial problems.'

'The black arts,' Goodfellowe smiled as though sucking lemons. 'The Chief Whip will be proud of you, Lionel. You're making your point extremely well.'

'Look, Tom, don't rock the boat. You're the only one who'll get soaked. It can be a lonely voyage out there on the back-benches, without friends.'

'And without a licence,' Stalybridge growled.

'I value you as a friend, Tom. Don't push me away.' Lillicrap took his arm, gave it a reassuring squeeze, while Stalybridge withdrew. All smiles.

It was only as Goodfellowe was filing past the clerk's desk, having his name scratched on the voting register, that it came to him. A simple point, one which didn't mean much, probably, but which nevertheless nagged at him.

He'd never told Lillicrap about Corsa's offer. But somebody had.

*   *   *

The British still do it best, Lillicrap mused, as he nestled into the softened Connolly hide at the back of the Silver Dawn. Pedestrians and drivers stared,

172

craning necks, trying to catch a glimpse of who was in the back seat. Somewhere, deep down, old class instincts still stirred, forcing that innate snatch of deference to the surface before it was replaced within seconds by lingering resentment. Rather in the manner they elected politicians.

He had lunched with Corsa in Jermyn Street, the newspaper man's shout, with the offer of a week's Christmas skiing from the chalet in Gryon thrown in as a digestif. Corsa had emphasized that the week involved no measurable cost to himself so it was difficult to argue there was any measurable pecuniary benefit to Lillicrap. A gesture of friendship, between the two of them, nothing more. Take it or leave it. Not the sort of thing the Register should be interested in, any more than they would be interested in the bill for lunch. In the circumstances it would have seemed an act of churlishness on Liliicrap's part for him to have refused. So instead they ordered another armagnac.

Corsa had insisted on driving the Whip back to the House, but even for a Rolls-Royce the traffic in Piccadilly wasn't parting. Lillicrap was in no hurry. He sat back and let the stares tickle his ego.

'What's all this trouble I hear about the Standing Committee?' Corsa enquired, staring out of the window as if it mattered less to him than the weather prospects at Wimbledon.

'No trouble really,' Lillicrap responded, a stirring of unease beginning to dispel the after-effects of the armagnac. 'It's simply that your friend and mine, Tom Goodfellowe, has been screwing around. Being difficult. So the Opposition are beginning to treat him as a semi-detached samurai and have withdrawn his pair.'

'What does that mean?'

'Effectively it means that, if he decides not to turn up for a vote, we lose our majority and have to rely on the Chairman's casting vote. An inconvenience, no more.'

'And if he were to vote against on any matter?'

Lillicrap examined his shirt cuffs, trying to imitate Corsa's accomplished air of insouciance. 'That would be more of a problem. It would delay matters.'

'You mean you might not get the Bill through?' Corsa's tone had not changed and he was smiling ruefully, for all the world as if it were a game, but the lips were pulsating like a stretched membrane, as though something of great menace were trying to escape from within.

Lillicrap hesitated, ill at ease. 'No. In the worst case we could always bring the matter to the Floor of the House, get any Committee vote overturned there. Inconvenient, no more.'

Corsa reached across and placed his hand on Lillicrap's, adopting the manner of a doctor reassuring a worried patient. Lillicrap shuddered. The hand was freezing cold. To him it was more like the gesture of a Victorian surgeon about to operate, without the benefit of anaesthetic and caring none too much about the patient's chances of survival. 'Lionel, let me spell it out for you. I'm a friend of this Government, you know that. A very good friend. None better. I'm also a businessman. Business can't thrive on uncertainty. Doubt is like a dose of clap or a Royal exclusive, highly contagious, does the rounds. Can infect the whole neighbourhood. I wouldn't welcome that, neither would any other newspaper. The Government has said it will push this Bill through, and that's precisely what it must do. No delays. And no damned excuses. Seems to me a Government that allows itself to get screwed by a single backbencher is scarcely a Government with a future. A Government due for one hell of a ducking at the next election. That's what the editors would say.' The hand withdrew and he sat back to admire his handiwork, debating with himself whether it was necessary to cut deeper still. 'There. I appear to have made a little speech. Forgive me, I don't have your training in the arts of oratory. But I hope I've been able to make myself clear.'

'Perfectly. You don't need to worry. The Bill will be law by the end of this session. Have no fears.'

'But I do, Lionel. I lie awake at night, worrying about my shareholders. And about you, Lionel. I think it's unfair that everyone should be put to so much trouble by a parliamentary fossil like Goodfellowe. God, the man's practically unemployable outside of politics.'

Lillicrap had half a mind to object on behalf of his kind, but decided this was not the moment.

'Lionel, we can't have you and the Government being held to ridicule, Wouldn't you agree it's time to give Mr Goodfellowe some—how might I put it? —gentle encouragement to remind him whose side he's on?'

'I'm trying, believe me.'

'You're not trying hard enough.' Corsa's voice had filled with scalpels. 'You need a little help. My help. And I think I may have just the right thing.'

'Your help is always appreciated, Freddy.'

'Can you meet me in my office at about six this evening? I think I'll have what you need.'

Lillicrap bit his lip. 'Six? Aahhh. Touch difficult. Conflicting duties.'

'More important than nailing Goodfellowe?'

'Good point. Can I use the phone?'

Corsa lifted the leather-bound armrest to reveal the car phone inside. Lillicrap punched out the number.

'Hi, it's me,' he announced with a clandestine air. 'Something's come up. I might be a little late for our appointment.' He looked at Corsa. 'Perhaps about an hour?'

Corsa nodded in agreement.

'That's fine with you? Great. See you then.' He handed the phone back. 'A party contributor,' he smiled. 'Wants to offer us more help for the next election. We have to keep 'em sweet.'

'My political editor tells me you need all the help you can get.'

Lillicrap didn't contest the point. They were drawing into Parliament Square and the evening newspaper boards were already announcing another Ministerial squabble, this time one the media hadn't invented. They exchanged farewells, Corsa waving his habitual salute, like a general inspecting his troops in the trenches, bidding them good fortune while he withdrew. Until six.

Not until Corsa had crossed the river and left Westminster behind did he pick up the phone again. He pushed the redial button, making a mental note of the number which appeared in the display.

'Hello, Jennie Merriman,' a voice replied.

Corsa offered no more than a brief smile of triumph before killing the call. Next he rang the editor's number at the *Herald*.

He didn't bother with introductions. 'A Jennie

Merriman ...' He gave the telephone number. 'I want to find out more about her. Who she is. What she does. Put a ferret down the usual holes, will you. Apparently she's of considerable service to the Party, and I'd like to find out more about what sort of services she provides. A little insurance policy.' He moistened his lips. 'And while we're discussing insurance, there's another task. You'll remember Tom Goodfellowe, the Honourable and Upright Member for Shanghai? He's becoming inconvenient. I want a full set of those pictures on my desk within an hour. Then I want to find out all there is to know about him. Usual form. Money. Mistresses. Mistakes. Where he buys his underwear, where he leaves it. Run through his bank accounts and credit cards. Then run a hand over his friends. And of course his family. If I need to, I want to be able to barbecue the bastard. In a hurry.'

It had been a very necessary lunch, he reflected. Good to know his allies, and his enemies. Although politicians were scarcely sport. Like cabbages, really. Practically indistinguishable from one another, all set out in their neat green rows. Waiting to be dug up and boiled, whenever it suited.

                    *   *   *

Lillicrap's invitation had been offered in the old spirit, before life in the Whips' Office had dried his veins. It was in that same spirit that Goodfellowe had accepted. Lunch on the Terrace with Lillicrap providing. It was that cusp between spring and summer when warming breezes made music through the leaves and the Palace of Westminster seemed to melt into honey cake beneath the sun, and they had found a small table overlooking an

177

ebbing tide. They turned their backs on the rest of the Terrace, discouraging interruption.

To Goodfellowe's amazement, lunch appeared out of Lillicrap's document case. A pack of smoked salmon, a couple of rich yellow lemons, whole grain rolls with little tubs of butter, a pepper grinder, every item was produced in the manner of a conjuring trick. The crowning moment came when Lillicrap extracted a bottle of cooled Rossendale Chardonnay, a wonderful New Zealand confection of gooseberries and cream and even a hint of corn. Enticing but not ostentatious, and the whole meal for less than a tenner.

'And not an ounce on the waistline,' Lillicrap enthused. He'd become tediously figure-conscious recently, and taken to visiting the gym.

They discussed old times and families, reminiscing about their first campaigns, their last unmarried loves, and a shared Whitsun break when the kids had raced their donkeys along the sands of Watergate Bay.

'We go back a long way together, Tom. I'm always conscious of that,' Lillicrap remarked, wiping the last of the crumbs from his lips.

'I assume I'm due another formal bollocking, Lionel. Thanks for dressing it up so nicely.'

Lillicrap fed the last of his roll to the tangle of sparrows which flocked eagerly around. 'Nothing formal about this. OK, so I'm a Whip and a bloody ambitious one, as you know, but I'd like to think I can still be your friend.'

'Again, I'm grateful. Hadn't realized sentiment was permitted to creep past the Chief Whip's door.'

'Don't be too condescending, Tom. We've been supportive of you in the past, in your times of trouble.'

'I suppose I should have known there would be a price to pay.'

'Not at all. You were desperate to find a nursing home for Elinor, we were happy to help. No strings. You're not the first colleague to find himself on a few financial hooks. The loan was all part of the service.'

Goodfellowe nodded. At the time he'd have danced with the Devil, and the Whips knew all the right steps.

'I'm here as a friend today, Tom,' Lillicrap continued, adjusting his carefully groomed hair that had slipped in the breeze, 'and I'll hope you'll take what I've got in that spirit. A little bad news amongst the good.' His frame tensed and he leaned once more towards his document case. The sparrows flew away in alarm. From the case he extracted a large manilla envelope which he weighed in his hand, as though having final misgivings, before pushing it across the table. 'I think you'll agree this is much better coming from me than from the Chief.'

Inside the envelope Goodfellowe found only one item, a photograph. Of himself with Jya-Yu, outside the police station. She was stretching up towards him, her small but well-formed figure clearly outlined, and she appeared to be kissing him full on the lips. One brief, tantalizing, devastatingly distorting moment, frozen in time. The custody sergeant had warned him, so had the inspector. Don't get involved. 'This is a stitch-up!' Goodfellowe spat.

'Freelance photographer, apparently. Been trying to hawk it around.'

179

'There is nothing in this, Lionel.' Goodfellowe was willing himself to keep calm, trying not to protest too ardently in case it lent the matter a sense of gravity, but his heart was racing. The photograph trembled slightly in his hand.

''Course not. But you'll have to admit it doesn't look too good. Nothing indecent, but the sort of thing which encourages people to think we're all at it.'

Goodfellowe examined the photograph for a considerable period as though hoping it might fade in the sunlight. It only seemed to grow more compromising.

'Wonder what dear old Beryl would make of it all?' the Whip muttered, twisting the knife a little too keenly.

'Are you trying to intimidate me?' Goodfellowe barked, shoving the photograph back into the envelope.

'Precisely the opposite. I said there was good news as well as bad. The photograph has been bought by a friend and won't be appearing. Freddy Corsa, Tom, is a friend of this Government and doesn't want to embarrass us. Or you.'

'Is this the point where I'm supposed to fall down on my knees in gratitude? I've done nothing wrong.'

'Don't be so bloody sanctimonious. Tread carefully, Tom. Not every newspaper would be as generous as Freddy Corsa. Westminster is a rosebed over which the media regularly deposit large amounts of manure. Don't get smothered in it. I say that as a friend, and it seems to me you need a few friends.'

'Sorry.' Goodfellowe chewed his lip. 'Bad day. Feeling a bit sensitive. Letter arrived this morning

180

to tell me that the fees at Elinor's nursing home are going up again. Small deluge over this particular rose bush.'

'Oh dear.'

'We talked about some other parliamentary consultancy. What do you think are the chances?'

'Now you're talking to me as a Whip.'

Goodfellowe understood. 'And at the moment I'm regarded by the Whips' Office as the loosest piece of elastic in the knicker factory.'

Lillicrap began packing away the remains of their meal. Duty in the Chamber beckoned, time for sympathy had run out. 'Stop pushing everyone away, Tom. Look, there's got to be an election sooner or later, and maybe sooner. Grasp the logic of that. We need to clear the decks, get rid of this Bill. Make sure we have the press on side. It's as simple as that. There's no great conspiracy.'

'I never said there was.'

'Speaking as a friend, you've got no Ministerial job, no money, few obvious prospects. And no licence, not even to bark.' He pushed the envelope across the table. 'You need this like you need ovaries.'

Goodfellowe looked upon the envelope, reluctant to touch it.

'Keep it,' Lillicrap added. 'The *Herald* will have plenty of copies.'

It sounded like a threat.

The Whip was retreating now, disappearing away from the sunshine and through the doorway that led to the shadows within. 'Think about it, Tom,' he shouted over his shoulder.

'I shall. Every word you've said, my friend.'

Lillicrap vanished, leaving Goodfellowe to

181

ponder on oblivion.

'And with friends like you providing the shovel, a man might dig himself all the way to damnation.'

*   *   *

Goodfellowe walked into the large open-plan basement area which housed some two dozen House of Commons secretaries—the Dragonaria, as Mickey called it, in recognition of several of its older inhabitants who seemed to breathe fire every time a male researcher or unmarried Member dallied around her desk, which they did often. For the moment the area was quiet, some secretaries were still at lunch, others only worked half-days. Mickey sat at her desk, almost hidden by a dozen red roses.

'Lucky girl. From Justin?' he enquired.

'That cannot be a serious question.'

'Then who?'

She sucked the end of her pencil, almost like a schoolgirl in the midst of an exam. Finally she asked, 'Don't you find that life can be complicated?'

'Tell me about it.'

'Well, the roses are from one of life's little complications.' She smiled brightly, all innocence.

He shook his head, genuinely puzzled. 'How on earth does Justin put up with it?'

'Because I give him a hard time, which he has been brought up to expect. And also because when I give him a great time, it's better than anything the poor darling's ever found elsewhere. The benefits of experience, Tom, aren't necessarily confined to old men with grumbling prostates.'

'Not necessarily my area of expertise,' he offered guardedly, concerned that one of the more elderly

182

dragons might be tuned in. His concerns were interrupted by the ringing of the telephone, which Mickey answered. Her face lit up.

'It's for you.' She held out the phone. 'One of your little complications, I think.'

He took the phone. 'Goodfellowe.'

'Hello, Tom. It's Elizabeth. Haven't seen you for a while. Just calling to see if everything is fine.'

He could have sworn it had grown suddenly warmer in the basement. Goodfellowe turned his back on Mickey. 'Sorry about that, Elizabeth. It's simply that . . . to be honest, I've had a real struggle this month to pay Sam's school fees. 'Fraid I haven't had much scope for entertaining.'

'Tom Goodfellowe, men don't have to pay to see me. Why, what sort of girl do you think I am?'

He'd missed her; she was rebuking him, and he would happily have been flayed by her until dawn.

'No excuses,' he apologized. Anyway, how could he explain the most significant reason he hadn't called, which he had trouble admitting even to himself? He was plain scared. Of his emotions, rusted and seized as they were, and of where they might lead. For too long that mighty machine which drove his lusts and his feelings had been silent— longer than four years, he realized with a pang of guilt, since well before the accident—and he was no longer sure he could control it if it started to turn again. He had made a conscious effort to put Elizabeth out of his mind, and failed. Now that he could hear her voice, the fire was being stoked once more. 'I was going to call you,' he offered. It was only half a lie; he spoke to her every night once the work had ceased to crowd his thoughts and he was alone in his bed of sorrows. 'Elizabeth, I wonder . . .

183

I've got to come back up to town next weekend. I'm reviewing the papers for one of the Sunday breakfast programmes. Because of the Bill, I suppose. I know you'll be busy for much of Saturday evening with the restaurant but . . .'—here goes — 'if you're free later, perhaps we could have supper. Then spend some time together on Sunday. All day, really. If you'd like.'

He waited, twisting in the silence, his throat dried by the sudden heat. A part of him, that part which yearned for a return to the simple and straightforward life, hoped she would say no and leave him rusting in peace.

'I'd like.'

The great engine trembled. 'Me too.' He looked behind him. Mickey was pretending to be busy. 'I don't want to embarrass Mickey by discussing the sordid details in front of her. I'll call you later.' He rang off.

'Just as long as you make sure there are some sordid details,' Mickey muttered, loudly enough so he would be sure to hear.

On the floor at his feet he noticed a pile of pencil shavings. Like flakes of rust fallen from a great but neglected machine. 'It's been quite a day,' he sighed.

'Try and show a little more enthusiasm by the weekend,' she advised.

'I'm not even sure I'm going to make it through to then. More bills for Elinor. My dear friend Lillicrap has told me that I'll only get another consultancy if I behave myself. And then this.' He threw the envelope across the desk at her and waited as she opened it to reveal the photograph.

'What's this?' she said in alarm.

184

'It's an attempt to blackmail me into being a good boy.'

'You sure?'

'Without a doubt. I could live to be a hundred and never see another photograph like that. And Freddy Corsa is sitting on it, refusing to publish. Why? Because he, like my Government, wants me to behave myself and help on the Bill. He's not been able to buy my co-operation, so now he tries a rather less subtle approach.'

'But why should he be so . . . eager? Anxious?'

'That's the question of the day. And I haven't the slightest idea. The Bill will go through eventually, all I can do is get in the way. Delay it a little. Like lying down in front of the bulldozers.'

'So what are you going to do, Tom?'

'I know what any sane and sensible man would do. Get on with my life, take care of my wife, accept that my Government knows best and take up trainspotting.'

'You've already got the anorak and woolly gloves.'

'And doesn't that about sum me up.'

'Look, do you really want to become the scourge of Fleet Street?' She was standing in order to command his attention. She had a very direct stare which some men could find intimidating.

'Trouble is, I rather think I do,' he mumbled mournfully.

'Then for pity's sake do it properly,' she replied sharply. 'Find out what Corsa is up to. And why. Stop being so emotional about the bloody thing.'

'And what about my financial woes?'

'Tom, I love you dearly but you are the most financially incompetent man I've ever met. Give you a million and somehow you'd let it all dribble through your fingers. You're never going to change, so why worry about it? But please.' She took both of his hands in her own, squeezing them urgently. 'Don't sell yourself.'

A proper Joan of Arc, he thought, clad in clinging cashmere. He wanted to rejoice for her commitment, share in her enthusiasm, rail against his misfortunes, above all to fight back with her. Instead he found himself twisting his lips, puckering as Elizabeth did when she concentrated. And remembering what had happened to Joan.

'You really think one man can make a difference?'

'If he's surrounded by some good women, he might have a chance.'

'Even if he's the most financially incompetent man you've ever met?'

'So long as I still get paid at the end of the month.' In any event her salary was met directly by the House authorities, not by Goodfellowe. The same could not be said of her out-of-pocket expenses. Last month the cheque he'd signed for her had bounced. 'Refer to drawer', the bank had instructed imperiously. She never had, and never would. 'Anyway, my mother always warned me not to get involved with older men who plied you with gifts and compliments. I suppose I'm safe with you,' she added.

He laughed. It was the first time that week he had laughed. It was like a fond memory, warming his spirits. One of the dragons, returning from lunch, stared at them holding hands. He laughed all the more. 'Time to prepare our defences. Two things you will do for me, Miss Ross. I need to get a feeling for what the *Herald* is up to, so get me back copies for the last three months.'

'But you can find whatever answers you need on the computer network.'

'Trouble is, I don't know what questions to ask. I've got to have the original pages, not a computer index.'

'And the second?'

'Find Betty Ewing and see if she can break bread with me in the Tea Room this afternoon.'

'Don't you want somewhere a little more discreet if you're going to sup with the Opposition?'

'Discretion isn't likely to feature prominently in this campaign.'

'Perhaps it should.' Mickey picked up the photograph lying on her desk.

'I take your point,' Goodfellowe acknowledged a little bashfully. 'What do you think I should do about that?'

'She's not even a constituent. Stop seeing her, for your own sake.'

'Trouble is, old duck, I can't.' He glanced at his watch. 'We've got to surrender to bail in a couple of hours.'

*   *   *

The Charge Room resembled an out-take from the latter stages of a Rocky movie. A fight had burst into life in the far corner between two motorcycle couriers and was continuing well beyond the point of futility. In spite of the presence of three police constables who were attempting to smother their enthusiasm by lying on top of them, the leather-clad pair were still managing to exchange punches and insults. Jya-Yu blanched. How could she be here, with such animals?

She had arrived at Charing Cross police station to be met by the sight of Goodfellowe attempting to shake the creases from his trousers and, after a wait of ten minutes, a representative from the firm of Crabbie & Gill, Solicitors. Mr Gill himself had been expected but had been detained on some more pressing issue, and in his stead had sent a junior colleague who attempted to conceal his lustreless youth and inexperience behind an air of profound superiority. He offered no apology for his lateness and could barely muster a handshake for Goodfellowe, while his client seemed scarcely to exist for him beyond the pages of a slim blue file. His smile was tight, like a piece of plucked elastic, with leaky eyes and an unfortunate case of acne which reminded Goodfellowe of a discarded oyster shell, an impression of emptiness which was reinforced every time the youth opened his mouth.

Jya-Yu, by contrast, appeared incapable of speech. The toll of sleepness nights had swollen her eyelids so that they had all but closed, her head was held low and her hands clenched tightly together, knuckles showing white, as if at any moment she expected to be thrust into handcuffs and was resigned to her fate. Throughout the preliminary interview with the arresting constable she maintained a rigid silence, speaking only to acknowledge her name, even when he told her of the damning lab report. Her fear was evident—fear which only increased as she was led into the Charge Room to be confronted by the heaving mass of bodies and abuse. Not until a fourth constable had added his substantial weight to the pile did the fight slowly subside, the motorcyclists flapping like fish on a river bank until there was no air left in their lungs for incitement. They were dragged away nose-down in the direction of the cells.

'Sorry about that, miss,' the custody sergeant offered jovially from behind his desk, attempting to defuse the atmosphere. 'Not our usual service, I assure you. I don't normally allow fighting before my second cup of tea.'

The mild humour had no effect on Jya-Yu.

'Now, what have we got here?' The sergeant straightened his glasses as he examined the Charge Sheet.

'She's not having any of it, Sergeant,' the arresting constable volunteered. 'Not a word, in spite of the forensic. She's keeping schtum.'

'Nothing more to add. Is that correct?' the sergeant enquired.

Jya-Yu didn't move a muscle, seeming scarcely to be breathing.

'It doesn't help, miss, staying silent. It may be used against you in court. The lab report confirms that the substance was the bone of a large cat which we believe was tiger bone, yet you're offering no explanation for it.'

Still she would say nothing.

The solicitor decided it was time to intervene, rising on his toes. 'You sure now? Nothing you want to add by way of elaboration or elucidation, Miss ... er?' Oyster Man began to rifle through his file, he didn't even know her name. 'Miss Yu?'

'Your client's name is Pan Jya-Yu,' the sergeant rebuked, pronouncing the name perfectly and making it clear he considered the solicitor to be a waste of public funds and, still more exasperating, a waste of space in his crowded Charge Room. He returned his attentions to Jya-Yu who stood before his desk, doll-like. 'Well, miss, you've got no previous and you're not an illegal immigrant. There's no hard evidence to support the allegation of soliciting. And the constable's nose we can consider an accident.' For a moment, Goodfellowe's heart began to rise in optimism. And in vain, 'But although this is a first offence, it's a very serious offence,' the sergeant continued, 'dealing in an endangered species. So I must tell you that you will be reported for being in possession of a restricted substance which we believe to be tiger bone, for the question of prosecution to be considered. Have you still got nothing to say?'

'What does this reporting mean?' Jya-Yu uttered her first words in a voice which sounded as softly as a sparrow's.

'It means they will formally charge you and may prosecute. Bring you to trial,' the solicitor replied. At least he'd got that bit right. Jya-Yu fell silent once more.

'Very well,' the sergeant sounded resigned. 'Wait over there on the bench, miss, and you gentlemen, please.' He began to prepare his papers and summoned the inspector who had managed to free himself from mayhem further down the long custody desk. Rapidly, Goodfellowe intercepted him.

'Inspector, what's going to happen? To Miss Pan?'

'Mr Goodfellowe,' the policeman greeted, but with no more than adequate enthusiasm. 'I did warn you on your last visit. This is a serious matter.'

'All the more reason for me to try to help then, Inspector. What's going to happen?' he repeated.

'Depends very much upon the young lady. What she decides to do.'

'But if you're charging her, what choice does she have?'

The inspector hesitated. He was a busy man, little time to spare for unnecessary complications, let alone public figures who got themselves wrapped up in this part of town with girls half their age. Yet at the first whiff of gunsmoke most such figures disappeared behind the protective fire of their lawyers and PR advisers. Not this one. Something in the mettle of the man encouraged him. 'What about a quiet word, sir? Off the record? Just the two of us?' He led Goodfellowe to the quietest corner of the Charge Room, away from the bodies and their bustle. 'Mr Goodfellowe, your young friend has been found in possession of an illegal substance. No question about it. And she refuses to offer any explanation. She's been no help whatsoever. Leaves me with little choice. We'll recommend that she be prosecuted and she will have to take her chances in front of a jury.'

'Chances, Inspector? Is that what justice has become?'

Goodfellowe's tone was concerned, sharp. And ill-advised. The inspector was well armed. 'You should know that better than me, sir. It's politicians who are always pressing us to take a stronger stand against the smuggling of rare animals. Some ordinary people might argue that we'd be better off targeting burglars and muggers, but animal rights are the flavour of the month. That's where the pressure is. The political pressure, Mr Goodfellowe, to secure convictions. Even outside the court you get political pressure. Banners, demonstrations, picket lines—that's what happens to those sort of trials once the activists get their hands on them. Don't care for that myself, not at all. Trial by pressure group. But that's what Miss Pan is facing.'

'I apologize, Inspector. Moralizing is a trap politicians fall into at their peril. I don't often do it. Not even on Sundays.'

'No need for apologies, sir. I think we both understand each other. And the pressures of public life.' The ripple of tension subsided. 'There's another practical point which the lady ought to consider if it goes to trial. We'd probably have to raid her uncle's premises in order to show we've taken the matter seriously. Who knows what we'd find? It all becomes very messy, even if she's not found guilty.'

'Is there no alternative? Even you appear to accept that a trial may not be fair.'

'This is the difficult bit, Mr Goodfellowe. I'm not applying pressure, not suggesting anything, you understand. Not my job. Could get me into trouble, even the slightest hint that I was applying pressure. I'm merely outlining the options.'

'Please go on.'

'Since this is her first offence, I could give her a formal caution instead of pushing for prosecution. If she accepted the caution it would be the end of the matter after three years so long as nothing else came up. It wouldn't even count as a criminal record.'

'Then why not caution her?'

'Because in order for me to do that she has to accept the offence. Admit her guilt.'

'You're suggesting that accepting a caution is the easy way out?'

192

'I'm not suggesting anything. Merely outlining the alternative. As you asked. Man to man.'

'And I'm grateful.'

'A caution isn't even declarable on employment forms. No fine, no fuss. How can I put it tactfully? Yes, I've known of more difficult solutions.'

'Even though it's a formal admission of guilt.'

'That's the bacon in the butty.'

Goodfellowe pondered. Her only guilt was that of loyalty to her uncle. Her devotion had deprived her of her innocence yet nevertheless he knew she would remain loyal. Not compromise him. 'She doesn't deserve this, Inspector. I think she's a victim. But the Chinese have a saying. Never set to sea in a borrowed junk. I'm afraid that's what Miss Pan did and ran straight into a storm.'

'If she were able to accept the caution, I think the waters may grow a little calmer for her.'

'The quiet life? Or justice?'

The inspector offered no response.

'She doesn't deserve this,' Goodfellowe repeated. 'But I'll put it to her.'

'It might save everyone a great deal of time. And torment.'

Thoughtfully Goodfellowe returned to the bench on which Jya-Yu was sitting. Oyster Man sat sulking beside her, complaining that she had refused to say anything to him, but as Goodfellowe drew near she sat up. 'What must I do now, Mr Goodfellowe?'

While the solicitor snorted in frustration, Goodfellowe began to explain. About prosecution. And the alternative. Admission of guilt and acceptance of a caution.

'If I accept, will there be any more ... procedures?'

'You will be photographed and fingerprinted,' the solicitor interrupted, trying to get his own back.

'Like a criminal?'

'It's a serious crime you are charged with,' he admonished, as though trying to justify his fee.

She sat very still for a few moments, concentrating, forcing out from her mind the distractions which filled every corner of the Charge Room. Her nails dug deep into the flesh of her hand. But to Goodfellowe's surprise there were no tears. She was putting up a fight, struggling hard for her dignity. Then her features softened. The taut muscles around the mouth seemed to relax and an expression of acceptance took control, wiping away the dread. She turned to Goodfellowe. 'For Uncle Zhu,' she whispered, and forced the smallest of smiles. 'The best way, I think. The easy way out.'

He shook his head in wonderment as, moments later in the company of the solicitor and the constable, she returned to the Interview Room to record her admission of guilt on tape.

As he watched her tiny back disappear, something rattled at Goodfellowe's bones. Perhaps he was becoming a natural pessimist, maybe his own experience had taught him that life rarely provided an easy way out. Not where he was concerned. In spite of the inspector's reassurance, instinct told him that the only plain sailing to be found was usually in the eye of the storm, at the moment before the skies were about to darken and the hurricane to hit. And Goodfellowe's instincts were usually remarkably accurate.

*   *   *

The late-afternoon sun spread sheets of amber

194

across the market square of Wooton Minster. All day it had blazed upon the ham-stone shops and painted doorways that huddled around the rim of the square, and now the shadows of the lichen-clad steeple of St Maud's began to spread out, pointing like an elegant finger across the cobbles and almost to the doorstep of the coffee shop. Around the table that stood in the window the conversation was ebullient. Talk of summer holidays, the boys they might meet, the boys they had already met, and of indiscretions both planned and performed. The senior girls of Werringham were on town time, enjoying their cappuccino.

The door opened and a light breeze entered bearing on its back a young woman. She was in her early twenties with a tomboyish face and cropped hair, and wore a red AIDS ribbon. She was alone, seating herself at a small table near the window to catch the last of the sun. For a few moments her presence inhibited the conversation of the five schoolgirls but by the time the newcomer had started on her pot of coffee the ripple of gossip had once more grown to a bubbling cascade, only to be interrupted for a second time as the young woman stood up and approached.

'Hi. My name's Jani. I'm involved with Oxfam. And I couldn't help noticing you were from Werringham. Were any of you by chance involved in the recent fashion show?'

Three of the girls indicated that they were.

'Great. That's a stroke of luck,' the woman enthused. 'Look, I need your advice. Please, may I join you? Perhaps order some more cappuccino all round? A bit of cake?'

They needed no extra encouragement. They

195

shuffled round and made a place for their new friend.

'You see, we were planning to do something very similar at Oxfam, then we heard of your success here. It's a brilliant idea and you got there first. So I thought I'd come and see what we could learn. Pinch a few of your ideas, if that's all right. Perhaps even get some of you to help. We want this to be big, plenty of television coverage, lots of personalities. We're hoping one of the Royals might even do some of the modelling.'

The woman found herself surrounded by excited chatter.

'I understand the show was organized by a Samantha Goodfellowe. She's not one of you by any chance?'

'Bet she wishes she were,' one of the girls chirped as the cakes and coffee arrived. 'One-Sip Sam would love all this.'

'One-Sip Sam?'

Some of the girls wriggled in discomfiture. 'It's a sort of ... nickname. She doesn't have a lot of money so she makes a drink last all afternoon. One sip at a time.'

'I'd like to meet her. Perhaps outside of school where we can be a bit more relaxed, not bothered by class timetables. Any idea where I would find her? Trouble is, I'm only in town for a couple of days.'

'You could try Red Hot Dutch—the local disco,' one suggested, giggling.

'No, not until the weekend, stupid,' a second responded.

'Anyway it's Tuesday. She gets late leave on Tuesdays to go to her art classes,' a third added.

'She has an art class?'

196

'Yes. She's rather talented, really. Gets special permission to go to local evening classes. In the Methodist village hall just outside of town. Even draws at life classes sometimes.'

The shared thought of all those bodies brought the schoolgirls to life. 'Some of the men have gorgeous muscle definition, Sam says.' —'They're usually ancient.' —'Sometimes they're below fifty.' —'She says they often have varicose veins.' —'Yes, but where?' Youthful laughter gripped them all. The sun had slipped sadly away behind the steeple, casting the market square into a sudden monochrome gloom, but no one seemed to notice.

By the time the cake had been reduced to crumbs and there was nothing left of the coffee but dark dregs, Jani had learned considerably more about Samantha. Much was of no consequence but there were valuable insights into a talented yet unhappy teenager who broke school rules on occasions and boys' hearts at every opportunity. Opinionated, direct, an individualist. The sort of girl who stood out from the crowd, even if only to shower it in red paint. As the pieces began slowly to fit together, Jani made a decision. She determined to make a visit to Red Hot Dutch to see whether she could find out more about a girl who made a drink last all night, and she would also drive out to the Methodist village hall that evening. There may not be too much to be gained from an art class, but it would justify the good meal she was planning at a four-star restaurant she'd found in one of the guides. It was an extravagance, of course, at a time when all expenses were being put under the budget manager's microscope, but it would seem unquestionably as though they had been incurred in the course of duty. She felt sure her editor back at the *Herald* would approve. After all, he'd said this Goodfellowe story was top priority.

*   *   *

The nightly exodus of MPs after the ten o'clock vote had left the corridors of the House strangely silent as Goodfellowe paced his way wearily back to his office. He'd almost not made it past the Speaker's Chair. A small cabal of colleagues had waylaid him with an invitation. Whisky and wickedness.

'The next election is drawing close. Too close,' one had suggested. 'We thought a few of us should discuss the problems. And possibilities.'

'Very privately,' emphasized a second.

'A free discussion. Frank exchange of ideas,' suggested a third.

'You mean whether we turkeys should try to save our own necks by plucking and stuffing the Prime Minister,' Goodfellowe had responded.

'Nothing should be ruled out.'—'For discussion.'—'If that's what you think should be discussed, Tom.' They had huddled around him, seething discontent from the shadows, whispering like witches at their cauldron.

'Why me?'

'We know you've had run-ins with the Whips. You're on their list of bad boys. We thought you'd welcome an exchange of ideas. With no inhibitions. No rules. And no minutes.'

He had considered the proposal briefly, but had declined. 'My reputation is in sufficient peril without being seen in the company of free thinkers,' he declared, turning away.

'Better a man of any reputation than a forgotten
198

one,' they had retorted, intentionally cruel.

So . . . He had been marked down by the trouble tendency as one of their number. Goodfellowe hadn't realized that, but he knew the Whips would have, and come to their own conclusions. Politics was a team game and he seemed to have no home any more. He felt very alone.

As he opened the door to his office a shaft of high moonlight found its way through the mullioned window and splashed eerily across the floor. In the middle of the puddle, where Mickey had left them, lay the back copies of the *Herald*. He picked up an armful and spread them across his desk.

'So, Mr Corsa, let's see if we can rake through the ashes and find a few sparks.'

*   *   *

The pub was hot and stuffy in spite of its size. Customers crowded in like battery hens, pressing into every corner, sweating mildly, spilling their beer and wine in their eagerness to get served and, of course, to get a better view. The music from the sound system was not the usual pub fare. They were playing an aria from *The Magic Flute*, which felt painfully loud in the cramped quarters, forcing all conversation to be brief and bawled. Not that many of the customers were there to talk. Most of their attention was focused on the point where two spotlights, battling though the rising smoke and heat, focused on the small raised platform next to the emergency exit. Upon that platform a woman was standing.

She wore a blonde wig. Slowly, and with only a suggestion of boredom, she was miming eloquently to the music. She was also taking off her clothes.

199

It was showtime at Mozart's, Covent Garden's newest and most fashionable watering hole, which, after the theatres and cinemas had disgorged their multitudes onto the streets, performed a public service by taking a remarkable number back off again. Mozart's was far more fun than the gastric obstacle courses offered by most late-night hostelries, and the supply of well-formed RADA students and resting actresses who needed a little extra cash appeared limitless. Mind you, it was all conducted with what Kenny, the Liverpudlian proprietor, regarded as being commendable restraint. Some only stripped as far as the waist, bearing their breasts in the authentic manner of an abused handmaiden or abandoned wife, but after ten o'clock the punters knew that poetic licence would hold sway and Pamina, driven to despair by Sarastro, would go all the way. They also knew that at this point in the evening the price of drinks would double, but still they queued.

The sole exception to the discipline of double-price drink was Curt, who leaned on one of the quieter corners of the bar. Curt was the local beat officer and Kenny, Scouser to his roots, knew that he'd better take care of the local police or, in a turning world, they would be sure to take care of him. So Curt and his guest got not only their drinks at standard but also the corner with one of the best views in the house. What was even better from Curt's point of view, tonight the guest was paying. Oscar Kutzman had called, wanted to meet in a hurry, as soon as he came off duty. Fair enough. Oscar was a bearded little creep with tight jeans and unfortunate personal dispositions but in addition to being a sodomite the photographer had other uses.

He had a photographer's sharp eye and was always on the street, taking in much of the London low life which had a habit of vaporizing at the approach of blue uniforms, and Oscar would usually pass on the information. He'd once helped smash a wholescale immigration racket, and all he asked in return was the opportunity to take exclusive photographs and to buy officers a few drinks in return for their tips. Yes, Oscar was all right. Ish.

Two pints of bitter arrived and Curt gratefully took the head off his. Oscar sipped. He preferred Dubonnet, but felt forced to play it butch with the local constabulary. No one was fooled, of course, but the boys in blue talked more freely when relaxed.

'So what is it this time, Oscar?'

Oscar quickly put down his glass and made a dive towards an inside pocket of his windcheater, but before he could complete the move a new aria had begun, a duet this time. He knew he'd have trouble capturing Curt's attention. He'd have to wait, and sought solace in examining the women with professional detachment. It was the only way he ever examined women. Curt stood smiling, tapping the bar with his fingers in time to the music until the soprano hit a High C when, accompanied by expressions of desolation and a ripping of Velcro, the costumes tumbled. The punters roared, banging bars and tables in approval. Culture could be such an inspiration.

'You were saying, Oscar?'

Oscar felt nervous. This was important. If it worked the *Herald* had promised instant happiness, perhaps even a staff contract. From his poacher's pocket he withdrew a large envelope and placed it

201

on the counter. Wiping his fingers on his jeans first, he proceeded to withdraw three photographs. Enlargements. Of Jya-Yu. Showing her face from different angles. 'Recognize her?'

Curt studied them. 'Why do you want to know?'

'I don't, my editor does. It's important to me, Curt. Can you help?'

The policeman was in genial mood, basking in the reflection of a week which had seen him put away not only plenty of overtime but also the station's newest WPC. A week for sharing. He smiled. 'Oscar, my old sweetie, if you feel the temptation to kiss me, please restrain yourself. But tonight you are in luck.' After all, he'd been in the Charge Room at the time, sitting on top of the pile of trouble.

'You know who she is?'

'I can even give you the number of her charge sheet.'

*　　　　*　　　　*

Big Ben struck four. From across the river, the famous silhouette of Gothic towers and pinnacles stood out clearly against the glow of the urban night. Only one light pierced the facade, from a window so small that it might have been no more than a reflection of the street lights along the bridge. Goodfellowe was still at work. His office resembled a waste tip on a windy day. Sheets of newspaper were strewn everywhere, covering almost every available surface. Draped over the small sofa. Washing over the desk. Laid out on the floor. Pinned to almost every part of the walls. Goodfellowe stared bleary-eyed. An image, an understanding, kept falling in and out of focus. At

202

some points during the night it had been close enough almost to touch, then he would reach out and it would fade.

He had started with the Earth Firm exclusive. He knew that the timing, if not the story, had been fixed, Lillicrap had admitted so. It had been reported and exaggerated for purposes that were more than simply journalistic. To help the Government, to help Corsa's friends, but most of all to help Corsa himself. So Goodfellowe had pinned the front page up on the wall and begun to surround it with others from the last months. Eventually he was lost in a blizzard of white paper that pounded him from all sides until he grew snow blind. Until he could no longer see and everything was gone.

His head dropped. He felt weary of this world, a world that had turned against him and had tried so hard to hurl him off. Yet as both eyesight and insight faded and his very thoughts began to ache, words kept repeating in his mind, words which Jya-Yu had spoken as he lay on Dr Lin's treatment couch. 'Look at things all round about, not just little bit at a time.' He had tried. It was pointless. The headlines kept shouting at him but he was too exhausted to hear.

CHAPTER SIX

'He's taken up puppy training.' Mickey tossed her head in concern as she entered Goodfellowe's room to discover it strewn with sheets of newspaper. 'Or maybe he's planning to become a tramp.' She had noticed all the signs. The growing anxieties and sleeplessness. A loss of weight he attributed to cycling, but which was in fact pure acid tension. His battles with Sam and his inability to express his emotions to anyone other than in the form of excuse and anger. They were beginning to mutter about him in the corridors and around the Dragonaria. Flaky. He'd lost it. And every morning's post seemed to bring more torment about his money, or lack of it. Pain and pressure everywhere. A cup which had long ago overflowed was now all but drained dry.

Goodfellowe lay slumped across his desk, breathing heavily. By his side was a bottle of Bulgarian blanc, opened and empty. He had now come to resemble his life, which was a mess.

'Tom.'

He started, roused from a world of vivid dreams and wild thoughts which somehow never seemed to connect.

'What the hell is all this, old love?' she asked tenderly, waving at the white wreckage of the room which surrounded him like the walls of a padded cell.

He scratched his stubbled chin. 'It's the answer. It's here. Somewhere, I'm sure. Just haven't quite found it yet.'

'Tom, I think you should . . .'

'Look, Mickey,' he insisted, cutting through her, rising to pirouette across the paper carpet and point an accusing finger at various sheets. 'Look at these exclusives Corsa has plastered all over the front pages. Like the Earth Firm campaign. Blown out of the water the moment it was launched because one of its members was caught playing sexual hopscotch, despite the fact that everyone knows the rules of that particular game were invented by the

Environment Secretary's husband.' The finger pounded another sheet. 'Then there was Wonderworld—another piece of over-blown nonsense. A huge commercial organization brought to its knees because on one particular day Corsa published a story which could have been written at any time about almost any place. Ludicrously weak stories of no substance published at the moment they would cause maximum damage.'

'Yes, but Tom I . . .'

'Here's another.' He moved the empty wine bottle in order to retrieve the front page which lay beneath. **'Killer Coal'**, the headline screamed. 'Some obscure academic produces a paper suggesting he's found more cancer clusters around coal-fired power stations than around nuclear stations. Nine months later —nine months, Mickey, if you look at the small print—the *Herald* goes ape about it. Why? Why is Corsa going out of his way to harm these groups? Why are they . . .'

'Tom!' It was her turn to interrupt. 'You're the one in imminent danger of harm. Have you forgotten you were supposed to meet Beryl in Central Lobby?'

'Oh, pig's wind. When?'

'Twenty minutes ago.' She looked at him. 'I'll go fetch her, bring her round slowly. Give you time to sort out your hair and this mess.' She began pulling a page from its fixing on the wall.

'No!' Goodfellowe's tone was sharp with menace, like a dog confronting a burglar. 'Don't touch anything. It's here, Mickey, the answer is here somewhere. I don't want anything moved.'

'But you can't bring her in here,' she protested.

'Then I shall talk with her out there,' he

instructed. He rubbed his feet tenderly before lacing up his shoes, retrieving his jacket from the back of the door and running a hand several times through his hair. 'How do I look?'

'Like something that didn't quite make it at Battersea Dogs' Home.'

He took two deep breaths to summon up the spirit. 'She'll never notice.'

Oh, but she did. Miss Hailstone was not a happy lass. She was important. As important, if not more so, in her opinion, than the Member of Parliament. She should not have been kept waiting. And she should not have been set upon by a man who looked almost deranged with darkened chin and blood-rimmed eyes and hair like the sea front at Frinton during an autumn gale.

'Mr Goodfellowe . . .' There was the formality again. She was rising up onto her toes in indignation in order to train her sights better on him. He knew he was in for a full broadside. 'I have come all the way to London specifically to meet with you because I thought it was a matter of such importance. To you. Yet I find you discourteous, dishevelled—have you slept in those clothes?' she asked, incredulous. She was angry with him, still angrier with herself for ever having been such a fool as to want him in her bed.

He decided there was little to be gained from the truth, particularly with Beryl. 'My humble apologies. How can I help you?' He guided her to a small alcove where they might find a little privacy.

'It's more how you might be able to help yourself.' She smoothed out the folds of her dress, preparing herself. Her bosom heaved. 'I have come to inform you . . .'—it sounded a little too starched,

206

even for her—'to let you know that the Committee has decided to begin our election preparations and to bring forward the time for us to choose our candidate.'

'My reselection.'

Another heave. She was wearing a large cameo brooch, a flower cluster which moved towards him with the menace of a Triffid. 'The reason I have made this trip especially is that I thought it only fair to tell you that some members of the Committee are not happy. With you. We were sad to lose you as a Minister, with all the kudos that can bring to a constituency. We haven't had a member of the Cabinet visit us in months. And little things, like invitations to Downing Street or garden parties at the Palace, matter to some people. I'm not speaking personally, you understand, I'm far too busy, but others do talk about such things.'

'I'll try to do better,' he offered weakly.

'They also talk about your unfortunate problem with the police. We all enjoy a drink, I'm sure, but getting arrested as a result is not what the party workers in Marshwood expect. What on earth are they going to say on the doorstep?'

'You told me that would be forgotten in time.'

'We move but slowly. Memories die hard in Marshwood.'

'Then why bring the selection procedure forward? Why not give it a little more time?'

'We must be ready whenever the call comes. And you are doing yourself no favours with your anti-party activities.'

'What on earth . . .?'

'We expect you to support our party and our Government, not to keep driving under whatever influence on the wrong side of the road.'

'I have my conscience.'

'And we have our selection procedures.'

'Are you telling me I may not be reselected? That you'll look for other candidates?' This was beginning to sound like a declaration of war.

Miss Hailstone paused, deliberate, painfully long. Once again she smoothed out non-existent creases in her dress. Then the Triffids advanced with murderous intent. 'I hope it won't come to that. But perhaps you'll allow me to give you a little advice.'

Goodfellowe braced himself. Beryl never gave advice, only instruction.

'You'd be wise to smarten yourself up, both your appearance and your politics. You're going to have to start playing the team game, if you want to remain the Member for Marshwood.'

* * *

Goodfellowe woke from his usual shallow, tormented sleep knowing that his time was fast running out. He was aware of what was happening to him. During endless nights he searched for answers but found only darkness. During his days, acid and alcohol ate away at his resolution. He was destroying himself with doubt. He had to make a decision, for no choice was a terrible decision in itself.

Corsa? Career? Conscience? Yet in a sense it all came down to Elinor. Their life together had started out in such pleasing pastures, surrounded by the fruits of their abundant success. But the seasons had turned, as they always do, with summer slipping almost unnoticed into autumn, a mild and colourful time, and certainly still comfortable. No complaints. Autumn was a favourite season, for some people, and Goodfellowe himself had found it balmy enough. Then the mighty storm had struck and winter had arrived more harsh than he could ever have imagined. He had always seen himself as a provider, competent to deal with any eventuality, able to look after his family. But he had failed. And as he looked at himself in the mirror, he knew he was no longer even able to take care of himself.

While watching Elinor's decline he had told himself that it might have been worse. What did love, physical commitment, mean to him anyway? His marriage had survived contentedly for many years with little of either. And he was perhaps approaching the age when the need for such things begins slowly to fade, so he had thought—he had wished it, almost, because that would have been the easy way out. Not to have needs. Not to have desired with a passion and an urgency that turned his stomach around so fiercely he couldn't sleep. He had a pride, and a sense of guilt, and no idea of what he should do. It was destroying his body just as it was flogging his soul and there was not a single facet of his life that was capable of surviving in such a manner. He had to decide what sort of man he was to be, or soon he would be no man at all.

It was a difficult journey to Elinor's nursing home without his own transport. It required a slow train to Salisbury followed by a lengthy taxi drive with the driver inevitably proceeding in silence once he had identified the destination. He tried to make the trip every week but it had become less regular recently since he had lost the car. At least, that was the excuse he made to himself. Elinor needed no excuse. She had grown oblivious to the time or the season, her world slowly becoming confined to the grounds of the clinic and, ever more closely, to her small room and particularly its television. She would receive messages from the television, she used to claim. And from the radio and car number plates, too. Messages of guilt and of damnation, blaming her for the accident that had drowned Stevie. But as she had begun slowly to realize that others didn't understand, that they couldn't hear or share the messages, she had stopped talking about the voices, simply sitting in front of the screen, surfing constantly between channels, even in the middle of the night when the station had gone off air and provided nothing but an electronic blizzard. That's often when the voices spoke loudest, were most insistent. The people around her didn't know, didn't hear, didn't care, so it had become her secret, a life shared with no one but the devils in the television.

She was in bed when he arrived. Inevitably, she was watching television. 'Hello, love.' He bent and kissed her forehead, noticing once more how dank and lifeless her hair had become, hair which had once been a match for the bubbling personality within. Now her aspect was blank, the skin grown thin and stretched like parchment. Around her the room was simple and utilitarian. And safe. No locks, except on the window. No glass or ceramic, nothing that could be made sharp. Even the fresh flowers he always asked should be at her bedside were standing in a vase of plastic. Her few personal possessions amounted to no more than a box of tissues and a few unread magazines. No sign of character. This was a room which, without her, would say almost nothing about the patient that had occupied it full-time for nearly eight months, with perhaps one exception, a small candle which stood on the windowsill in front of the dull protective metal mesh. As he always did when he arrived after dusk, he took a booklet of matches from his pocket and lit the candle. It was a family ritual that Elinor had begun while they still allowed her matches, a light to guide their lost son back home.

She turned from the candle to stare blankly once more at the television.

'Please, Elinor, I want to talk.' Was it too much to hope that she could listen? He sat beside her on the bed, lifting the remote control from her coverlet and switching off her television. Slowly, as though making the difficult passage back from another world, she turned to look at him. He held her hand, all bones, her eyes as glassy as those sewn on a rag doll. Occasionally he thought he could detect a flicker behind them, but of what he could not discern. Indifference? Suspicion? Apprehension? Perhaps contempt. He could no longer tell, she seemed barely sentient. So he sat and talked. Of his new apartment. Of Sam and her fashion show and how she was growing up. A little of his own turmoil and more of his problems in the House. He massaged her hand as though he might rub into her some understanding of what he was saying and through its heat generate some response, yet there was nothing. Glass eyes stared back.

'Try to understand, Elinor. I have come to a crossroads in my life, and I need your help to decide which direction I should take. I'll probably be damned if I take on Corsa, and I'll certainly damn myself if I don't. I feel my whole life is changing and somehow everything depends on this. There are risks everywhere. For me, for us. Do you understand?'

She turned away to look at the blank television screen, her movements tortuously slow, as though the brain was sending out instructions by way of the moon. Then, before he even realized it, the rag doll was staring back at him, eyes flickering vividly in the candlelight. Or was it a light within?

'There's another woman, isn't there,' she said slowly. They were the first words she had spoken in almost a month.

How on earth could she tell? What insight did this warped and half-buried brain of hers retain? Could she smell his guilt, was that it? Was it so damned obvious?

'But I love you, Elinor.'

'You can't love me.'

Not mustn't. Not didn't, not shouldn't, but couldn't. And with a sadness and a sense of relief that appalled him, he realized she was right. There was loyalty still, and in abundance, but not love.

Elinor turned back to her television screen, and would say nothing more.

'What are you trying to tell me, Elinor?' But he already knew. 'What should I do?'

But she had already spoken. A door had been closed in his life which would never be reopened.

He held her hand for a long time before laying it down. Then he snuffed out the candle and left.

He had been paired and released from voting in order to visit his wife, so when he returned to London he went straight back to Gerrard Street. He was in no mood for company. He prepared a simple supper, nothing too messy, he'd only have to clear it

212

up himself. With some reluctance he switched on the television for distraction. That reluctance grew as he watched the evening news unravel. He became tetchy at the coverage given to a picket line thrown around an abortion advice bureau; it gave the protesters coverage they could never have bought through advertising but which on the news was both priceless and cost-free. He grew angry at the interviewer who showered insolence and interruption upon a Minister, and incandescent at the Minister who allowed such nonsense to continue. Then came the family standing in front of their garden gate, pleading, and Goodfellowe over-flowed with wrath. It was a story that had run across several days and all the front pages. The abduction, the abandoned pushchair, the demand for ransom, the speculation, the parental appeals, the search. Then the discovery of her torn and crumpled body in a car boot. A family's tragedy of unfathomable depth. Yet why was it so necessary, so damnably bloody obligatory, for the media to know how they all felt? To camp outside their house until, weeping, the parents had been forced to come to the garden gate to share their grief in the hope that, after this one photo call, they might be left alone to mourn. Their plea for privacy was lost in the clatter of camera shutters which sounded like machine-gun fire from the trenches. The public had a right to know, so it was said, no matter who became targets.

It was not a moment for restraint, either on their part or on his. As he watched, Goodfellowe's frustrations and anger took possession of him. He was on his feet shouting and cursing at the newscast, but no matter how much he cried out they wouldn't listen, would never apologize. So he shouted all the

213

more. Then, uttering a howl that resembled more the fury of a wild animal, he had launched himself at the television and smashed his shoe straight through the control panel. With an air of offended majesty the television rocked back, and forward. Then it toppled. The screen gave a flash of outrage and the news, with all its outpourings of misery, grunted and died. Goodfellowe was astonished into silence by his own actions. He stood beside the wreckage, studying it carefully, wanting to make sure that all traces of life had departed. Then he bent down to examine his shoe.

'So, you weren't such a waste of money after all.'

*   *   *

'Di, you were brilliant.' He dribbled iced champagne between her shoulder blades and watched it trickle in little spurts down to the hollow of her back, laughing as she wriggled in anticipation. Then he leaned down to taste it. Champagne and sweat. Nothing tasted so good.

Another hour of distraction passed by before Corsa decided to venture upon the real point of the evening, hoping the champagne would make her a little too relaxed to see it coming. Her body lay wrapped in a cocoon of satin, satisfied for the moment, and when he tugged at the sheet to roll her towards him her arms fell open in surrender. He hoped it was a sign of things to come. 'Had fun?'

'Did you ever doubt it? You seriously think I'm the sort of girl who fakes my fun simply to flatter your wretched male ego?'

'Scarcely. I only wish we could squeeze a little more fun out of it.'

'Why, have I exhausted you already?'

214

'I'm not talking about just this. I mean with the *Herald* and the consortium.'

'Ah, your other little *crime passionnel*. I thought your story today about a mole on the executive committee of Greenpeace was a particularly splendid piece of foreplay. Most thoughtful of you. It'll have them running around in circles for months.' Her finger traced a sympathetic line around his nipple but he was not to be diverted.

'We're still playing at the moment. I'd love to start taking it seriously.'

'We will, in time.'

'But why wait, Di? Why not get on with it? Right away.'

'How?'

'Get the consortium into action. Don't let's hang around for those wretched politicians to finish scratching themselves. Buy into the *Herald* now.'

There was a rustle of sheets as she withdrew into her cocoon, considering. 'It wouldn't work,' she said, her voice still as soft as silk.

'Why not?'

'All for one and one for all? I think not. To have the sustained impact you promised we need more than one newspaper, not just the *Herald*. We need the other titles. Collective firepower.'

'But why not get started?'

'We have. To be a fraction mercenary about it, you're having to work very hard on our behalf with the *Herald* just to keep us at the starting line. Doesn't cost us a penny.'

'In your own words, that's only foreplay.'

'At which you are really very good, Freddy. But we can't move to consummation until the Bill is signed and sealed and the other titles are shaken out of the tree. Until that time our little plan depends on politicians, hornless unicorns all. On their propensity for sudden elections. On their unique ability to disappoint. To screw things up.'

'The Bill will go through, of course it will.'

'And when it does, there we shall be, right behind you. Or, in my case perhaps, right beneath you. But until that time it's all birds in bushes, and for the moment the only bird you have in your hand is me.'

He rolled on top of her, looking down, allowing the firm contours of his body to adjust to the softness of hers and make their own argument. 'So let's make a start. Buy me. Let me be your slave.'

'Don't rush the foreplay, Freddy.' She placed a finger on his lips to still him, then began running the tip down slowly through the dark hair of his chest in the direction of his navel. 'In fact, don't rush anything.'

Damnation. It was always going to be a long shot but he'd had to try. He needed to create some breathing space. The bankers had been starting to catch up fast, to ask the questions he daren't answer, which could only be answered by the consortium and its money. He could feel the breath of dragons down his neck. He was back where he had started.

The Bill or bust.

* * *

The music had a headbanging quality, thumping out its message with insistent phrasing and encouraging them all to shake and sweat and drive their bodies onward. Rivulets of perspiration cascaded down the purple temples of the Health Minister. His lips twisted encouragingly at his private secretary, who merely gritted her teeth. She wasn't used to this. Maybe it would feel better next week.

Goodfellowe had never been to the House of Commons gym before. Buried in the basement of what used to be the police headquarters of Scotland Yard and now expropriated as an annexe to the Palace of Westminster, it was an emporium of effort fitted out in tasteful lime-green and had become a popular meeting place for the fashionably fit, like the Health Minister. Political minds were crowded with as much dirty linen as a laundry basket; it paid occasionally to wash it all out. And to prepare for the long nights of effort and distraction.

'Lionel, I was looking for you. Your secretary told me you were here. Are you unwell?'

Lillicrap raised a flushed cheek. He was on the rowing machine and the video monitor in front of him showed he was just about to overhaul the Oxford eight somewhere near the Hammersmith Bridge. 'Got you!' he exclaimed in triumph as the machine began to bleep furiously, Quickly, he switched it off.

'But you haven't finished,' Goodfellowe pointed out, not entirely helpfully. 'You've got half the Chiswick bend to row.'

'Bugger off, Tom,' Lillicrap replied, reaching for his towel. 'I'll not allow a middle-aged cynic to spoil my fun.'

'Oh, fun's the objective, is it? That might explain it, I suppose.'

'All in a Whip's work. Have to keep an eye on the place, make sure none of our merry men overdoes it and drops dead. You know what a caring bunch we are.'

'Not to mention the inconvenience of

stretchering a corpse through the voting lobby.'

'Anyway, I wanted to lose a little weight. Get the old jowls slimmed down. Look better on television. Just in case.' Lillicrap began to wipe down his damp shoulders, admiring the muscle tone, and smiled encouragingly at the passing figure of a female library assistant. 'You should get yourself fit, Tom. Clean up your sex life.'

'Dust it down, you mean. With a trowel.'

'Action or impotence. That's what my old man always told me.'

'Then your father was a wise man. I agree with him.'

'Oh?' enquired Lillicrap, plugging his hand into the pulsometer to check his rate of recovery.

'I've come to tell you that I have reached a decision. About the Standing Committee.'

Lillicrap's pulsometer hesitated, then crept back up several notches.

'The Bill deals with the size of ownership. But size isn't everything, Lionel. I want the Committee to discuss the quality of ownership, too.'

'What the hell does that mean?' Lillicrap scowled. He was still sweating.

'Many saints have chosen to own British newspapers, but I'm more concerned with the sinners.'

'Like?'

'You need a typed list? Try Maxwell.'

'A one-off.'

'If only he were. There are people we regard as being unfit to become company directors or British citizens, but they can own our newspapers. And manipulate our news and our politics. We hand over the most powerful weapons in the country to anyone who can borrow or steal enough money, and then we crawl cap in hand whenever we want their support. Shouldn't work like that, Lionel. Mustn't work like that any more.'

'You do talk crap at times.'

'We don't even tax them. The Government puts tax on almost everything that moves—electricity, clothes, cars. But not newspapers. Why, Lionel? Are we so scared we won't even make them pay their way?'

'Spare me the moralizing, Tom, I'm a busy man. What is it you are telling me?'

'That I've had enough. I've grown sick of watching innocent people being torn to pieces by newsmen hunting in rabid packs. They froth at the mouth about public interest when the only interest being served is their own. It's all about money, not morality, but money alone shouldn't decide who runs the media any more than it should decide who runs the country. The Bill goes nowhere near far enough. It's not just a matter of who owns newspapers, let alone how many they own. It's about accuracy. And privacy. And fairness. And protection for victims of the press. The whole package. Unless the Government allows these matters to be debated, as part of the Bill, I'm going to vote against it.'

Lillicrap turned on him. 'Haven't you made yourself enough of a pariah? The Bill's already behind schedule. That would screw it up even more!'

'I pray you are right.'

'You can't win, you know that.' Lillicrap's tone was sharp, unforgiving. 'We'd get it back on the Floor of the House. Outvote you there.'

'Maybe. But I'll get my day in court.'

'Before they bloody hang you. With every editor in Fleet Street condemning you and with Beryl pulling at the rope.' (So, realized Goodfellowe, Lillicrap and Beryl had been in touch . . .) 'And it would be over my dead body as a Whip. My career would go down the pan for your spotty conscience. It would take our friendship with it, Tom.' Anxiety was turning to anger.

'Then how easily political friendships are swept away.'

'I thought we had more than that,' Lillicrap spat in contempt.

'So did I,' Goodfellowe replied, sadly.

'Are you determined?'

'I am.'

'Even though Freddy Corsa has those photographs of you?' Lillicrap, still perspiring, was growing ever more heated. He had squared up to Goodfellowe, fists clenched, looking as though he might hit him.

'You know the photographs are entirely innocent.'

'So you say, but Corsa could do immense harm by publishing them.'

'Don't you understand? That's precisely the point I'm trying to make, Lionel. All the more reason to speak out.'

'Tom, we shall have to ruin you.'

The Whip's words swirled on a flood of emotion, along with the wreckage of their friendship. Goodfellowe left them there. He'd only come to tell Lillicrap of his intentions out of loyalty; it had been a waste of time. At the door he turned once more. Behind him, he saw Lillicrap standing in front of his

220

metal locker. He was pounding it with his fist until it bent.

*   *   *

Sam let the cotton dressing gown slip from her shoulders and allowed the course director to show her how they wanted her to pose. 'Just a quickie,' he smiled, indicating that she should place one foot on the small stool and reach up with her hand, as though carrying an Olympic torch. It was a tiring pose, stretching her body and lifting her hands and breasts high. 'Only five minutes,' they promised, throwing themselves into their sketching with enthusiasm.

It was a warm early summer's evening outside but it felt a little cooler than she had expected. A draught, almost. It tickled. She was glad of the heater nearby. She stood in the pool of light thrown by the overhead lamp like an actress or an operatic star, barely aware of the audience seated in the shadows around her but feeling the intensity of their concentration and appreciation. All eyes were on her and she was lost, relaxed in her own innermost thoughts, responding to the solitude and peace.

It was scarcely surprising, therefore, that none of them paid the slightest attention to the far end of the hall, which in any event was in deep shadow. It was the end of the hall which opened onto scrubland, overlooked by nothing, and it was here Oscar Kutzman had been busy. That afternoon, armed with no more than a glass cutter, he had waited until he was sure no one was around and deftly removed one of the small panes of glass, replacing it with plastic film. Later that evening, after the art class had gathered and the curtains had been drawn to guard against the prying eyes of the Boys' Brigade meeting in the church next door, he had been able to remove the film and cautiously draw back an edge of the curtain to allow a full and uninterrupted view of the entire hall. And it was a calm evening outside; only the slightest draught.

That girl reporter had been right. He could see the lot from here, and they'd even pre-lit it for him. Not ideal conditions for photography, but he had worked in far worse.

*   *   *

They met at Goodfellowe's favourite restaurant in Shaftesbury Avenue shortly after ten. He'd hoped that by keeping away from her, isolating himself from the charms he knew had such an effect on him, he might have been able to put his feelings for Elizabeth in perspective. No chance. They continued to torment him, along with all the other emotions over which he had lost control. He wanted not to want her, it would make life so much simpler. But as soon as she glided through the door, tall and elegant, and smiled for him, it started all over again.

They had much to catch up on—or, rather, she did, since Goodfellowe did most of the talking. He had become like an ancient knight sitting by the campfire on the eve of battle, doubts banished, full of nervous energy, keen to share, and like all Irish women she was trained to listen. And to pour. She sensed he needed calming, slowing, anaesthetizing against himself and his fire-eyed enthusiasms.

'Isn't it possible,' she enquired after she had listened to his analysis, 'that Corsa is publishing these attacks on The Earth Firm and the rest simply

222

to boost circulation, like any other newspaper?'

'It's more than that,' Goodfellowe responded, trying to transfer a helping of fried seaweed to his plate and missing. 'Not just maximum sales, but maximum damage. These stories could have been published at any time, but I think they were printed when they could do most harm.'

'So why does Corsa loathe The Earth Firm? Or Wonderworld? Even the coal industry? What's the connection?'

'I'm not sure.'

'Perhaps it's simply a macho male thing. Too much testosterone. Screwing them simply because they're there.'

'You've been reading too many parliamentary thrillers.'

'You think there's logic mixed in with all the Corsa loathing?'

'Maybe it's not so much who he hates, but who he wants to help—apart from himself. The Earth Firm story was clearly designed to help the Government.'

'But who was helped out by the others?'

'That's what I've been asking myself.' He licked the sticky remnants of seaweed from his fingers. 'Great brain food,' he muttered appreciatively, while she refilled his glass. 'But Government can't be the common link. Not in the case of Wonderworld. Certainly not with the entire coal industry.'

'So?'

He dug his chopsticks into a bowlful of noodles as though ransacking them in search of inspiration. 'It's power. But not political power. He doesn't give a stuff about politicians. For him they're just hired hands.'

223

'It's not politics. It's not sex. What's left?'

'Money. That's what matters to Corsa. It's warfare all right and he sends his editors in like the Marines. But the target is commercial, not political.'

'Yet how does Corsa gain commercially from attacking something like Wonderworld?'

'Because whenever some unfortunate bastard gets staked out in the sun there's another lurking in the shadows waiting to pick his pockets. Losers, and winners. And you can bet that whoever won from staking out The Earth Firm or Wonderworld or the entire coal industry is a good friend of Freddy Corsa's.'

'Corsa has friends?' She was having trouble with the concept.

'Allies, then. Money men. This mystery group of backers the newspapers have talked about. Waiting to get in on the action after the Press Bill goes through. Maybe they're getting a bit of the action up front.' It fitted, he knew it was right, but Goodfellowe's elation immediately subsided into a frown. 'Still doesn't tell us who they are. Could be anyone. Absolutely anyone.'

'Maybe I can offer a clue.' Elizabeth's lips puckered thoughtfully. 'I belong to the Indulgents. It's a small dining club of res-taurateurs who get together to gossip and be disgraceful. We had an excellent little gossip last week about Freddy Corsa.' The lips moved from side to side as though performing sentry duty. 'He's dined in three of the restaurants recently with the same woman. Something of a feature. An attractive and very senior oil executive named Diane Burston.'

'She's well known, a player of substance. She'd

make an excellent member of any consortium.' He picked up a final stray piece of seaweed from the tablecloth. 'Tell me, what were they at? Business or pleasure?'

'Are there different types of sin, Tom? With those people surely it's all the same.'

'Elizabeth,' he whispered, 'you are a remarkable as well as very beautiful woman.'

'Tom,' she smiled in surprise, 'what has brought that on? Business or pleasure?'

'I almost forgot,' he stumbled, reaching into his pocket. He withdrew a small leather-bound edition of poetry by Yeats. 'Not particularly valuable. Something I found in the Charing Cross Road. While I was thinking of you. A sort of good-luck charm, I thought. It seems to be working already.'

She blew him a small kiss, the lips no longer puckering to one side but pointing straight in his direction. It had become a very special moment for Goodfellowe. He ordered a new bottle of wine to celebrate. And as he relaxed, his conversation turned to more personal matters, feelings he had difficulty in articulating but which now, with her encouragement and the benefit of wine, he attempted to explain to her. Feelings he had tried to bury. Of loneliness. Of his overwhelming sense of duty, which he still confused with love. Of how his life had become dominated by all its forms rather than its substance. He talked and shared, explaining not only to her but also to himself. Outside, the first thunderstorm of summer was turning the streets into dark rivers but, as she poured the wine and he poured out his heart, he didn't even hear it.

'The forms of life are important to me, Elizabeth. I owe responsibilities as well as love to Sam and

Elinor. And I could have met those responsibilities simply by saying yes to Corsa and to Lillicrap. It was the easy way out. But it would have left me emptied inside, and what goes on inside a man—the passions, the ambitions, the very personal comforts—surely they matter too?'

'You're asking that question of an Irish girl?' She poured once more, wanting to encourage him.

'I've been alone for a long time now. And I found a simplicity in loneliness which got me through my days, if not the nights. Then you came along and spoiled it. I tried to hate you for it, for walking into my one-dimensional world and ruining it, but that didn't work so I decided I had to start fighting back. Listening to the man within. Even poor Elinor recognized it. You can't love me, she said. And she was right. I want to love her, I should love her. But I can't. All I can do is my duty to her. Form without the substance. I need something more.'

'What do you need, Tom?'

'I need you, I think. At least I need to find out whether I need you. Do I make sense? Sorry, I'm not very good at this. Out of practice. Think I've drunk too much. But I need to open up my one-dimensional world, Elizabeth. And what I feel for you has had an extraordinary effect in broadening my horizons.'

'Broadening your horizons? Back home that's called lust. Are you propositioning me, Tom Goodfellowe?'

'Think I am.'

'And about bloody time.'

'I feel a bit of a fool.'

'Ah, but you're a passionate fool. An Irishman at heart.'

He began to laugh, rather wearily. 'Trouble is, old duck, I needed a bit of Dutch courage to blurt it all out.' He looked at his oft-emptied glass. 'I think I've overdone it.'

At a nearby table a waiter was gesticulating to the diners. 'One hour taxi. One hour taxi,' he shouted as the gutters outside overflowed. It was almost two a.m.

'Well, if you think I'm walking home in that cloudburst, you truly must be drunk.'

'My apartment is just round the corner.'

'Now isn't that a coincidence,' she laughed mischievously. 'But so much for lust. Seems to me it's not so much a case of you inviting me home, but me getting you home.'

Happy, clutching, soaking, with him trying to provide shelter for her beneath an old menu card, they had scuttled the short distance back to his doorway in Gerrard Street. Outside lay a pile of Sunday newspapers which had already turned to papier-mâché. 'Whoops. Completely forgot I was supposed to be reviewing the newspapers in the morning.'

'All the more reason for you to get a few hours' sleep,' she chided.

'Guess I'll have to make it up as I go along.'

'Is that the passion or the review?' she whispered. He declined to answer.

So they had dripped their way up the stairs, fumbled with his keys, and arm-in-arm had poured themselves inside his apartment. By the door, the red light on his answering machine was blinking belligerently. Twenty-one messages. This had happened once before when an automated message machine on call-back had pestered him all day, mistaking his number for a fax line. He took the phone off the hook. He wasn't in any fit state to be disturbed.

'Bath, kitchen,' he pointed out to her. 'Barry Manilow tapes,' he added, waving at the stereo system. 'My little vice, but only ever in private,' he confided, swaying a little.

'Anything else to declare?' she enquired, trying to stifle a giggle.

He became instantly maudlin, taking her hands. 'Only that I haven't been in the arms of a woman for more than four years and I can't wait to sober up.'

'And in the meantime?'

'You,' he waved at the bed on its mezzanine platform. 'Me,' he pronounced, flopping across the small sofa. Smiling, she leaned down to kiss him, but already he was asleep.

He was dragged back from the depths of senselessness by the insistent rasping of the intercom. The cab had arrived.

'Damned lies! It can't be,' he squealed, shaking his watch in disbelief, unable to accept it was already six fifteen. 'Ten minutes,' he shouted to the driver. He was nearly twenty. Elizabeth watched in amusement from the bed-platform above as he scuttled about the apartment trying to balance haste against modesty, a scramble perforated by a bout of drawer-rattling indecision as to what colour shirt to wear, and all the while battling to plaster down hair which spoke eloquently of the night on his sofa.

Finally he stood at the door, breathless. 'I'll be back by nine. Be here?'

'Get lost, Goodfellowe,' she smiled.

He had hoped to find another set of newspapers in the cab but the back seat was empty. The aerial

228

had been wrenched away, the radio was inoperable and the driver spoke unintelligible West African, so Goodfellowe had spent the journey tucking in his shirt and conducting further hostilities with his hair. By the time he reached the studios he felt uninformed, but almost fit.

'Mr Goodfellowe. Brilliant! So good of you to come.' An agitated young executive had swung open the passenger door and was hopping from foot to foot like a fire walker.

'My pleasure.'

'Thought you wouldn't make it. We tried to call last night. Several times. Really quite brave of you, in the circumstances.'

'What circumstances?'

The hopping stopped, the legs suddenly grown leaden. 'You haven't seen the newspapers?' It was a comment offered in awe.

'Not had a chance. Not yet.'

The television executive uttered a very bad word he had learned at public school and placed his hands together, putting them to his face as though reciting the rosary. 'I think you'd better come with me.'

Inside, in a small private room, away from the other guests who were gathering for the morning programme, they sat him down with a cup of muddy tea and a copy of the *Sunday Herald*.

'MP CAUGHT WITH CHINESE VICE GIRL.'

Below the screaming headline was the photograph of him with Jya-Yu. It seemed, more than ever as he studied the photo once again, that they were engaged in a passionate lip-spreading kiss.

229

The future of Tom Goodfellowe, the former Minister who was recently found guilty of drink-driving, was thrown into further doubt yesterday when it was revealed he was having an association with a Chinatown vice girl. Police sources confirmed that Pan Jya-Yu, 18, was recently arrested on suspicion of prostitution and drug handling. She also attacked her arresting policeman. She has since accepted a caution—effectively pleaded guilty—to possession of a restricted substance, believed to be an Oriental sex drug.

At the time of her arrest the vice girl, instead of calling for a solicitor, telephoned Goodfellowe. Police sources indicate he was at the police station within fifteen minutes of the call being made, missing a series of vital House of Commons votes to be there. He was also present at her side when she returned to answer bail.

Goodfellowe describes himself as a friend of the attractive teenager, who is only two years older than his own daughter. Our exclusive photograph, taken outside Charing Cross police station on the public street a short while after her arrest, suggests their friendship will come as a grave embarrassment to the Government in its attempts to rebuild its image on family values after other recent sleaze scandals . . .

Constituency sources in Marshwood indicated this latest scandal, coming on the heels of Goodfellowe's own arrest and conviction for drunk driving, could result in his being thrown out by his local party. 'We

230

wanted an MP. Instead we seem to have got a jailbird,' one senior local official commented.

Last night the Member for Marshwood was not answering his telephone and was believed to he in hiding.

Only the shivering of the newspaper in his hand revealed that Goodfellowe had not turned entirely to stone.

The executive coughed timorously. 'What can I say? I'm sorry, I suppose you won't want to go on with the show, not after this. Perhaps you'd like to go straight home, I've kept the car.'

Goodfellowe turned, with the eyes of a wolf in winter. 'I'll go on.'

'You will?' The executive brightened.

'An entire division of Hitler's Waffen SS couldn't keep me off your bloody programme. This is evil.' He flung the newspaper away from him, across the room, where the pages divided and settled like falling snow. 'I want to be straight on there so I can tell everyone what a miserable piece of filth this is. I demand you let me on!'

'Yeah, sure. Great. Really great,' burbled the executive. 'Would you like make-up first?'

As preparations for the programme rushed around him, Goodfellowe had difficulty controlling the anger that was causing both hand and voice to tremble. He practised breathing exercises to calm himself as sound-men and make-up women fussed around, wiring him up and attempting to keep the eruptions of hair battened down. Maxine the make-up woman stepped back from him to pass a professional judgement on the result, sucking her teeth. 'Would you like eye-drops,' she offered, 'to get rid of some of the red?'

But it was too late, he was on. He was seated on the sofa opposite Jeremy, the show's host. They hadn't turned on the full studio lights yet but already he could feel the beads of perspiration gathering along his hair line. Too much wine, too much anger. Maxine rushed to give him a final despairing wipe. Then it began.

'We start as ever with our review of the morning papers, and our guest today is Tom Goodfellowe, Government MP and former Minister, And a man much in the news himself. Eh, Tom?'

'It's filth.' Suddenly so many thoughts were scraping around inside his head that he found it difficult to slow them down sufficiently to express them. 'It's filth,' he was reduced to repeating.

'For those who don't know what he's referring to, the *Sunday Herald* has this front-page story devoted to our guest this morning. Never say we're not timely.' He held up the *Herald* for the inspection of the watching millions. Goodfellowe felt his muscles tighten with tension. He was screaming at himself to relax, to take control, but the commands seemed to be being issued by a voice from an entirely separate body.

'So, what about it? Is it true?'

'It is a collage of innuendo and lies,' Goodfellowe replied, scowling. Relax, you fool! the voice insisted, but Goodfellowe ploughed on, 'This is a most shameful article.'

'But you do know this girl?' Jeremy interrupted.

'Of course.'

'She's not a constituent?'

'Just a friend.'

'A very good friend, it would seem from the

photograph. Is the photograph false, have they doctored it in any way?'

'Who can tell? But it is certainly . . .'—last night's indulgences were clouding his mind as he struggled for the phrase—'unrepresentative.' What a bloody stupid word, the voice argued with him. 'It implies we have a relationship way beyond the reality.' The voice groaned.

'OK, let's deal with the facts one by one. The story states that this young lady, your friend, was arrested on suspicion of prostitution and being in possession of drugs, and assaulted the arresting police officer. Is that true or false?'

'It was all a mistake. She's a very decent girl.'

'But she has, according to the story, accepted a caution for possessing a controlled substance.'

'Yes, but . . .'

'A sex drug. An aphrodisiac, I suppose you might call it.'

'The case is not what it seems.' He felt heated, in more ways than one. The perspiration was beginning visibly to trickle and he knew his eyes looked puffed and blotchy. Damn, he could feel his hair springing up in defiance, pushing through the pavement of lacquer. He would look like a Christmas turkey. Behind the cameras Maxine winced. This wasn't going to be one for her portfolio. 'This is nothing more than a newspaper's disgraceful attempt to distort a confused personal situation in order to damage my reputation,' Goodfellowe continued. 'The young lady in question is a sweet girl. Not involved in vice.'

'Well, I'm not sure about that. She's involved with sex drugs and I suspect that many people would accept the description of vice girl as fair comment.

233

But if she's not a constituent, why did you feel the need to help her? Not once, but repeatedly?'

'Because she asked for it, she was being arrested and was frightened. There doesn't have to be any other motive.'

'Fair enough. I can understand that from your position, since as the article points out and many people know, you're not a total stranger to the problems of being arrested yourself. But is it true that you missed important Commons votes to rush to her side? Was she that—what's the word?—significant to you?'

'At the time I scarcely knew her.' Try not to look so stiff and guilty, the voice whispered, but it was pointless, his hands were clenched to stop them shaking.

'Forgive me, I don't mean to doubt your word, but the photograph suggests something entirely different. You were kissing her, that's correct, isn't it?'

'It was no more than a gesture of gratitude on her part.'

'It was her fault, then?'

Goodfellowe struggled. 'No. Don't twist my words. It was nothing more than gratitude, I tell you ...' The voice was suggesting it had a train to catch.

'Then she's obviously a very grateful type of girl. So what is your relationship with her?'

'It is tea. I buy my tea from her.' The truth sometimes sounds so damnably inadequate. And unconvincing.

'I won't bother asking whether you take it with one lump or two.'

'Really...' His anger was beginning to show, binding his tongue. The interviewer was quick to

234

take advantage.

'And remember, folks. That's something you heard first on the Morning Programme. Tea for two. So let's recap. What about the story is inaccurate?'

'The whole wretched thing.'

'But we've just gone through the relevant details and you've pretty much confirmed them,'

'They have disfigured the facts and come up with a completely false and possibly libellous conclusion.'

'Oh, so you'll sue?'

'I . . . I haven't had time to consider.' It was too evasive, and too late. He could hear the sound of a closing door as his judgement and its voice gave up and left. 'This is not a situation of sleaze, it's only an example of the kind of support politicians provide every day. It's been deliberately distorted.'

'The road to Hell, it would seem, is littered with used tea bags. Well, I want to thank you, Tom, for coming in this morning and clearing up the confusion. You've been a sport.' Jeremy reached across and extended a hand to thank him. Only then did Goodfellowe become aware of how wringing damp his own had become.

Jeremy turned back to the camera, his interest in Goodfellowe obliterated. 'And as you enjoy your morning cup of tea, friends, remember—keep practising safe sipping.' Someone on the floor crew sniggered. 'Our next guest this morning refuses to become involved in politics and knows nothing of vice. She's a missionary who has recently returned from . . .'

And it was over. Finished. Before millions of viewers. His reputation ruined. He'd had a wealth of experience at dealing with the media and defending every aspect of policy in the teeth of the storm but this had not been politics, it had been all too personal. And he had been too angry, too emotional, too uptight. Taken by surprise. Even had he handled himself less than disastrously they would have congratulated him on his performance yet still assumed the truth of the story. A man of his age, a politician no less, and a young girl. Obvious, wasn't it?

He decided to walk the three miles home. He needed the fresh air and the space, time to gather in the pieces of wreckage. To relieve the heaviness of his hangover. It was only as he reached Covent Garden that he remembered Elizabeth and began to quicken his stride, feeling a sense of urgency, ignoring the new blister he could feel swelling on his heel.

As he hurried into Gerrard Street he half-expected to find a posse of newsmen camped out on his doorstep but the street was empty. They hadn't caught up with his change of address. As he bounded up the stairs the blister burst and he found his hands shaking so uncontrollably that he had trouble getting the key in the lock. Mercy, at last he was home.

The volume of Yeats was lying on the kitchen counter. Elizabeth was gone.

CHAPTER SEVEN

He had tried to telephone Elizabeth but got only her answering machine. She had surrounded herself with an electronic wall of silence. He thought of rushing round, then held back. Perhaps she needed a little time. In any event, his feelings towards her had grown confused, anger mixing with apprehension. She had jumped to conclusions, like all the rest. No benefit of the doubt, no time to listen. And he had other pressing matters to deal with. He telephoned Jya-Yu but the phone was constantly engaged, scarcely surprising, so he phoned the apothecary. He got Uncle Zhu. In the background he could hear the noise of chaos and Goodfellowe wondered whether in response to the publicity the police had decided to raid the premises after all. Zhu was curt, evidently harassed, and didn't want to talk, putting down the phone before Goodfellowe even had a chance to say sorry.

He took his own phone off the hook, made himself a cup of strong black tea and took it to the bathroom. He looked at himself in the mirror. The face staring back at him seemed to have withered. On occasions recently when middle age had pressed upon him he had found himself studying old men, imagining what he himself would look like in twenty or thirty years, if he lived that long. They all looked the same. Bent, helpless, unkempt, and his reflection told him he was catching them up. Many also had rheumy, dissolving eyes, he had noticed, as his own now were. Tears fell. He soaked in the bath for a long time until his mangled feet stopped hurting, trying to wash away the rest of the pain.

As he towelled himself down he made a mental list of all the people he needed urgently to contact—the Press Complaints Commission, a reliable lobby correspondent, a libel lawyer perhaps, the Chief Whip (no, why bother? Undoubtedly the Chief was already trying to contact him). But first priority was to telephone Jya-Yu once more. He put on his bathrobe and reconnected the receiver, but no sooner had he done so than the telephone rang of its own accord.

'Daddy?'

He was flooded with remorse. The very first call he should have made, with not a second's delay, and she wasn't even on his list. She was away, not a daily part of his life, and part of him still thought of her as a child, to be protected and kept apart from problems. How twisted his values had become.

'We knew you were going to be on television this morning. We all sat down to watch you.' Humiliation hung on every word. He could hear her tears. As he could feel his own.

'I'm so sorry, my pet. Please believe me. None of it is true.'

'Who is she, Daddy?'

'A neighbour here in Chinatown. A young lady I scarcely knew.'

'But you made time for her. You were kissing her.'

'She was embracing me. In gratitude, nothing more.'

Great Buddha, not even Sam believed him.

'There are reporters and photographers at the school gates. They asked me what it was like to have a father who goes with Chinese prostitutes.' She had grown suddenly breathless as though she were having another of her childhood asthma attacks.

'Jya-Yu is not a prostitute . . .'

'They asked if you took sex drugs, too. They started asking me if I had ever taken drugs. Or read the *Karma Sutra*. If I had a boyfriend. Whether I was allowed to bring him home during the holidays.

238

To sleep with him.'

She couldn't continue. The brazen, even defiant young woman of recent months had disappeared, in her place was a frightened child whose emotions and resolve were melting, all because of him. He had failed her more than he could ever have feared.

She gulped, summoning her courage. 'I think I know now why you sent me to boarding school.'

'Why was that, darling?'

'You wanted me out of the way so you could be free to do these things. You sent me away not to help me, but so you could help yourself.'

'Please let me . . .'

'I don't mind that so much,' she cut across, determined to force her point through. 'In a way I can even understand. But do you know something?'

'What? '

'You know why I hate you so much?'

'Sammy . . .?'

'I hate you, Daddy, because you're such an awful bloody hypocrite. That's it.'

I hate you, Daddy. He had never wanted to live to hear those words, never dreamed even at his darkest moments that he would. Then Sam was gone, had fled, abandoned him, and in her place another voice. It was Miss Rennie.

'I require a frank word with you, Mr Goodfellowe, if you please.' The tones were Edinburgh prim, brooking no debate.

'Headmistress, let me explain . . .'

'I think there are many other people who require an explanation ahead of me, Mr Goodfellowe. What I require you to do is to listen.' Bare rock was showing through the heather. 'Poor Samantha is in a most wretched state and normally I would suggest

239

she return home for a few days. However, in this case I suspect we might both agree that sending her home would be the last thing to bring her any comfort. So, unless you have strong objections, she will go to the home of her art teacher, Mrs Ashburton, for a few days.'

'You're taking her out of school?'

She took it as an accusation, which perhaps it was. 'Mr Goodfellowe, let me tell you what you have done. Even as we speak reporters are invading the school grounds, accosting my pupils, trying to bribe information out of them.'

'Truly, Headmistress, you can't blame me. This is all a misunderstanding. Let me explain . . .'

'I have only one interest, Mr Goodfellowe, which is in the good name of my school and its pupils, to both of which you are causing immense damage. Heavens, man, they're even sifting through the dustbins! This must stop. You must stop it. Otherwise I shall have no option other than to ask you to take Samantha away from this school in order to protect the others.'

He could scarcely believe it. He sat stunned.

'I hope I have made myself perfectly clear, Mr Goodfellowe.'

He sighed, a blue-black sound of immense despair. 'In all this, Miss Rennie, I can find only one consolation.'

'Which is?'

'That matters cannot get any worse.'

Yet already he was out of date.

*   *   *

Machines, even the great machines of state, have at

240

their heart some small and seemingly insignificant part, a simple spring or a ballbearing perhaps, without which nothing would run. The Downing Street switchboard was such a part, that vital component which kept the channels of government open by being able to get hold of anyone on any occasion other than during seduction or surgery, it was said, and even then they had a better than evens chance. Lillicap discovered it was a reputation thoroughly deserved. He had tried every number he knew to find Corsa, but either the phone rang unanswered or the janitor who picked it up had little idea who Mr Corsa was, let alone where to find him on a Sunday morning. In desperation he had tried the *Herald's* editor, but ran into the stone wall. He had tried to pull a little rank but was brusquely reminded how little rank a Junior Whip had to pull. Corsa valued his privacy. So it was not until Lillicrap had greased the ballbearings and asked with an uncharacteristic lack of bluster for the assistance of the Downing Street girls that he made any form of progress. Within ten minutes they had not only got Corsa but, by the sounds of things, even got him out of bed. There was a distinctive 'I don't want to be ready for this' tone in the proprietor's voice, and another voice in the background, female. Traditionally Whips were trained to assume that everyone was sleeping with the vicar's wife and beating his dog, although nowadays it was just as likely to be the other way around. At least Corsa was clear about his orientation. And his annoyance.

'Lionel, this had better be important.'

'Important enough for you to splash it all over your front page. What the hell was that in aid of? And why didn't you warn me?'

'I didn't wish to compromise your principles.'

Lillicrap failed utterly to grasp the sarcasm. 'Was it truly necessary? To go public?'

'There speaks a man used to dark corners and shadows. I have only the straightforward ways of a press man. A spotlight and my front page.'

Lillicrap thought he heard a giggle and the sound of bare flesh being slapped. 'You told me you wouldn't use the photograph.'

'I had no choice.'

'No choice?'

'He must be destroyed. Whatever it takes.'

Lillicrap's heart caught. The candour was unmistakable, he thought they were the most sincere words he had ever heard Corsa use. That frightened him.

'Hold up, Freddy, you're getting this out of proportion.'

'I've got nothing out of proportion. This Bill is everything. It must go through.'

'And it will. I'll deliver.'

'And you'll deliver the Opposition too?'

'What? '

'Don't you know that Goodfellowe has been taking tea with that harridan Betty Ewing? Planning how they can frustrate you. Delay the Bill.'

'How do you know that?'

'Because I have friends in low places, lower even than the Government Whip's Office.'

'In the Opposition?'

'Know thine enemy, Lionel. And he is the enemy. Plotting in the bloody Tea Room, for God's sake. He's not even trying to make a secret of it.'

Lillicrap flustered. This was getting out of hand, he was losing his hold on circumstance. And a Whip

242

who loses his hold on circumstance soon finds it tightening around his throat.

'Even if we take a drubbing in Committee we'll get it all back later. Might delay us a couple of months, three or four at most.' Lillicrap attempted to generate some enthusiasm in his voice but every part of Corsa remained shut away.

'I don't want later, I want now. No risks. No delays. All I want is what the Government promised me. What you promised me.'

'I can fix him. Without all this publicity. I promise. He won't cause any more trouble.'

'If the Bill goes down, Lionel, you go down with it.'

'I'll fix it. Don't worry.'

'But I do, Lionel. And so should you.'

*   *   *

It was near the summer solstice and the shortest of nights, but it had come as little comfort to Goodfellowe who slept not at all. He was shaking inside, every particle of him at odds, his sense of guilt doing warfare with his sense of grievance and twisting him about as though he were being stretched on the rack.

He had tried calling Jya-Yu several times but she wasn't answering her phone. Maybe it was a blessing. If he couldn't get hold of her, perhaps no one else could. Elizabeth wasn't answering, either. He thought of going on a hunting expedition for Jya-Yu then prevaricated. The press had finally sorted out his change of address and there was a pack of them outside his door. They might follow him, which would only mean more photographs. Better to stay. Perhaps.

Sooner or later, however, he would have to make an appearance. He couldn't hide, didn't want to hide—hell, he'd done nothing wrong. Or had he? He was no longer certain about anything. So at around nine he made his way down the cold stone stairs to his front door and opened it with the best smile he could find.

'Good morning. Gentlemen.'

The pack closed in on him, thrusting at him with their tape recorders and cameras. And their questions.

'Got a statement for us, Tom?'

'Only that I have never had any form of improper relationship with Miss Jya-Yu. Therefore the implication of the story in yesterday's *Herald* is entirely incorrect. I shall be taking professional advice to see what redress I might have.'

'So were the facts in the story inaccurate, Mr Goodfellowe?'

'Facts are like bricks. You can build a house with them or use them to mug an old lady. It's the way you use them that matters.'

'Why did you choose to come and live in a red-light district?'

'Chinatown is not a red-light district . . .'

'It's spitting distance from Soho. So have you ever paid for sex, Tom?'

'That question is a disgrace.' He shoved his hands in his pockets, hoping to look nonchalant, in truth wanting to ensure they didn't reach out and throttle the bastard.

'Was that a yes or no?'

And the impromptu press conference had rapidly degenerated as he was asked whether he would sue, what he knew of Oriental positions both

244

philosophical and physical, if he would be resigning, had he spoken to the Prime Minister, did he like Indian tea, too, until it all began to be lost in a sea of innuendo and aggression. Then, as though from a scene in a Hornblower film, the stormy seas parted and through their midst under awesome sail came a battleship. It was Beryl. She was wearing a dress of bright floral motif and as she advanced she looked like two stray mongrels having a scrap inside a hydrangea bush.

'Mr Goodfellowe, a word please.'

By her manner it seemed as if at least two would be necessary. But it gave him an excuse for turning his back on the press. He took her inside.

'Care for a cup of tea, Beryl? I'm sure I can find some English Breakfast.'

'No thank you.' She also refused his invitation to proceed up the stairs to his apartment, clearly under the impression that it was a den of depravity from which lady visitors were fortunate to emerge with either honour or underwear. She stood resolutely on the doormat, one hand wrapped around the latch to effect a rapid departure. 'What I have to say is very brief.'

'A relief to us both. You could have phoned.'

'I tried. The phone was off the hook. Anyway, some things one prefers to do face to face. As a matter of honour.' She made it sound as if he would have no personal experience of such things. Her cheeks flushed. 'Is it your intention to resign your seat?'

'Of course not. I've done nothing wrong. I shall stand for reelection as we discussed.'

'Not,' she emphasized, 'as we discussed.' The hydrangeas rustled in the quickening winds. 'That

245

was before. If you are not going to resign and insist on standing at the election, then I have come to tell you that I will be opposing your nomination as the official candidate and I feel certain that a majority of my Executive Committee will support me.'

'You're going to throw me out?'

She had already begun to open the door. 'You've thrown yourself out. You're arrogant. You show no loyalty. And you spend far too much time inside police stations.'

'You're trying to destroy my life.'

'You are the one destroying it, Mr Goodfellowe. No one else.' She turned for one final, defiant glare and found it returned.

'You know, Beryl, when they handed out the milk of human understanding, you got the sterilized skimmed.'

*   *   *

In its haste to deliver its cargo of newspapers the Transit van veered sharply as it came off Trafalgar Square and made a dash into Whitehall. Its wing mirror brushed Goodfellowe's shoulder; another couple of inches and it would have had him off his bike and wrapped around the railings. He shouted a protest. The newspaper van responded with a black cloud of noxiousness as the driver accelerated away, leaving Goodfellowe too busy coughing even to curse.

He was still coughing from the effects of the exhaust as he passed the diminutive statue of Sir Walter Raleigh outside the Ministry of Defence. He'd always thought the two of them had much in common. Raleigh had been another West Country MP, an adventurer who had sailed off into the unknown in search of El Dorado and came back instead with potatoes and tobacco. Something, at least, to show for the effort. But instead of reward, a fickle nation had lodged him in the Bloody Tower, dragged him to a scaffold in Old Palace Yard beside Parliament and, in front of a large audience, struck off his head. Much like breakfast television, Goodfellowe reflected.

As he cycled into New Palace Yard he noticed the duty policemen looking in his direction, conferring and nodding, as they might have done when Raleigh's tumbril passed by. Goodfellowe sighed, guessing it was going to be one of those days. He stared them down and with determined step made his way directly to his office.

'Where's the post?' he demanded, as Mickey walked in. His desk was preternaturally bare.

'You don't want to see it, believe me. A yard-high pile of righteous telephone messages, abusive faxes, notes scribbled on pieces of card and toilet paper, you name it and you've got it.'

'You all right?' He noticed the uncharacteristic grey smudges under her eyes.

'Only if you are.' She gave a brave, defiant smile which didn't quite convince. 'Don't explain, I know it's not true. If only it were, at least you could have gone down with a grin on your face. What are you going to do, Tom?'

'Dunno. Keep trying to fool myself that it can't get any worse. The constituency wants to dump me, Elizabeth has walked away. And I am in the most dreadful trouble with Sam.' Quickly he brought her up to date. 'Whatever else happens, I must keep Sam. Without her, there really wouldn't be much point in going on.'

'She'll come back. Don't worry.'

'How can I not worry? Tell me, what do you think she would want me to do about this mess? Should I pack it in? Become a librarian?'

'Is that a serious question?'

'As serious as . . . I was going to say, as serious as sin. After all, if Beryl gets her way I'll have no choice.' He had slumped in his chair, like a punch-drunk prize fighter between rounds. 'Maybe I should just accept it and give in.'

'Sam wouldn't. The reason she's upset is because she idolizes you.'

'Me?!'

'Of course. You're her father. She thinks you've let her down, let yourself down. She would want you to prove yourself, to carry on what you're fighting for. Not to hide away amongst boring books.'

'But she says she hates me. As hell is hot I just can't figure her out.'

'Sixteen-year-old girls can't figure themselves out. Life happens too quickly for them. She still needs you to help show her the way.'

'Are you sure she would want me to fight?'

'Absolutely certain. And for what it's worth, so do I.'

He hurt all over, bruises everywhere, but in spite of his trepidation he began to haul himself off the stool. The bell was ringing for the start of a new round.

'Well, I can't afford to sue and I've got no money for one of those PR crisis managers to arrange pretty photographs of me with my family. Even if I had a family. But I think we may be close to the truth. Is that enough?'

'Truth isn't one of my specialities, Tom. But I

248

could give it a go.'

Limbs that had felt numb, that had stopped shaking simply because he no longer had the energy to tremble, began tingling again. 'You see, it's all commercial. The *Herald* attacks a company or an industry or a pressure group, and in the shadows someone is laughing all the way to the bank. One of them may be Di Burston. We need to know who the others are.'

'How?'

He began pacing back and forth, the enthusiasms returning. 'Try your computer thingy. The Internet. Look at all the dates of the *Herald* exclusives for the last three months, and see if anybody's share price benefited as a result. It may not provide the full picture but it could give us a damn good idea.'

'Done.'

'Meanwhile, Fate has dealt me an interesting card.' He clapped his hands. 'I've got Question Number Three to the Prime Minister tomorrow. So I shall go right to the top. Time to see who holds the aces. And . . . why, Miss Ross, you're smiling.'

'Why, Mr Goodfellowe, you're fighting.'

'I don't pay you to sit around smirking. Go back and dump all those wretched letters in the bin and get on with what I've asked. After you've made me a cup of tea.'

'Get your own bloody tea,' she responded, retreating with a laugh.

And he did. He decided to spend only a little time around the House that day, enough to be seen so that people knew he wasn't hiding, but it was a disillusioning experience. It felt as though he had a large placard hung around his neck with a Government health warning proclaiming he had contracted an incurable social disease. Colleagues found excuses to shuffle away, even many he regarded as friends discovered a litany of reasons for rushing off and being unable to talk, or to support. He hadn't the stomach for a parade around the Dragonaria. There were a few people, seemingly mostly from the Opposition, who had a moment for genuine sympathy, yet none believed his association with Jya-Yu was innocent. But, he tried to console himself, what the hell did most of them know about innocent association? The only people who displayed genuine eagerness to talk with him were lobby correspondents from the national press. Several offered sympathetic coverage in return for exclusive details of the inside story. Not one would accept his word that there was no inside story.

So Tuesday had dawned and he had prepared himself for his part in the pantomime of Prime Minister's Question Time. In the normal course of events Downing Street would have contacted him beforehand, eager to find out what he would ask, anxious to ensure that the answer appeared as spontaneous as it did authoritative. But not today. Silence. Perhaps they assumed he would not be bothering. Or perhaps their answer was already prepared, no matter what he asked. He did not have long to wait. The House was crowded, as usual, and he had to squeeze along the narrow morocco leather benches to find a place. Members were usually jealous of their territory but, as he sat, those on either side seemed to retreat and allow him a few extra inches. Like measuring out no-man's-land. No smiles, none of the customary greetings. Further along the House, from the bench immediately behind the Prime Minister, the Parliamentary Private Secretary leaned forward to touch his master on the shoulder and whisper. The Prime Minister looked round, noted the presence of Goodfellowe, and returned glassy-eyed to his briefing book.

Robin Chissum had a style in answering prime ministerial questions which reflected his non-political, safety-first approach to government. It could be summed up as tedium relieved by occasional flashes of arrogance. Not for him the sweeping ideology which condemned whole classes at a stroke; if he didn't know what to say he would talk about consensus, knowing that the issue would have moved on by the time those who struggled to reach that elusive harmony had argued themselves to a standstill. It caused those in his party who regarded themselves as keepers of the ideological flame to stamp in frustration, but it meant he could pick his enemies selectively. And deal with them ruthlessly. For the House is like a great carved wood sailing ship, with its crew under orders and a captain who stands visible on the quarterdeck. The weather may be unpredictable, the seas often violent and the ship reluctant to handle, yet it is built to survive all perils but one. That of a mutinous crew. Against that danger the officers and coxswains guard with ceaseless vigilance, and the response to rebellion is automatic. Retribution.

'Number Three,' Madam Speaker cried. 'Mr Goodfellowe.' The time had come. He rose, calm. Too tired to shake. Anyway, he thought he knew what to expect.

'Will my Right Honourable Friend turn his attention during his busy day to the problem of the
251

treatment meted out by the press to people in public life? Not just politicians but Royalty, judges, generals—why, even soccer managers. How many times has the press twisted the facts, indulged in deliberate exaggeration and invention, for no better reason than to sell their products? It amounts to nothing less than wholesale pollution of public life by the press. The destruction of people for profit.' He paused. A trifle pompous, he reflected, but a useful soundbite. 'Is he aware that no other industry in the country—no asbestos factory, no chemical plant, no sewage facility, no nasty little waste tip— could get away with what they get away with? So will my Right Honourable Friend now agree to amend the Press Bill in order to give proper protection to innocent people against this growing menace of the media?'

He had wanted to say so much, yet had so little time. He hoped at least he'd made the point. He was about to find out. The Prime Minister rose thoughtfully, looking down at his red briefing book in the manner of a captain consulting his charts. Then he dispensed with it, closing it abruptly as though he already knew which course he wished to steer, and placed both hands on the Dispatch Box for support. Goodfellowe, from two rows behind him, was having difficulty seeing clearly but Chissum seemed to be displaying a rueful smile.

'It's a novel proposal for winning elections, I must say, to suggest we lead the press to the slaughter. Can't imagine why it's never been tried before. I'm always looking for new ideas, Madam Speaker, but I'm not sure I'm the man brave enough to attempt such a—how shall I describe it?—an *exuberant* approach to winning friends and influencing electors. Something like fourteen million newspapers are sold in this country every day. Wish I had as many friends as that.'

Quickly he had captured the mood of the House. Members chuckled, waiting for his next words. 'I am a firm believer in freedom of speech, Madam Speaker, particularly in the run-up to elections . . .' That was cheeky. He clearly thought it cretinous to consider tangling with the press when he was looking for every ounce of support. Even the Opposition responded with laughter to his nerve ' . . . and I appreciate the advice and the support which members of the press have offered me. May it long continue.' He leant on one elbow, turning from the body of the House for the first time towards Goodfellowe. 'I must also tell my Honourable Friend that I am suspicious of calls for reform which are generated in the heat of the moment. Such calls frequently lack wisdom or objectivity.' Ouch. 'And while I am talking to my Honourable *Friend* . . .' —he gave the word a gentle ripple of emphasis—'let me tell him that I am a great believer in the bonds of friendship. Friendship is a two-way street.' He was staring directly at Goodfellowe. 'And some people seem to have trouble identifying who their friends are.' Goodfellowe could hear the collective breath of the House being drawn in at the public rebuke. With carefully timed drama Chissum turned his back on Goodfellowe. 'Sadly, Madam Speaker, in politics you never know where the opposition is coming from.'

Those immediately around Goodfellowe cringed with reflected embarrassment; others at a little greater distance sucked their teeth nervously, like seamen witnessing a Sunday keelhauling.

Opposition Members jeered. The Prime Minister resumed his seat with a grim satisfaction. He wasn't going to have any bloody nonsense this side of the election, and anyone foolish enough to step out of line would be handled without pity. The others deserved a little encouragement.

The Government at its highest level had set its face against Goodfellowe. He was bait for barnacles. To be tossed aside as the great ship of state sailed on. Yet as the tide of chatter began to flow once more around him, leaving him like bones on a beach, he found it hurt less than it might. He had been expecting it, there had been plenty of signs along the way, but he'd had to make certain, to find out exactly where he stood. Now he knew.

Alone.

*   *   *

'Good news.'

'The boy stood on the burning deck when all but he had fled, and you think there's good news?' Goodfellowe eyed Mickey with more than a dash of scepticism.

'Something to fight the flames with. I've run the check of share prices against the *Herald* stories you wanted. There's a match. Not in every case, but in enough to make a damn fine liverwurst. The Wonderworld fiasco sent the share price of its only real rival soaring. That's Hagi Entertainments. It's a Japanese number. And the only ones to benefit from the attack on Killer Coal seemed to be the nuclear industry, no specific firm but there are only a handful anyway and one of those, Nuclear Reprocessors, has been getting a lot of favourable coverage in the *Herald* recently.'

As they huddled closely together in conference, Goodfellowe became aware of an unusual hush. The eyes of the Dragonaria were upon them, the man of marked morals and his altogether too young, too attentive and too impertinent assistant. Suspicion sat in every stare. He straightened up and waved an extravagant arm. 'Good afternoon, ladies. My apologies for not greeting you all personally as I came in. Are you well? Would any of you care to join me and Miss Ross for tea?' Instantly heads dropped and the noisy clatter of typewriters and correcting tapes resumed.

'What about Diane Burston?'

'More difficult,' Mickey replied. 'No direct correlation, but the environmental groups like Greenpeace and The Earth Firm have been a pain in her purse for years. The *Herald* has certainly taken some of that pressure off.'

'Any more?'

'I think we can show a link with one of the drug companies.'

'What a tangled web he weaves. But perhaps not quite twisted enough.' He sat close beside Mickey for an hour, watching intently as she brought up information on her screen and demanding more, promising that one day he'd gather up his courage and take that computers-for-muddled-Members course himself. It all made him late for the start of the Standing Committee, and when he arrived Betty Ewing was in full swing. He slipped into his seat and was spreading his papers when a voice whispered in his ear.

'I did warn you. You're playing in the big boys' league.'

Goodfellowe examined Lillicrap as though he

were a debt collector asking directions, then went back to his papers.

'For one last time, Tom, don't turn away from us,' the Whip persisted. 'You need us. Don't reject the hand of friendship.'

'The Prime Minister's hand of friendship just shoved me overboard, Lionel.'

'There's still time to climb back on,' the Whip insisted. 'But the way you're going, they'll even take your lifebelt away.'

'Meaning?'

'I told you this was the big league, Tom. No walking wounded. Outside groups don't normally like their parliamentary consultants splashed all over the front pages of the newspapers. They want advisers who can work within the system, not Members who wander round this place like a dose of salmonella.'

'As you say, Lionel, we are all big boys. After all this I was scarcely expecting your help to find another consultancy.'

'I'm talking about your existing deal. The Caravan Park Owners' Federation.'

'So you'll take that away, will you?' The light was beginning to dawn.

'Not my call, Tom. They may insist.'

Goodfellowe grunted in defiant understanding, then returned to the study of his papers as proceedings droned on around them.

Lillicrap bit his lip in exasperation. 'You're a bloody fool, Tom. I've given you every chance. So now you listen, and listen damned well. You were in trouble a couple of years ago and we bailed you out. Arranged a loan so you could take care of Elinor. I was happy to do all that. But you never knew where

256

the money came from, did you?'

'Didn't it come from you? You gave the very clear impression it did . . .'

'How the hell can I afford to throw around fifteen thousand pounds on a Whip's salary, for Christ's sake? Look at my frayed cuffs.' He shook a sleeve in front of Goodfellowe's face, to whom the cuff and the rest of the suit seemed to be in perfect order. 'Be real. This job is costing me a fortune. Overdraft Alley. I can scarcely afford the water for the whisky any more. No, it wasn't me, old chum. The loan came from a wealthy supporter, someone who wanted to help the party. I was merely the channel. The honest broker.'

'Who is it?'

'You'll never know. That's the way to keep the system smelling sweet. Blind bail. We get you out of trouble, you owe us, yet you can't be accused of selling favours to the real donor.'

'But now I know he exists.'

'More to the point, he knows you exist, too, and what you've been up to. A slip-up in the system, I'm afraid. Shouldn't have happened . . . And he wants his money back.'

'You're kidding,' Goodfellowe gasped in surprise.

'He wants the loan repaid, Tom. He says he intended to help the party, not—and I quote—a freeloader.'

'This is nothing short of blackmail.'

'It's business, Tom. Satan's teeth, can't you see what you're doing to yourself? Pull back. Stop. Even now it's not too late.'

Betty Ewing had sat down, her denunciation of the Bill for the moment completed, and a vote on her amendment was about to take place. 'As many as are in favour say Aye!' the Chairman was demanding—'Aye!' the Opposition benches responded in ritualistic chant—'Those to the contrary?'—'No!' the Government supporters shouted in their turn—'Division!' the Chairman declared.

They would wait a few minutes for stragglers before locking the doors, but the Opposition was already present in full number. If Goodfellowe insisted once more on abstaining it would be another drawn vote, another pothole on the road to progress. As the minutes dragged on Lillicrap spent the time fretting, nibbling at his nails.

'You're not as tough as you pretend, Lionel.'

'You think I enjoy this? I'm your friend.'

'Really? And when friendship collides with your conscience, Lionel, which would you choose?'

'Don't preach conscience to me, Tom, it's little more than an excuse for prevarication, for doing nothing. For letting others take the blame.'

'You accuse me of allowing others to take the blame? I seem to have piled a mountain of it upon my own back.'

'That's the trouble with your type of conscience. You can't control it.'

'And you can't buy it, either.' Goodfellowe's tone had grown sharp.

'Tom, I'm only doing my job.'

'As I am trying to do mine.'

'And it will dance you all the way to the scaffold.'

Their exchanges had grown rapidly more heated, but now Goodfellowe held back, taking stock. 'I see how little we understand each other, Lionel. I thought we were friends, but perhaps our friendship was nothing more than idleness.'

258

'For friendship, for self-interest, for loyalty to the party—whichever speaks loudest to you. Listen to it. Just don't sit on your brains and abstain, Tom. Vote.'

'A wise old Chinaman once said that if you sit by the river long enough, the bodies of your enemies will float past.'

'Sit by the river long enough and you become fish bait. For God's sake start playing the game.'

'Lock the doors!' the Chairman instructed. The attendants complied and the Clerk began calling the vote in alphabetical order. Sheila Fagin and Barry Gedling had voted, now the Clerk was looking towards Goodfellowe, pen poised.

'Lionel, I think you're right. It is time to start playing the game.'

The Whip sighed in relief. 'You won't regret it, Tom.'

'I dare say. But you will.'

With that, Goodfellowe voted against the Government. The Opposition amendment was passed. The Bill was grinding to a halt.

*   *   *

Corsa had telephoned at six thirty the following morning, twenty seconds after spotting the report in the final edition. It was only a small item tucked away on the *Herald's* parliamentary page, but even a short piece about a Government defeat in committee had been enough to curdle his enthusiasm for breakfast. He didn't know that Lillicrap had been working until two, and even if he had he wouldn't have given a damn.

'Lionel, dear boy. You and I must meet.'

The instruction was delivered in the manner of a

259

concrete block dropped from a great height. In normal circumstances press and politician exercised a mutual caution which disguised their underlying battle for supremacy, but these circumstances were not normal. Within forty minutes Corsa was stationed outside Lillicrap's Notting Hill home leaning impatiently on the Rolls' horn for attention. Three minutes later the Whip appeared on the steps, tieless, wild-eyed and munching a piece of toast, a smear of stale shaving cream still stuck behind his ear, scurrying as though the block of concrete had caught his toes.

'Bloody hell, Freddy, can't it wait until the percolator's finished?'

'No.'

Reluctantly Lillicrap climbed in. A Dire Straits tape was playing, loud to the point of intimidation, scraping irritatingly upon Lillicrap's raw eardrums, but he felt disinclined to interfere so he sat silent and felt small. Which was just as Corsa had intended. Corsa made no attempt at conversation as he drove in the direction of Hyde Park, turning off towards the Serpentine. He parked beside the lake in a secluded area which at night-time was the favoured haunt of lovers but which at this time of day was empty apart from the occasional dog walker and duck feeder. The still waters reflected a glorious, glistening early summer's morning. Lillicrap shivered.

Corsa switched off the tape, and suddenly the car was bathed in an oppressive silence. He turned to face Lillicrap. The eyes were utterly without compromise.

'You said you'd fix him.'

Lillicrap came out fighting. 'Freddy, have you

ever thought that maybe we never needed to fix him? That it's the pressure we've been putting on him that has made him so bloody stubborn? If you hadn't done the things you've done, and I like a fool hadn't done the things you wanted, he would probably have come along with us for the ride, helped us, rather than pissing in the petrol tank. It's *our* fault—*your* fault, Freddy. Have you ever thought about that?'

'You think too much. All this introspection and self-analysis isn't good for you, Lionel. You won't like the things you find, believe me. And nothing changes the fact that it's just one man set against a major piece of government legislation and your entire future. Your neck or his. He still requires fixing.'

'The man's incorrigible. There's no way through to him. I've tried everything. Friendship. Blackmail. Even a public flogging from the Prime Minister. He won't budge.'

'He will. Everyone has their point of persuasion.'

'I haven't found it.' Lillicrap sounded morose. He had tried to the point of shame to bring the man around. What the hell did Corsa expect?

'You just haven't looked hard enough. So we're going to go over everything, you and I, right now. Every scrap of gossip, every speck of dirt. I want to know everything about his wife, his children, the accident, anything that might do damage. We are going to squeeze this man dry until there is nothing left.'

Lillicrap looked aghast at the press man. 'Now hold on, Freddy. I don't mind putting around a bit of boot leather but I'll not get involved in that. He is—was—a friend. There are limits.'

261

Corsa smiled, relaxed, back on familiar territory. 'There are no limits. And Lionel, dear boy, you will help. Unless, of course, you want me to tell your wife about Jennie Merriman.'

'You complete bastard.'

'Believe it, Lionel. I have the details of your goings and your comings at Miss Merriman's flat for the last five weeks. She's a considerable party contributor, you once told me, but it seems as if you've taken it upon yourself to collect most of the contributions. Although not all of them, you might be interested to hear. Anyway, I heard you'd promised your wife you'd given her up. Would never see her again. Clumsy.'

Lillicrap emitted a mournful groan.

'You see, Lionel, everyone has his point of persuasion.'

'But he's a decent man. He may be a pain in the arse with a lousy sense of timing, but he's fundamentally decent.'

'No women? No drugs?'

'A drink-drive, but that's all public.'

'And what of his daughter? I understand they have a difficult relationship.'

'Sure, but who doesn't with a sixteen-year-old? She's a good kid.'

'A virgin?'

'God's teeth . . .'

'Doesn't he neglect her? Send her away to school? Or maybe he's been paying her a little too much unpaternal attention as she's been getting older? Let your imagination flow freely.'

'You simply don't understand. Get your mind out of the sewer. He loves her, always has. After Stevie was born they couldn't have any more kids but they

262

both desperately wanted another. So they adopted Sam. Now that's one hell of a commitment. In spite of everything, no matter how much he's crossed me, I rather admire the man.'

'Lionel, you're not being helpful. A piece of mush on the woman's page about Goodfellowe and the adopted daughter? I can't print that.'

'You couldn't print it anyway. So far as I'm aware she doesn't know. He's never found the right time to tell her, not after the accident and her mother's illness. I only know because he discussed it with me over a bottle some while ago.'

'Are you serious?'

'Perfectly.'

'She doesn't know she's adopted?' Corsa's hands came up to his forehead as though his hair had caught fire. 'But that is absolutely wonderful.'

'What is?'

'Spilling the story on the adoption. If she doesn't know. What could give him more pain?'

It all but took Lillicrap's breath away. 'But that's evil. You can't print that stuff.'

'What's this? An outbreak of innocence? Let's pray it's not infectious. Of course I can print it. It would be handled very tastefully. I'll kill him with his own kindness.'

'It violates every guideline on privacy,' Lillicrap protested, his face contorted with indignation. 'It would be a disgusting intrusion, there'd be one hell of a price to pay.'

'You may be right.' Corsa hung his head in apparent resignation. 'In order to preserve the good name of the *Herald* I suppose I might be forced to sack the reporter, even the editor.' The head slowly rose. He started to smile, like a coffin lid beginning

263

to crack. 'And in order to preserve their good names I would be forced to re-employ them elsewhere within the organization. At greatly inflated salaries, of course. Everyone would be happy.'

'Except Tom and Sam. She doesn't know.' Lillicrap was shouting. 'Do you hate him that much?'

'Hate him? Why no, Lionel. I think I like him.' God, he'd said it. What was even more extraordinary to Corsa, he thought he probably meant it. 'I almost regret having to tear him apart. He's one of the few politicians I actually admire.' Corsa laughed, a sound full of coffin dust.

Lillicrap had never mistaken himself for being overly fastidious, but suddenly he felt sick. Bile was in his throat and he found himself swallowing hard. 'I need some fresh air.' He pulled savagely at the door handle. 'Think I'll walk back home.' He tumbled out into the arms of the summer morning, feeling as though he had brushed with death.

As the door slammed shut, Corsa began pounding the steering wheel in triumph. The horn began to blare, staccato, echoing across the lake, proclaiming victory. The ducks flapped and scattered in alarm, a dog howled in protest. The horn was still blaring as Lillicrap stumbled away in shame.

* * *

Goodfellowe picked up the phone again, as he had begun to a hundred times. This time he dialled. He had tried to put Elizabeth out of his mind, to concentrate on the other pits of disaster that had been dug across the pathways of his life, but he never fully succeeded in shutting her out. He

264

remained angry with her, bitter that she should have deserted him, run off, taking with her so many of his hopes. Yet still he missed her, more than ever he wanted to. She would enter his thoughts, his stomach would start to spin, he'd run to the phone, then hesitate, forcing away temptation. But not this time.

'Elizabeth? It's Tom.'

'Tom.' Said softly. A pause. 'How can I help?'

'By letting me explain.'

'You don't owe me any explanation, Tom.' Another pause, a silence of sadness. 'I think I saw it explained in considerable detail on television.'

'There is nothing between me and Jya-Yu. Please believe me.'

'I'm not a jealous woman, I have no claim over your loyalties.'

'Whether you like it or not, you do.'

She sighed, an expression of resignation. 'Perhaps I'm not what you imagine I am, Tom. Not the woman you think you care for. Try to understand. Beneath that extravagant exterior of mine there are still too many bruises. No children. No husband. A restaurant instead of a home. Deep down I suspect I'm rather traditional about those things. And I simply expected something much simpler from you. Not so complicated. I suppose it was only a matter of luck that I managed to leave your place without running a gauntlet of television cameras and finding myself all over the Nine O'Clock News.'

'I apologize. It's not what I intended. But so much of my life seems to have been not what I intended.'

He paused for a response, but she said nothing.

265

'I seem to be going through one of those periods of my life when everything is warfare, Elizabeth, whether I want it or not. All I know is that there are things for which I have to fight, no matter what it costs me. I have to find out the truth about Corsa. About so many other things, too. It may leave me without a job, a career. But I can't run away from it, not any more.'

'But is there any pleasure in the search for truth?'

'So far, only pain. Yet I have to go on. It's not just the truth about Corsa I'm looking for, but the truth about myself. Who I am. What I'm about. I've grown confused about so many things in my life and I need more answers than ever. I had hoped you would help me find them. I still hold to that hope, Elizabeth.'

She offered only a silence, both hurt and hurtful. He wanted to press her, to force some commitment from her, to say anything that would bring her back, smiling, through the door. Yet he hesitated, held back, knowing that by pressing her he might find only the rejection that he feared.

'Whenever this is over, may I give you a call?'

'I'm not changing my number. Not just because of this.'

'Then I will call. I promise.'

'Goodbye, Tom.'

His heart sank, the words seemed so achingly final.

'I am so sorry, Tom. And I wish you luck in the search for your truth,' she added. Then the phone went dead.

What did those last words mean? Hope? A final flicker of grace in farewell? He didn't know and wasn't going to find out, not until everything else had been resolved. The swirling in his stomach began again, like a persistent ulcer. He sat in his office, struggling to control the pain.

He was glad it was Mickey, not anyone else, who came through the door some twenty minutes later. He wouldn't have to pretend with her, there was no point, she could read everything in his face.

'You practising for a misery of the month competition?'

Immediately she forced a grudging smile from him. She was distraction. The pain was pushed to one side.

'Your luck may be changing,' she encouraged. 'Either that or you've sold out like the rest.'

'Meaning? '

She held up a copy of the *Herald*. 'And I quote: "Goodfellowe is a politician whose private life has come in for considerable criticism after it was revealed he had a close association with a young Chinese girl recently arrested on suspicion of prostitution and drug possession . . ." '

Goodfellowe was about to curse but Mickey raised an agile eyebrow to demand his continued attention.

' " . . . but like an increasing number of parents he took the step which counts for so much more. He and his wife, Elinor, adopted a daughter, Samantha. Now sixteen and strikingly good-looking . . ."—it's a lovely photograph, Tom—"Samantha has helped sustain the Goodfellowe family through periods of great difficulty, particularly when their only natural child, Stevie, was drowned in a tragic swimming accident".' She passed the newspaper across to him. 'I never knew Sam was adopted! You never told me.'

267

Goodfellowe sat haunted. Mickey was right, it was a wonderful photograph, taken recently at school, full colour and reproduced very large across the page of what was entitled an 'Adoption Special'. Other well-known families were mentioned, many at greater length, but the visual impact was all Sam. 'The *Herald* salutes these parents of caring and courage,' it said. (Corsa had particularly liked that touch. They might be accused of an accidental invasion of privacy, of a sad and unfortunate mistake, but no one could find proof of malice . . .)

Goodfellowe's voice was hoarse, the words forced out like those of a man dying of thirst in the desert. 'He is the Devil!'

As Mickey watched, astonished, a physical change came over Goodfellowe as though he were being leached within, leaving him ashen.

'Corsa. The Devil,' he repeated. It was scarcely more than a croak. 'Sam doesn't know. But Corsa does. This is his message to me. A sign.'

'Of what?'

Goodfellowe shook his head savagely, once, twice, three times, as though trying in vain to rid himself of a yoke that had been cast around his neck. 'A sign that there is no hiding place. Not for me. He will pursue me behind the locked doors of my home and even into my soul. For him there are no limits. He will use Sam, destroy everything I have with her, if that is the only way he has of destroying me.'

He gazed once more at the photograph, of a smiling, darkly serious young woman with an expression of worldly concern she always thought she had inherited from him. As he stared it grew

268

smudged with tears.

'There is only one thing in this world which I want more than to have him grovelling in misery at my feet.'

'What's that, Tom?'

'That one day she will find enough courage to forgive me.'

*   *   *

'Drive! Drive, man!' Goodfellowe shout.ed from the back seat, urging the taxi on.

The cabbie had decided it was his lucky day when he had been stopped in Parliament Square and asked to drive to Wooton Minster. The passenger had agreed the fare without a quibble, stopping at a cash machine for funds. The driver thought the man had looked unusually tense as he had waited for the money and, when it flooded into his hands, he seemed to have gone through some form of release. Rather like sex. People have strange relationships with their cash dispensers, the driver decided. Yet this was a weird one. No conversation, just overbearing anxiety and constant exhortation to go faster. Was he chasing, or being chased? The cabbie couldn't decide. He thought he recognized him, too.

The driver was surprised when he discovered that the passenger's ultimate destination was a girl's school. There were still further surprises in store. No sooner had they pulled into the drive than the man began tugging at the door in great agitation, shouting for the lock to be released, running for the arched red-brick entrance.

It was there Goodfellowe was intercepted by Miss Rennie. She stood squarely in front of him, arms crossed defiantly, barring his way and making

269

it clear he would have to bowl her over if he were to get any farther into her school.

'I must see her. Has she heard?' he panted.

'I went looking for Samantha as soon as you telephoned this morning. I'm afraid she had already read the article.'

A spark of hope dwindled and died, leaving only ashes inside.

'How could you not have told her, Mr Goodfellowe? You owed it to her, surely.'

Goodfellowe closed his eyes, exhausted, trying to recollect every false step he had taken along this road. 'We had always agreed, her mother and I, that we would tell her when she was twelve. It seemed the right time. On her birthday. But a few weeks before that Stevie was drowned, there seemed more than enough turmoil for her to deal with. Then Elinor became sick, we always hoped she would recover, still be able to tell Sam together. Trouble is, Miss Rennie, I can't think of a moment in the last few years which hasn't been filled with some upheaval, some pain for Sam, some good reason for putting it off for just a little while longer. Some moment when I wasn't drowning too.' It sounded like a confession, an expiation of guilt. If it had been offered in any expectation of forgiveness, he was rapidly disabused.

'Did you never think of the greater harm that would be done to the poor girl by her finding out in this manner? She is sixteen. Girls of that age find themselves in a world which seems to be inconsistent and hypocritical, their lives constantly changing. For Samantha that's been more true than most. It wasn't enough that she should lose her brother and her mother; on top of that she felt she

270

had lost you. Now she's lost herself, her very identity, the only thing she had to hold on to.'

'I must see her, put it right.' He advanced towards the Headmistress with the clear intention of passing. With maternal ferocity she held a hand out against his chest.

'If you will take my very profound advice, Mr Goodfellowe, I tell you that trying to see her now is not a wise course of action. She needs a few days to recover. Time to think.'

'But I must . . .'

'You must? For whose sake? Hers? Or yours?'

Flakes of Lothian granite filled her voice. He backed off, bemused.

'In any event, I'm afraid you cannot see her at the moment. She has disappeared. Run away. Oh, it's not as bad as it might seem,' she instructed, waving away his rising alarm, 'I have a good idea where she might have gone. But I must warn you, Mr Goodfellowe, that if you burst upon her in her present frame of mind she might well run away again. Then no one will know where she is.'

'I can't see my own daughter?'

'If you insist on knowing, I must tell you where I believe she is. But I don't advise it. Most strongly I don't advise it. You've done enough harm to her already.'

'I never meant . . .'

'Nevertheless it happened. And now my concern is what is in the best interest of Samantha. That should be your concern, too.'

His shoulders heaved. 'I've lost her.'

Miss Rennie examined him carefully. To her eyes he looked ragged, almost second-hand, like something pushed to the back of the shelf and long

271

forgotten, but there could be little mistaking the genuine mournfulness that now spread across him. His arms were clutched about himself, his breathing was rapid and shallow, the dark eyes, so expressive, flickered like a meteor shower that was burning itself out. He was a man of very little hope, which troubled Miss Rennie greatly. She was the proud grand-daughter of a crofter, to whom hope was life, and it was dying within this man. 'Perhaps you should come with me, Mr Goodfellowe,' she suggested, her tone softening. She led the way into the school, up a staircase polished dark by the passage of a thousand young hands and through the fire doors of institutional corridors that brought them to a distant wing of the building unknown to Goodfellowe. They came to a room with a large bay window in which stood six beds. 'Samantha's dormitory,' Miss Rennie explained, leading him over to the bed which stood nearest the window. The coldest in winter, the brightest in summer. Extremes. Much like Sam. Beside the bed there was little except for a bookshelf, a locker and a small wooden wardrobe with three drawers beneath it. Miss Rennie kneeled to open the bottom drawer.

'I found it this morning as I was looking for clues to Samantha's whereabouts,' she said, withdrawing a battered black tin a little larger than a shoe box. It was—had been—Elinor's, a simple hideaway for her most sentimental pieces which she had kept under the bed. It had disappeared some time ago, when she became ill, and Goodfellowe had assumed Elinor had simply forgotten about it or thrown it out, like so much of the rest of her life. Now it was back. He sat on the bed and opened the lid.

Inside he found memories. Stevie's bronze St

Christopher. A much-handled pink envelope in which was a letter, probably the last, written to Sam by her mother. There was a bracelet he had given to Sam two Christmases ago. And photographs of her with two boys, young men really, neither of whom he recognized. But most of the box was filled with cuttings from newspapers and magazines which had one thing in common—Goodfellowe. They started some five years previously while he was still a rising Minister and tracked almost every turn of his career since then. If career it could be described. It was noticeable how few items were included for the last two years.

'Apparently at the end of every week she collects the newspapers from the Library and cuts out every item which has any mention of you.'

'I had no idea she was even interested.' There was no disguising the tremor in his voice.

'She takes very great pride in what you do.'

He spread out the most recent cuttings on the bed cover. Small items from parliamentary reports. A photograph of him dedicating a new maternity ward. His last election address. A letter he'd had published in *The Times*. The drink-drive case, of course. And the front page of the *Sunday Herald* with the photograph of Jya-Yu. It didn't amount to very much, recorded here for posterity.

'Some of the other girls can be cruel. She's even got into a few fights defending you.'

'Fighting? For me? But I'm the one she's always fighting with.' The words caught at the back of his throat.

'For a sixteen-year-old, love scarcely equates with unquestioning obedience.'

'I seem to have let her down rather badly. There's

273

so much of her life at school I don't really understand.'

The headmistress sighed. 'It's a tremendous pity, Mr Goodfellowe, that you seem able to appear at our school only when there is trouble ...'

CHAPTER EIGHT

As the taxi drove him back to London Goodfellowe felt much like a comet that had disappeared around the far side of the sun. Obliterated. Cast into impenetrable darkness. The fire gone. Without Sam he could not fight, without Sam there seemed no reason, nothing to fight for. She was the last thing that truly mattered in his life; now she, too, had walked away from him, just like so many others. Like Elizabeth. Like Elinor, even. And as his own father had done. Memories of his father returned to haunt him, as they always did when the ebb was at its lowest. Goodfellowe's father had not been born to wealth, but he had found it, or rather it had found him, during the shortages that gripped the country in the aftermath of the war. He had been a small-time black marketeer in Yeovil, always finding the petrol to drive up to London with a van full of fresh farm food produce, and back again to Somerset with the batteries, tools and nylons needed by the local farmers and their daughters. At war's end he had accumulated a little cash, which he used to buy up surplus military supplies left behind in great quantity by the Americans as they hurried home. This surplus was sold off in job lots, whole ware-housefuls, always cheaply and usually in a hurry.

Goodfellowe Senior often had little precise idea of what he had bought but at such knock-down prices he didn't have a care. The deals would always pay their way, even as scrap.

One fresh spring morning in 1946 he was woken by an insistent pounding at his door. Outside he found a US Air Force general and three full colonels, and for a moment he thought he might be under arrest, the consequence of one of his many deals too far, but instead of waving arrest warrants they produced a cheque-book. There had been a problem, they explained. American factories were turning to peace-time production and a sudden and quite desperate shortage had developed of Mustang engine spares. They had sold him a warehouseful. Could they buy them back? Please?

The deal made Goodfellowe a rich man and the proceeds, for once entirely legitimately obtained, had transformed his life. In the aftermath of war such things as manor houses, green rolling acres, even Bentleys, were cheap, and he had been able to buy his way into West Country society, though not without incensing the newly impoverished aristocracy. In the end, however, cash spoke louder than ancestral escutcheons. And life had been good. Goodfellowe had married, son Thomas had been sent away when he was old enough to one of the finest provincial schools, and the family had attempted to ignore the many whispers of jealousy and to fulfil their assumed roles amongst the Somerset landed gentry. Goodfellowe sat on the committees of many local charitable endeavours while Mrs Goodfellowe busied herself with bazaars and flower-arranging at the church, and although she could still sense the lingering traces of

275

resentment she remained steadfast in her confidence that time would wear away the last of the barriers. Until, that is, Mr Goodfellowe was found to have 'borrowed' a large sum of money from one of his charities to finance another of his business deals. He always maintained that it was no more than a loan and that he intended to pay it back, every penny, and was still protesting his good intentions when they sent him down for five years. It was justice not solely for the crime, local society gloated, but for the family's effrontery in usurping the proper order of things. The car went, so did the house along with its many trappings. They couldn't pay Thomas's school fees, and the school made it clear they had never truly wanted 'his type' around. They gave him less than an hour's notice to pack his trunk. In full view of the other schoolboys he had dragged his belongings out across the gravel of the courtyard to where his uncle was waiting in a small Austin van to drive him away, never to return. More than thirty years later he could still remember every step of that tortured walk to the van, and his final look back at the school he had loved, to see every window crammed with the staring, pitiless faces of his schoolmates. The humiliations piled upon a fifteen-year-old boy had inevitably left their scars, made him cautious about both fortune and friendship. Good training for a political life. But they had also left him with resolve. His humiliations were the reason he had spent his life trying to reclaim the honour of the Goodfellowes. They were also the reason he had fought so hard to keep Sam at the very best of schools. He had failed in both.

Yet, inexorably, comets reappear. As the miles passed in silence towards London and the friction

276

of his memories grew all too fierce, the innate Goodfellowe stubbornness that had always been both his strength and his folly began to reassert itself. What was the point of stopping the fight at the point where he had lost everything and had nothing more to lose? And should he let others mock him, as they had mocked his father? Was he simply to shuffle away with his head bowed like a fifteen-year-old schoolboy dragging his life behind him? No, not then, and not now. Not Goodfellowe.

'Back to Parliament Square?' the driver enquired as they came off the motorway.

'Granite Towers,' Goodfellowe growled. The comet was set on collision course.

Yet Corsa wasn't at the newspaper office. He was at the Foundation, Goodfellowe was told—in the penthouse, as it turned out. Goodfellowe had intentions of staging a dramatic, sense-stunning entrance, but the idea led only to frustration, foiled by the computerized security lock on the lift. Corsa kept him waiting for twenty minutes, deliberately, until eventually a flunky escorted him up in the glass-sided lift and, as they stepped into the penthouse, directed him to the balcony overlooking the Thames. The sun was glorious early July but a sea wind was blowing up the estuary, ruffling Corsa's hair as he turned. He seemed relaxed, in shirtsleeves, no tie.

'Tom! Delighted to see you again. And I'm so glad we were able to carry something good about you this morning. A fine story. You came out of it particularly well.'

That smile again, the eruption of teeth, like the welcome of a cobra. But the eyes remained dissecting tools. Corsa refrained from offering a handshake.

Goodfellowe began slowly. 'There are no limits, no rules, in your game. No part of my life or the lives of those I love that is allowed to remain untouched by you. Nothing that lies beyond your appetites. Or, it seems, your grasp.'

Corsa turned to look down the river towards Canary Wharf, which was sparkling like a Roman candle in the sunlight. 'I thought politicians welcomed coverage. Most of them come crawling to me on their knees for a favourable mention. You'd be surprised how pathetic some of them can get.'

'I shall fight you in every way I can.' It was said almost serenely, as though to emphasize that this was no idle threat, but Corsa responded with passion.

'Don't. Don't try and fight me, Tom. You won't win, you can't. Haven't you realized that yet? You don't run things any more, and you know you'll get no help from your friends. That's if you have any left. Surprising how fast friendships fall away in politics, isn't it? Particularly with a gentle push from the media.'

'Division. Destruction. Is that all you see?'

'That's all that sells newspapers. Tits and trouble, that's where the money is.' Corsa sighed patronizingly, as though dealing with a recalcitrant relative. 'I hope you haven't come to give me a moral lecture? '

'You wouldn't understand, even get close.'

Corsa seemed lashed by Goodfellowe's evident contempt. His expression creased with anger, an expression that for once was not merely for effect. Somehow Goodfellowe's words—or was it Goodfellowe himself, the man's stubbornness, his

278

petulant refusal to be like all the others?—had an unsettling effect upon the proprietor. His control slipped. 'Don't you, bloody politician, set yourself up as being so superior. Don't you dare. The whole lot of you are of no more moral consequence than a shoal of fish. You chase the current, mouths open, constantly changing your position, your lives torn between emotions of greed and fear. Swallow the other bastard before he swallows you. Parliament has the moral sensibilities of a pool of piranha. Except you don't have the teeth.'

'And you are any better?'

He shook his head in vigorous denial, struggling to regain his composure. 'I never suggested that. I'm a press man, I let my editors do the moralizing. And when they begin to irritate me, I fire them. No, I never suggested we were any better. But we do have the teeth.'

'And friends.'

'Yes, we have many friends. Honourable, dishonourable, quite a few Right Honourables too, in all shapes and sizes.'

'A size ten? Like Di Burston?'

Corsa was back in control of himself. Suddenly he realized he had once again underestimated this man and he would need his wits around him. This was going to be more interesting than he had thought.

'Or perhaps you were thinking of your friends at Hagi Entertainments, particularly when you took an axe to Wonderworld,' Goodfellowe continued. 'Or would you prefer to discuss your special friends in the nuclear industry.'

'Such as?'

'Nuclear Reprocessors PLC.' Goodfellowe took

279

the gamble, he didn't know for certain, but he could see from Corsa's rumpled brow that he had played the right card. 'And the other members of your little consortium. I think the piranha pool will be interested to learn how you've used the Herald to promote the commercial interests of your backers. Make quite a splash.'

'You've done well, Tom. Very well.' A hint of genuine admiration hung in his voice. 'But it will do you no good. They were all legitimate stories.'

'Published and promoted way beyond their significance.'

'An editorial judgement. You can't legislate for editorial judgement.'

'It wasn't editorial judgement. It was corruption and commercial dishonesty, stories to show favour to your friends.'

'But that's what newspapers are about,' Corsa mocked, shrugging his shoulders with Mediterranean extravagance, 'doing favours to your friends. The *Guardian* sucks up to pressure groups, the *Telegraph* is the house magazine for the Church, *The Times* flogs satellite television and the *Express* is astonishingly nice about their chairman's wife. Everyone's at it, and there's not a morsel of law to stop it.' He shook his head disparagingly. 'Tom, you really have a lot to learn.'

'It was corruption,' Goodfellowe repeated defiantly, irked at the glib logic. 'As has been your attempt to buy the loyalty of members of the Standing Committee, including its Chairman.'

'Oh, the waters are deep where you have been swimming. Deep enough to drown in, unless you can prove what you're saying.'

'You paid for Breedon to go to Las Vegas, and
280

with his girlfriend. It must have cost thousands yet not a penny is recorded in the Members' Register.'

'Correct. Could cause the Chairman a flutter of embarrassment, I suppose . . .'

'And I'll bet that a large number of members of the Committee have accepted your money,' Goodfellowe interrupted, anxious to pursue his advantage.

'I said a flutter of embarrassment, no more. And the same goes for any other member of the Committee with whom I might have had an understanding.' Yes, an understanding. He savoured the word. 'You've forgotten your own rules. The Register is for interests that have a political bearing. Boxing matches in Las Vegas can scarcely be described as being fundamentally political. Any more than a travel article written from Saas-Fee or Bali would have been. I will swear on a dustbin full of bibles that I bought his article, not his vote. Breedon will be all right, as you would have been. The arrangements are precisely the same as we offer to any guest writer, politician or no. All you have is a far-fetched conspiracy theory with no one to support you. You couldn't prove a thing.' The breeze had dropped, the balcony was warming. Corsa rolled up his sleeves nonchalantly as though he had not a care in the world. 'And any suggestion of a grubby motivation would look extraordinarily hypocritical coming from a Member who took the trouble to write to me asking for just such a favour.'

Goodfellowe kicked himself. He'd entirely forgotten about the note.

'It would look even more bizarre when it came out—as I assure you it would—that the very same

281

Member some time ago accepted a fifteen-thousand-pound loan from me. A loan that has still not been fully repaid.'

'You?' Goodfellowe stepped back, aghast.

'I still have all the original documentation, a trail leading from my bank account to yours.'

'I never knew. But why . . .?'

'Never wanted to become a politician myself, but I decided it might be useful to own a few, So I'm outstandingly generous when the party asks for help to bail out someone in financial difficulties. Gives me leverage. Opens doors.'

'I never knew,' Goodfellowe repeated.

'And there's not a sparrow between here and John O'Groats who'll believe you. Start accusing me and they'll think you're trying to wriggle out of repaying.'

Goodfellowe seemed to deflate. He had been living off Corsa, taking his shilling after all, and plenty of them. He felt mucky. 'Nevertheless, I shall fight you. Someone will listen.'

'Will they? You really think they will, Tom? Or do you think they'll simply step back and fold their arms, and wish you on your way. Your way out, that is. And the reason they'll fold their arms is to hide their own soiled hands. In politics the line between friendship and corrupting influence is so difficult to see, yet so easy to cross. You don't know you've crossed it until it's too late, by which time there's no way back.'

'I can only be grateful I haven't joined the rush.'

'Don't stand in the way of the crowd, Tom. You'll only get trampled.'

A silence ensued. Corsa stared out across the reaches of the Thames as though he had lost all interest in the discussion, while Goodfellowe struggled to comprehend all the many ways in which Corsa seemed to have rustled his arguments and tied his options in knots. Eventually Corsa turned.

'What are you going to do?'

Goodfellowe didn't know. He had been searching his mind for the fault line in Corsa's defences, but had found none. 'You'll win in the end, of course. Even if I found some excuse for kicking the Bill out now, it would only come back next session. The best I can do is to delay, be an inconvenience.'

The smile flickered back to Corsa's face. That irritated Goodfellowe. Irritated him to hell.

'But I think I shall try to keep my principles a little longer.'

'Meaning?'

'By opposing the Bill. In Committee. On the Floor of the House.'

'On what grounds?'

'On the grounds that if you want it, I'm against it.'

For the first time during their encounter Corsa's lips appeared to lose a little of their flexibility. They narrowed, became stuck. 'That would be foolish. And utterly pointless.'

'It's all I have. You've left me with no other choice.'

'You have every choice. To survive. To prosper even. Or to destroy yourself. I never wanted this quarrel, you picked it.'

'Nevertheless we have a quarrel. And unlike some of my colleagues, you can't buy me.'

'Oh, but I believe I can.' Even the pretence of humour had disappeared. 'Wait,' he instructed.

Goodfellowe watched as Corsa returned inside

283

the penthouse to stand in front of a Howard Hodgkin hanging in the centre of one wall. The picture swung back on hinges to reveal a wall safe from which Corsa removed a handful of slim folders. He flicked through them, extracted one, replaced the rest, and returned.

'Every principle has its price,' he muttered, handing the folder across.

Goodfellowe opened it. Inside was a series of photographs, some in colour, most in black and white, of a young girl posing unashamedly for the camera, lifting her breasts, stretching her long legs until the muscles stood taut, relaxing full length on the floor, one leg gently crooked to provide an avenue for the eye leading to her naked navel. It was Sam.

'She's a beautiful girl. And very popular,' Corsa continued. 'Underneath the photographs you'll find the transcripts of interviews with three local boys who have been out with her. They have one thing in common. They've all screwed your daughter. They all claim she's exceptionally—how can I put it?— wholehearted in her approach. One also says he got her to smoke a little dope, but that was only once.'

'Lies! All disgusting lies!' Goodfellowe all but choked on the words.

'Perhaps. We shall see. Although some of it was corroborated by the doorman at the night-club. Red Hot Dutch, I think it's called.'

'You're not going to print this filth?'

'If I have to. If you make me.'

'You can't print it. This violates every code, every agreement . . .'

'We'd find a way. Just as we did this morning.'

'You want to buy me off. With this?' Goodfellowe

284

waved the folder defiantly. But as his eyes caught the photographs of Sam once more, his strength of purpose failed him. He snapped the folder shut and buried his head in it.

'Not to buy you off, Tom, merely to persuade you of my good intentions.' Corsa took a pace forward, drew closer. 'I offered you the hand of friendship, I even loaned you money. You have shown in return nothing but enmity. You have brought everything on yourself. Your reputation is in shreds, your finances are a shambles, your career probably at an end, your family falling apart, and yet—and yet it can still all be put right, every bit of it. If you, even at this late stage, would become my friend. Stop opposing me.'

'You mean stop opposing the Bill.' Goodfellowe's head was up again.

'It's what your Government wants. It's why you were put on the Committee in the first place. Nothing more. Come with us all, for friendship. And in return you may have the dossier and the original photographs.' It all sounded so reasonable, so simple. The easy way out.

Goodfellowe clutched the folder to his chest as if he would never give it up. 'I know I can only be a pinprick in your plans. But I'm curious. Why does it bother you so much that I might delay the Bill, even for a few months? Why is it so damned important to you?'

'Business hates uncertainty,' Corsa replied. 'No one will gain by delaying reforms which even you agree are inevitable.'

'But it's more than that, it must be. You need this Bill, now. You need it in a hurry. Or else why go to these lengths?' He banged his fist upon the folder.

285

'It matters, doesn't it, the delay? Very much. And the only thing that matters to you is money. A lot of money. Which means...' He rubbed his hand across his scalp as if to encourage the blood supply to the brain. 'It's the consortium. You need their money. For which you need the Bill.' The pieces were beginning finally to fall into place.

'Let me put it this way. I would welcome your co-operation.'

'And if I don't co-operate?'

'Then, with regret but without a moment's hesitation, I will ruin your daughter's reputation. Utterly. Is that what you want on your conscience?'

Goodfellowe could find no answer. As he struggled with his thoughts a silence ensued during which the tension seemed to evaporate from Corsa's body. The shoulders came down, the fingers unclenched, the jaw relaxed. Only now with its disappearance did Goodfellowe realize how tense Corsa, too, had been. How much it all mattered to him.

'Strange,' Corsa began, 'I hadn't understood before now how much alike we are. Oh, yes,'—he cut short Goodfellowe's protest—'you and your bike and me in my limousine. We both seem to spend our lives driving the wrong way up the street. We find the challenge irresistible. A matter of our natures, perhaps. And I guess we both have something to prove.'

'To whom?'

'Mostly to ourselves, I suspect. Who else matters? After all, neither of us gives a damn about the good and the great, our so-called superiors. I see them bend their knees too much, to me. You see it, too. Submissiveness and weakness all wrapped up

286

behind their old-boy arrogance. That's something neither you nor I suffers from, Tom. We should be on the same side. Allies. Even friends. I think that's why I let you up here. Why you disturb me so much.'

Goodfellowe bridled. Corsa had tried flattery, bribery, blackmail—was friendship simply another ploy in their game? But something in him said that Corsa's confession was genuine. 'There's a difference between us, Freddy. You seek to smash the system, take it over for yourself. I prefer to try to make the system work.'

'It doesn't. It won't.'

'There you may be right. But once you and your headline writers have knocked over everything that's good and the world around us is laid flat, where are people going to find shelter from the storm? In bingo halls and brothels? Because that's all you'd leave us with as you sailed away in your luxury yacht.'

'You'd have me dragged off in chains.'

'For what you have tried to do to me, and so many others? Yes.'

'I'd prefer to be friends, Tom, truly I would. But you know I'll use the material about Sam if I have to.'

'I know you will,' Goodfellowe whispered.

'Just as I know you'll never give me cause to. That's the trouble, you see, with a conscience.'

*   *   *

Lillicrap strode along the Committee Corridor with steps full of purpose in the direction of Committee Room 10. These were the dog days of July and everyone was impatient for the long summer recess that lay ahead. The temperature had risen steadily

287

during the last week, leaving the atmosphere inside this part of the Palace with an unmistakable masculine ripeness, but it would soon be over, they would all be gone. So long as he could get this wretched Bill out of the way.

'Are you going to make us sit till all hours, Tom, or shall we get it over with and enjoy a Pimm's on the Terrace?' The Whip's greeting to Goodfellowe outside the Committee Room door was genuine enough and he had no reason to expect the response he got. With no warning other than a guttural cry of rage, Goodfellowe had grabbed a handful of his shirt and thrust him fully across the corridor. Lillicrap hit the panelled wall with an impact that rattled his bones.

'Maggot!' Goodfellowe snarled, lifting the other man off the ground until he started to choke. 'You told Corsa about the adoption. It could only have been you.'

'Oi, steady on!' the policeman on duty in the Committee Corridor cried, setting off to quell the disturbance, only to be confused to discover that those locked in confrontation were two Honourable Members. Lillicrap waved him away.

'I didn't mean to, Tom,' he struggled, half-choking, astonished that Goodfellowe had the strength to continue holding him six inches off the floor. 'Let me down. Please.'

But Goodfellowe wouldn't, shaking him like a doll. There was an extraordinary look in Goodfellowe's eye, like a distant sun exploding. 'You ruined my family. I trusted you. As a friend.'

'For pity's sake,' Lillicrap cried hoarsely. His tie was slipping, choking him, his face had begun to ripen like a plum. At last Goodfellowe relented and

Lillicrap all but fell to the floor, struggling for breath.

'Tom, I never meant it, you must believe me. I would never do that, no matter how desperate I was. You have to believe me, as a friend.'

'That friendship is dead. You sold it to Corsa.'

'An accident,' Lillicrap panted. 'He tricked me. Truthfully. You know he can be evil. Tell me what I can do to make amends.' Struggling desperately to control his breathing, he began dusting himself down, rearranging his rumpled collar.

Then the light in Goodfellowe's eyes burned out and died, his energies gone. 'There's nothing you can do. The damage is done.' Without another word he turned for the Committee Room.

Lillicrap hurried after him, anxious lest further mayhem break out in the Committee itself, but Goodfellowe was already seated, head in hands, motionless. The Committee Room was sweltering in the morning sun that burned through the towering window blinds. Overhead the ceiling fans were turning despairingly. Most Members were already in shirtsleeves, their backs sticking to the leather chairs, trying to cool themselves from the water bottles and horrid plastic cups that had been laid out along the tables. On the public seats the designer jackets were coming off, the cool brows of the lobbyists beginning to burn, the briefing papers turning limp in their hands. But Goodfellowe appeared to be unaware of it all. He remained jacketed and oblivious, raising no objection, pursuing no argument, offering not a word all through the proceedings. Then a division was called. Betty Ewing was pressing another amendment and insisting on a vote. After all, with

289

Goodfellowe's agreed support she would win.

'Division!' the Chairman commanded languidly, perspiration soaking into his collar, and the wheels of democracy started to turn. When the doors had been locked, the Clerk began calling out the roll.

'Mrs Ewing?'

'Aye!'

'Mrs Fagin?'

'Aye!'

'Mr Gedling?'

'No!'

'Mr Goodfellowe?' A long silence. They all turned towards Goodfellowe, head still buried in his hands, as though kneeling before a headsman's axe. 'Mr Goodfellowe, are you in favour of the amendment?' the Clerk requested, more loudly.

Goodfellowe struggled to lift his head as though the effort drained his last reserves of energy. The face was set rigid, like a mask, the eyes rimmed with red, unseeing. Big Ben began striking the hour, muffled in the fetid air like a funeral bell.

'Mr Goodfellowe?'

The lips moved but no sound emerged for some moments, and then only in a whisper. 'No . . .' His head sank back down, but not so quickly that he failed to see the look of abject contempt thrown towards him by Betty Ewing.

* * *

She found Goodfellowe's office wrapped in darkness. All was silent. She was about to retreat when, in the shadows, something stirred.

'Whoever it is, go away,' Goodfellowe said simply. 'It's been one hell of a day and I don't wish to be disturbed.'

290

The figure remained silhouetted against the light.

'If that's difficult to understand, let me put it in plain English. Bugger off.'

Still she didn't move.

'Who is it? Who's there?' he demanded in rising irritation.

'Only me.'

A pause. 'Sam?'

'I came to London. I thought we should talk.' Hesitantly she stepped a pace into the room, as though fearing the need to make a rapid escape. 'We never seem to be able to talk, do we? Not about important things. Like adoption.'

'Sam, I . . .' He rose but her body language insisted he keep his distance. He slumped back into the chair. He shook his head, bereft of defences. 'I am so sorry, Sam. Your adoption was meant to be a thing of joy, not pain. The number of times I tried to tell you, somehow it never seemed quite the right moment. It was always something for tomorrow. And these last couple of years, you and I, we seemed to be fighting all the time. I guess I was frightened of what might happen if you learnt I wasn't your natural father.'

'Perhaps you should've spent less time worrying about whether you were my adopted dad or my natural dad and just got on with the job of being any sort of dad.'

'That's cruel.'

'So was reading about your Chinese girlfriend in the newspaper. You seem to have plenty of time for her.'

It was turning into another one of their sessions. In spite of himself his irritation rose.

'She wasn't a girlfriend and I was only doing my

291

job.'

'Great. Do I have to wait to get a vote before I get your attention? '

'Have you any idea what I've been going through for you?'

'How could I? The only way you ever talk to me is through the newspapers.'

That's when Goodfellowe remembered the memory box tucked away in the back of her drawer. All the clippings she had collected. And what they meant. In the reflected light she watched as he physically struggled to find the words.

'Saying sorry isn't really good enough. I have not been very good at being your father. But I have tried, believe me, tried so hard. And I've missed you. I'm very glad you came.'

'I just wanted to talk.'

He sighed, a cupful of sorrows drawn from the deepest well. 'I'm afraid we have more to talk about than you think.' He switched on the desk lamp. It threw a pool of light onto the leather top, and in the middle of the pool he placed a folder. 'This is what Corsa would have published, if I hadn't supported his Bill.'

Cautiously she stepped forward to the desk and sat opposite him, opening the folder and beginning to read.

'It's about your sex life, Sam. Or are you going to deny what it says?'

She looked up. 'Why should I? I'm not silly, I'm not a tart. I'm just growing up.'

He struggled to get his emotions around her admission before moving on. 'And what about the drugs? You think doing drugs is growing up, too?'

'For a little while I went out with a creep who

292

smoked dope. Nothing heavy. I tried it once. When I realized what a creep he was I dumped him. I haven't touched anything since.' She sounded very matter-of-fact.

'I never believed you would try drugs . . .'

'Dad, look at me and tell me you've never in your life tried drugs. Swear it to me.'

'I . . . It . . .' His sudden stumbling gave its own answer, 'But that was at university. A long time ago. In the Sixties.'

'And because it was so long ago that made it better? You must have been—what—all of eighteen? Very grown up.' She forced herself to bite back the sarcasm once more, this was not why she had come. 'You know, we may not be flesh and blood, but in many ways we are very alike.'

Across the lamplight their eyes met and made contact. She meant it as a peace offering, he could see, but it wasn't going to be that easy.

'I'd like to think so, Sam, that we are alike. But not in all ways.' He indicated that she should dig deeper through the file, to the photographs. They slipped into her hand and she placed them under the light, like exhibits. Goodfellowe looked away as she studied them, very carefully, one by one. If he had expected exaggerated emotion, harsh denial or despairing tears, none came. It was several moments before she spoke and when she did her voice was soft, matching the dark atmosphere of the room.

'I model at life classes, and these photographs were sneaked, you can tell. I'm angry about that. But I'm not ashamed. I draw at life classes every week. Men and women, old and young. It's been a fundamental part of any artist's training since

293

Michelangelo. So why is it supposed to be all right to draw a model, but not to be one?'

'Because, because, because ... if they had published those photographs and their story it would have done you great harm, no matter what the truth. You would probably have been sent away from school, and I couldn't have stood that. It happened to me, being thrown out of school, because of something my father did. I could never live with it happening to you for something I had done. That's why I have voted for this wretched Bill, done things I would never have done for any other reason, because you are the most precious thing in my life. And I'm terrified I might lose you.'

'You've never said anything like that to me before.'

'I always assumed you knew.'

'You can't assume love.'

'Sam, I've had to lock my feelings away ... bury them so deep over the last few years. To block all the pain. Selfish of me, perhaps. Doesn't mean I ever stopped loving you, not for a moment. And if ever I let you think that, then I have failed in everything that matters in my life.'

'Dad?'

That one awesome word.

'Yeah?' He was choking.

'I'm very glad I came to talk.' She reached across the pool of light, across the folder and the photos which separated them, to take hold of his hands. They sat like that for a long time, neither wishing to let go.

Eventually Goodfellowe spoke. 'Sam, is there anything you want? Anything I can do?'

'Perhaps one thing.'

'Name it.'

'Dad, can you kill this bloody Bill? Can we get our own back on Corsa?'

He groaned, his elation slowly sinking to the frost-hard ground. 'If only I could. But it's too late. The Standing Committee finished its work this afternoon, it's as good as over. That's why I was hiding here. In shame.'

'You've got nothing to be ashamed about, Dad.'

'I wish you were right. It's not true. But it is too late.'

*   *   *

Chance found Goodfellowe and Lillicrap entering the Chamber side by side.

'The final act of our little play, Tom.'

'I am sure you will go on to still more stunning performances, Lionel. Forgive me if I'm not around to applaud.'

'It hurts me that we've had such misunderstandings. I hope we can put them all behind us, remain friends.'

'Somewhere I seem to remember being instructed to forgive our enemies. It said nothing about forgiving our friends.' Goodfellowe ignored the proffered hand and turned away. Lillicrap, with a reluctant shrug of his shoulders, crossed to his appointed place at the end of the Front Bench.

The final act, as Lillicrap had described it and for which they had gathered, was the Third Reading of the Press (Diversity of Ownership) Bill. With Goodfellowe's capitulation, the Bill had made rapid progress through Standing Committee and was now to be brought for its concluding vote to the Floor of the House of Commons. The end of the line for the

295

Bill, and for Goodfellowe. His colleagues might forgive him, he'd never forgive himself.

The House was crowded, as were the galleries above. The Chamber was quietly bustling, like a concert house before the curtain rises. Up in the gods Goodfellowe could see Corsa and, beside him, Diane Burston, come to witness their victory and the *coup de grâce*. Goodfellowe could not hide an acute sense of humiliation and Mickey had encouraged him to stay away. 'What's the point in turning up? ' she had asked. 'A bit like staying away from your own execution,' he had replied. 'Somehow you just have to be there.'

The House was finishing off a half-hearted discussion of a Private Member's Bill—some twaddle about the need to regulate the size and sharpness of stiletto heels to which no one except the proposer was paying any particular attention— as Goodfellowe claimed a seat on the benches. He found himself directly in front of Frank Breedon, who pointedly ignored him as he continued with an animated discussion about plans for the forthcoming summer holidays. The House was growing distracted as the Private Member's proceedings droned on until, through the general clutter of noise, came a determined interruption. An Opposition MP had taken exception to the tedium of the Private Member's Bill and decided to liven up proceedings with an injection of remarks that were gratuitously sexist. Madam Speaker intervened to demand an immediate return to order but he continued undaunted to barrack and to press his spurious point, arousing both annoyance and amusement amongst Members on all sides. Over his shoulder Goodfellowe became aware that Breedon was holding his arms out as though firing a shotgun, with his sights trained on the interrupter.

'You shoot, Frank?' Goodfellowe turned to enquire of his Chairman.

'As often as I can. Glorious Twelfth almost upon us, can't wait. Going to blast away at a few on the Tullymurdoch estate this year. Alongside our beloved Committee Whip.' He fired another imaginary volley across the floor as those around him egged him on.

Goodfellowe felt his stomach churn, a sudden wicked turbulence that was a warning of still worse to come. Something was moving inside him, something unpleasant that left him ill at ease, as though he had been invaded by some angry parasite that was trying to force its way through his system. He turned once more to Breedon.

'Costs a fortune, doesn't it, Frank, the fishing and shooting game? '

'No problem,' he answered cheerily. 'Lionel gets us a very good deal. A very good deal.' He chuckled in satisfaction. 'Bright lad, young Lillicrap. He'll go far.'

But Goodfellowe had already gone. Even as Madam Speaker announced the start of proceedings for the Third Reading, the Member for Marshwood was hurrying back out of the Chamber.

*   *   *

The parasite got the better of him as he sat at his desk. It had entered his head, sending the blood rushing through his ears and agitating his thoughts to the point of incoherence. He was having difficulty catching his breath and seemed quite unable to find what he was looking for in the

297

Register of Members' Interests that lay open in front of him. He summoned Mickey.

'You all right?' she enquired, anxious.

'Don't worry about me.' He waved in the direction of the telephone. 'There's a hunting estate in Tullymurdoch. That's Perthshire. I want you to try and book me a week's shooting and fishing. From August the twelfth.' The parasite was multiplying, he thought he was going to burst. 'Do it. Please. Now.' He waved at the telephone again. He was visibly trembling.

Mickey perched on the edge of the desk and dialled. First directory enquiries, then another number, to which she chatted for several minutes while Goodfellowe could do nothing but suffer. Eventually she replaced the receiver and turned to him.

'There's good news and bad news,' she announced thoughtfully. 'The bad news is that you need to be in a party of eight and a week all-in at Tullymurdoch will set you back at least four thousand pounds a head, nearer five if you want the salmon fishing and other extras thrown in as well.'

'And . . .?'

'The good news, for you at least, is that they're fully booked. Always are at this time of year. A corporate reservation. And I don't know whether the rest of the news is either good or bad.'

'What is it?'

'It's booked in the name of a Michael MacPherson.'

'Who's he?'

'Apparently he's from the Granite Corporation.'

Goodfellowe sprang from his chair like a beaten grouse and flew straight into her arms. 'Mickey, you

298

are the most wonderful woman on my staff,' he enthused, planting a kiss full on her lips before rushing out of the door. The parasite had vanished.

*   *   *

When Goodfellowe returned to the Chamber the Minister was on his feet, defending himself and his Bill from the final desperate charge being mounted by the Indians of the Opposition. It was good sport. The result was already known, the Minister would escape with his scalp, the white men in grey suits would win. They always did. They had more guns. Goodfellowe bowed to Madam Speaker and sat down, not this time on the leather benches but on the carpeted steps of the gangway that cut across the middle of the Chamber. It put him directly alongside Lillicrap at the end of the Front Bench. Lillicrap was consulting the notebook which lay open on his lap, a small volume in which duty required him to record not the words but the performances of those who spoke from the Government backbenches, awarding them mysterious acronyms in the manner of military decorations, the meanings of which would be shared only around the Masonic brotherhood of the Whips' Office. MM: Ministerial Material. VC: Virtual Chloroform. MIA: Malice In Action. DFC: Destined For Catastrophe. And so on. He was scribbling when he noticed Goodfellowe's face appear at his elbow.

'Who is Michael MacPherson, Lionel?'

'Michael? We were at university together. Leicester. Why?' Goodfellowe gave the impression of a friendly retriever squatting on the floor beside him; Lillicrap, busy with his notes, had no sense of alarm.

'An old friend?'

'Sure. What's all this about?'

'What does he do at Granite?'

In an instant Goodfellowe had all of Lillicrap's attention. The Whip bent low in order not to raise his voice. 'What the hell are you talking about?'

'Lionel, tell me what he does at Granite. I can find out with one telephone call.'

Lillicrap's brow knotted. 'He's something in the Finance Department. The Director, actually. So what?'

'Tell me, why does he pay for your hunting trip to Scotland every year?'

The pen Lillicrap was using escaped from his fingers and rolled to the floor. Lillicrap's lips were moving, but no sound emerged.

'You've been going every single year, yet you can't afford that sort of money, you told me so yourself.'

With evident pain Lillicrap rediscovered his vocal cords. 'He's a friend, Tom. We go as friends, together. It's a friendly arrangement.'

'Oh, Lionel, you've been at it, you have.' Goodfellowe's tone was conciliatory, even indulgent.

'It's always been handled as friends, nothing more,' Lillicrap insisted.

'It must have been worth several tens of thousands over the years. Yet not a word of it in the Register. A straight gift. An inducement. You haven't even scribbled overpaid articles about the pleasures of the peat moors to justify it. At least Frank Breedon has that.'

'Michael and his family come to my house, as

friends. I don't charge them, of course I bloody don't.' He tried to sound offended at the thought. 'So when I go to visit him, as a friend, at his home or his hunting lodge, he doesn't charge me either.' At this point Lillicrap's bravado began to fracture, his tone grew less amenable. 'Look, I was nothing of importance in politics when it all started. We scarcely discussed politics. No one was twisting my arm. There was nothing to put in the flaming Register.'

'But then it changed, didn't it? Slowly the time together became more political,' Goodfellowe coaxed.

'Maybe we discussed mutual interests over a drink or two . . .'

'And he introduced you to Freddy Corsa. Who asked you to invite along some other friends. Political friends. Like Brother Breedon. And me. You started running his errands, handling the loans he made available, facilitating all his contacts, encouraging his schemes to buy friends with holidays and well-paid articles. In return he picked up your bills. You should have registered it all, Lionel.'

'Tom, you must believe me. It's not what you make it seem. This isn't sleaze. It all happened so gradually. Perhaps I should have registered it as an interest at some point, but it was so difficult to know when I had crossed the line, between friendship and . . .'

'Between friendship and corrupting influence. A line so difficult to see, so easy to cross, someone once told me. And he knew what he was talking about.'

'Look, perhaps I made a mistake. A genuine
301

mistake. I promise I'll register it from now on, without fail. I'll keep it all above board.'

'Too late. Too late,' Goodfellowe whispered, so that Lillicrap had to bend almost double to hear. 'Your fingerprints are everywhere, leaving their grubby marks. On my membership of the Committee, where you thought I would do as I was told by you. And as you were told by Corsa. They were all over my first meeting with Corsa, at the toyshop. They're on the loans, and on the money he offered me for articles. Worst of all, it was you who leaked the news of Sam's adoption to him.'

'I've told you that was a complete accident. I never intended . . .'

'No one is going to believe you, Lionel, not when you're blasting away at wildlife for free beside Freddy Corsa and the Chairman of the Committee which has just passed his Bill. They're going to say it stinks. That you are in the jampot beyond your elegant cuffs and right up to your elbows. They'll ask how you can afford the house and the big cars and the foreign holidays on the pittance you earn. They'll ask where it all came from. And when they find out, your colleagues will transform into a pack of moralizing hypocrites, and do you know what they're going to do?'

'What?'

'They are going to crucify you.'

'Tom, for old times' sake. As old friends. Please give me a chance.' Lillicrap made a desperate grab for Goodfellowe's arm. Their intense and sustained deliberation just below the Front Bench had begun to attract attention around the House, it was evident that something was afoot, but Lillicrap didn't notice. His eyes saw only the horror of

302

crucifixion and the dragging of his body through the dust of many streets.

Calmly, Goodfellowe bent to pick up the Whip's fallen pen, placing it carefully back into Lillicrap's hand.

'One last chance. Please, Tom. I beg you.'

'You should never have involved Sam in this,' Goodfellowe concluded, and rose to take his seat on the benches.

*   *   *

The Minister had finished his speech and the Opposition spokesman was gathering his papers to make his reply when Goodfellowe rose to his feet.

'On a Point of Order, Madam Speaker.'

'Point of Order, Mr Goodfellowe,' she intoned, staring at him through spectacles in an enquiring manner. At the end of the Front Bench, Lillicrap's face had taken on the appearance of warm wax.

'I must apologize, Madam Speaker, for being unable to give you any prior warning of my Point of Order. In all honesty, I am not entirely sure that a Point of Order is the correct manner in which what I have to say should be put. But I know it must be put, and before this debate goes any further.'

'You'd better put it then, and quickly,' the Speaker interjected, wary as always about self-indulgent Members who wasted both their own breath and their colleagues' time.

'Madam Speaker, it is well known that during the Committee stages I held serious doubts about the passage of this Bill. Those doubts have now become rock-hard certainties. For the House to approve the Bill at this time would be immoral, corrupt and probably unconstitutional.'

The atmosphere of the Chamber of the House of Commons does not travel well through television. The action can be seen and the words heard, but it is like experiencing sex through cartoons. The essence is missing. Yet for those who are there at the time, nothing else seems to matter. For many politicians, speaking from the Floor of a packed and attentive House is much like copulation. There is a tremor of terror and anticipation as you begin, and there is a mystery special to each occasion which decrees that no matter how many times you have gone through the motions before, you never know whether this time the earth will move or will simply fall in on top of you. That is the terror of failure, but it is risked time and again for the few elusive moments of fulfilment which leave a man, or a woman, exhausted and in triumph. Goodfellowe had begun with no teasing, no gentle anticipation but instead a full-frontal assault that left those around him gasping. Immoral? Corrupt? Unconstitutional? It was as though the fair maidens of the House were staring at the glinting point of a knife in some dark alleyway.

'It is with great regret that I must inform the House that the passage of this Bill has been sought by means of bribery and blackmail by those who stand to gain from it.'

Up in the visitors' gallery, Corsa turned to an elderly gentleman sitting next to him. 'Can he do this? Accuse people? Slander them?'

'Parliamentary privilege,' the old man whispered. 'In the Chamber he can say what on earth he likes and not a court in the country can touch him.'

Down on the Floor, Lillicrap began to squirm with dread. The end of the Front Bench was beginning to feel like the trapdoor on the gallows.

Goodfellowe continued: 'As a member of the Standing Committee, and solely because I was a member of that Committee, Madam Speaker, I have been offered bribes.'

A collective drawing-in of breath could be heard around the benches. The Prime Minister, who had been preparing to leave after his colleague's speech, sat transfixed as though nailed in position.

'I have been offered substantial inducements for the explicit purpose of gaining my support for the Bill so that I would help push it through Committee.'

'What sort of inducements?' an Opposition Member could be heard muttering.

'The inducements were of several kinds. Offers of free holidays.' Behind him, Goodfellowe could hear Breedon clearing his throat as though preparing to intervene. 'Most surprisingly, perhaps, I was offered an extraordinary sum of money in exchange for articles I might have written. Now, many Members of this House are gifted authors whose talents are justifiably rewarded when they contribute articles of substance to newspapers.' He had to get that point in quickly, before he lost half of his audience. 'But it is truly surprising that a man of my meagre literary talents should be offered any sum, let alone a King's Ransom of nearly twenty thousand pounds. In my case, Madam Speaker, I can confirm that the offer was intended as a bribe.'

Up in the gallery Corsa had arched forward, gripping the carved rail in front of him. Goodfellowe momentarily caught his eye.

'For a while, in an attempt to obtain documentary evidence, I played along with the idea.' A useful point. That would explain the note he had written to Corsa, should it ever come to light. But mentally Corsa was already resolving to burn it. 'And when I thought the matter had gone far enough and I refused to cooperate, the sources involved then turned to blackmail.'

The whole House writhed with excitement.

'But still I would not participate in their plans, so the sources turned to my family. Quite simply, Madam Speaker, they threatened my family in order to get at me.'

Further along the bench a female Member was all but swooning in emotion. She had never experienced anything like this before, not in the House, at least.

'They invented stories about my family, invaded their privacy, took photographs in their most intimate moments, to try to get me to change my mind on the Bill.' He had marked the photographs of Sam in the most public of manners. Corsa would never dare publish them now.

'And all this has been done simply to speed the passage of this Bill, because to certain interests this Bill means profit. Vast amounts of it. And they want it now, at any cost.'

'Who? Who is it?' Urgent moans and sighs of anticipation began to rise on every side, but Goodfellowe was determined to keep them unfulfilled, breathless for more.

'Behind the legitimate newspaper interests which this Bill seeks to regulate, there is a hidden network of money men who have little direct interest in newspapers, but great interest in news. They want to manipulate the news for their own benefit, and for the disadvantage of others. We thought the Bill

306

was about selling newspapers; they knew it was about selling news.' ('Who? Who?' the cries continued.) 'But sadly their identity will remain hidden under this Bill for, as we discussed in Committee, the ultimate ownership of a newspaper can be extraordinarily difficult to identify.'

'Hear, hear!' Betty Ewing was stamping her foot in agreement.

'Much to my regret, Madam Speaker, I have been unable to obtain documentary evidence of these matters, other than the photographs which, frankly, I would not care to have revealed.' He knew this was going to be the difficult bit, the unexpected withdrawal. It induced a perceptible sense of disappointment. Breedon was beginning to mutter. 'Charlatan. The whole thing's preposterous.' 'Name them! Name them! Parliamentary privilege!' others were beginning to demand. The House was beginning to wriggle out from beneath him.

'I shall not identify them,' Goodfellowe responded. 'Since I cannot as yet prove this matter in court, I will not mimic the practices of the press by naming people without hard evidence.'

In the gallery, Corsa released his grip on the wooden balustrade and threw himself back into his seat like a bowstring from which the tension had been released. Around the House, some Members began to scoff and mutter that it all amounted to nothing more than limp accusation and privileged posturing. 'He dreamed it up over his breakfast,' Breedon was claiming for all to hear. To start upon the act of love is always a step into the unknown, to withdraw at the peak of expectation is a leap towards certain oblivion. It was time for Goodfellowe to seize the moment once more. Time to take the gamble.

'Madam Speaker, the House will be aware that these matters have been of great concern to me for some time. That is why I urged in Committee that Members record every financial contact with the press—not that I believed any of them would bow to pressure, but simply because I knew there was a possibility that such pressure might be exerted. I wanted to gather as much evidence as possible.'

'You haven't got any,' Breedon was barking.

'It was always going to be difficult to prove these allegations, since we are dealing not just with money, but also with the motivations for giving it. But the House will understand that I felt I had to try.'

Goodfellowe was looking directly at Lillicrap, who seemed about to melt. He could gather enough circumstantial evidence to ruin the Whip in Parliament, but not to prove criminal misdoing on his part, even less on the part of Corsa. Yet ruining Lillicrap might be the only measure of justice he could guarantee. On the other hand . . .

'It is not my word alone that I ask the House to accept. Firm evidence was always going to be difficult to obtain, which is why at every step of the way I have consulted with and taken guidance from my Honourable Friend, the Committee Whip.'

As one sentient creature, the House turned to Lillicrap.

'It was his view, Madam Speaker, that the allegations were so serious and might have involved other Members in allegations of corruption that absolutely no one else should be informed. He decided that the business of the Committee should continue as normal while I tried to obtain documentary evidence. In that effort, sadly, we have failed. But my Honourable Friend has been aware of the bribery and blackmail which has been aimed at me. He will be able to confirm everything I have said today.'

The figure of Lillicrap now commanded the collective attention. His head had been buried in his hands in a manner most took to be studied concentration. Now the head came up, his features set grim but with a flush of hope filling his cheeks. He was alive. The trapdoor was still in place. There was a way out, a chance of reprieve. He straightened himself in his seat. As though his life depended on it, and very slowly, he nodded in agreement.

The House expelled its breath in a moment of most extraordinary passion.

'It is possible, Madam Speaker, that we shall never be able to bring these matters to court. But in the light of what I have revealed, I must ask the House not to approve this Bill today. It should wait until the next parliamentary session for calmer and, dare I say it, less corruptible consideration. The inconveniences of delaying a year are far outweighed by the penalties of proceeding. The public, and I hope the House, will demand a pause for thought. I ask, through you Madam Speaker, that this Bill be buried.'

Exhausted, feeling spent, he resumed his seat. He could feel the sweat trickling down the small of his back. Had he been a smoker he would have reached for a cigarette.

Cautiously the House came back to life, moving its limbs slowly, stretching, saddened that it was over, knowing this had been an experience that was unlikely to be repeated for a very long time. Even Madam Speaker spoke with a sigh.

'That was the most extraordinary Point of Order I think I shall ever witness. In light of what has been said, may I ask the Minister what his intentions are?'

The Government Front Bench looked bemused. Both Minister and Prime Minister were looking pale, drawn, like witnesses of some awful assault, but now they set to conferring, with Lillicrap's head nodding in a sustained fashion. They were all agreed. Moments later the Prime Minister was pushing his reluctant colleague forward towards the Dispatch Box.

'In light of the very serious allegations made by my Honourable Friend, the Member for Marshwood,' the Minister began, 'I believe we will need to consider afresh how best to proceed, indeed whether we should proceed, with the Bill at this time.'

There were formalities to pursue, other Cabinet colleagues to consult, but the exercise was academic. The Prime Minister was already shaking his head in surrender.

'With your permission, Madam Speaker, I beg to move that the House do now adjourn.'

They had no choice. They could not continue. The debate was over. The Bill was dead.

And so was Corsa. The bankers were already hammering at his door, the Fraud Squad would not be far behind. Goodfellowe glanced up into the gallery. Diane Burston had gone, and with her the support of the consortium. Corsa sat on his own, abandoned. He was looking directly at Goodfellowe. Their eyes met and fixed. Not even

Corsa was able to muster a smile, but with what Goodfellowe later considered to be surprising grace, the pressman began silently to applaud.

*   *   *

A few minutes later as he left the Chamber, Goodfellowe noticed for the first time that his shoes were no longer painful. How things change, he reflected. The House was still in turmoil and he thrust aside the outstretched arms and the questions, too exhausted to respond, but as he passed behind the Speaker's Chair he was grabbed by Lillicrap who hustled him into the toilet at the back of the voting lobby. The Whip stood with his back to the door, his arms spread, barring entrance to anyone else.

'What do we do now?' Lillicap all but pleaded.

'Get our stories straight. You know most of the details anyway. We'll meet tomorrow. Breakfast. At the Ritz. Your treat.'

'But Corsa will kill me!'

'Only by killing himself, and I doubt if he'll bother. I'll bet there are far too many alligators circling in his swamp for him to be concerned with small fry.'

'You saved me,' Lillicrap whispered gratefully.

'But the Chief Whip won't. He'll skin you alive because he thinks you've been holding out on him. Keeping secrets. You'll be out of a job. It's still better than you deserve.'

Lillicrap was all but sobbing. 'I'll be back. After the election. Don't you worry.' With that he rushed to the basin to bathe his face and burning eyes.

Goodfellowe walked away, driven by saddening memories of friendships past mixed with a nausea

311

of cold contempt. His strides were confident now, full of renewed purpose as he passed along the panelled corridors, feeling once again as though he belonged, that he was part of it all. Then he pulled himself up sharply. No, that wouldn't do, slipping back into the old ways. Getting sucked dry by ambition and disappointment. He had become something of an outsider, a pain in the collective butt, and he rather enjoyed it. Perhaps it was better that way.

Sam and Mickey were waiting for him in his office. They had watched the proceedings on the closed-circuit monitor.

'As a reception committee this is somewhat ... small. But very welcome.' He held his arms out wide and Mickey reached up to embrace him. Sam kept her distance, smiling reproachfully, deliberately coy.

'Daddy, weren't you telling a few lies in there about poor Mr Lillicrap? What sort of example is that to a young girl?'

'A father never lies. Let us say I was merely redistributing the truth. A little unevenly, perhaps. But very fairly.'

'You took a hell of a risk,' Mickey interjected. 'What if he had denied it?'

'Offer a drowning man your hand and he'll accept, even if it costs him a kick in the teeth as you drag him out. It was either that or Lionel knew I would push him under. It concentrated his loyalties wonderfully. Anyway, I had no choice. Without him I could prove nothing against Corsa directly, my word against his.'

'There'll be one almighty stink.'

'An inquiry, no doubt, but it's like a game of blind man's buff. No one will be sure who they'll bump

312

into. So interest will fade in the run-up to an election, they'll accept my word but say that firm evidence is lacking. They will issue a ringing call for sobriety and motherhood and insist on due care in accepting money from the media, then forget it while they all go poaching for editorial support and wondering why Freddy Corsa has disappeared from the scene.'

'A measure of justice, at least,' Sam suggested.

'Perhaps. But I can't help thinking of Jya-Yu. I feel I've let her down so badly, dragging her onto the front pages. I've never been able to get her on the phone, to apologize. And her uncle was furious. He would barely talk to me.'

Mickey began to laugh, clapping her hands. 'Wrong again, Goodfellowe. She returned your call this morning. She escaped from it all in Hong Kong but now she's back and she's fine. So is her uncle. He's not angry. He couldn't speak because he was rushed off his feet. Since the *Herald* article was printed he's been fighting off the crowds. Apparently they all think you're on tiger bone.'

'I shall recommend it for the entire Cabinet.'

'But what about you, Daddy? Do you think they'll be grateful? Make you a Minister again?'

He shook his head. 'Gratitude isn't one of the great foundations of politics. Anyway, I don't want that any more. I may be a mere backbencher, but I think I've shown there's some fun to be had. I don't want to be Prime Minister. And the press would never allow it.'

'But why, Daddy?'

'Because my name is far too long for headline writers. Eleven letters. Goes on forever. I'd have the longest Prime Ministerial name since . . . since

313

Neville Bloody Chamberlain, and a fine mess he got us into.'

Sam looked puzzled, greatly concerned, until he burst into laughter.

'You're impossible!' she shouted, and at last she was in his arms.

'Thanks for caring. But truly I want other things. I want a life. I want you, Sam.'

Her hug was enormous. 'And I want to celebrate,' she exclaimed. 'Can we?'

'Let's all three of us go out to dinner tonight,' he suggested.

'Anywhere special?'

'Perhaps.' He paused, as if it were the most difficult decision of his day. 'Mickey, at the risk of doing too much damage to your manicure, pick up the telephone and give The Kremlin a call. Ask if they will accept a booking. In the name of Goodfellowe.'